Ichabod

Seven Cows, Ugly and Gaunt

Book Two

Mark Goodwin

Technical information in the book is included to convey realism. The author shall not have liability or responsibility to any person or entity with respect to any loss or damage caused, or allegedly caused, directly or indirectly by the information contained in this book.

All of the characters, places, and incidents are products of the author's imagination or are used fictitiously. Any resemblance to actual people, places, or events is entirely coincidental.

Cover design by Deranged Doctor Design
www.derangeddoctordesign.com

Copyright © 2016 Goodwin America Corp.

ISBN: 1530704677
ISBN-13: 978-1530704675

DEDICATION

To the real Miss Jennie, a woman who, in all things, remained grateful to her Creator, and endured the hardships of the great depression by learning to barter, produce her own food, and make do with what she had; all of which are the essence of the modern preparedness movement. Thank you for being an inspiration to us all by showing us how to persevere to the end while always having a song of joy in your heart.

1913-2016

Make a joyful noise unto the LORD, all ye lands. Serve the LORD with gladness: come before his presence with singing. Know ye that the LORD he is God: it is he that hath made us, and not we ourselves; we are his people, and the sheep of his pasture. Enter into his gates with thanksgiving, and into his courts with praise: be thankful unto him, and bless his name. For the LORD is good; his mercy is everlasting; and his truth endureth to all generations.

Psalm 100

ACKNOWLEDGMENTS

Thanks to my wonderful wife, best friend and editor-in-chief, Catherine Goodwin.

Thanks to Ken and Jen Elswick, and Dutch Perry for their assistance with editing.

CHAPTER 1

Therefore as the fire devoureth the stubble, and the flame consumeth the chaff, so their root shall be as rottenness, and their blossom shall go up as dust: because they have cast away the law of the LORD of hosts, and despised the word of the Holy One of Israel.

Isaiah 5:24

Danny Walker opened his eyes.

"Daniel. Daniel. Wake up, Daniel." Nana's voice grew louder from the other side of the bedroom door.

Danny looked at Alisa, his young wife, lying next to him in the bed.

Alisa was awake also. "So much for letting us

sleep in, huh?"

"Better see what she wants." Danny rolled out of bed. It was so cold, he could see his breath. He grabbed his jacket and opened the door.

"Daniel, something has the cows all stirred up down at the barn; might be a coyote. You best go see what it is." Nana held out a kerosene lantern and the shotgun for him to take.

"Okay, let me get my shoes on." He tied his shoes then bundled up with a jacket, gloves and a toboggan. Danny considered getting his AK-47 rather than taking the shotgun, but took the weapon Nana handed him. It was too early to argue.

He kissed Alisa. "Be right back."

"Do you want me to come with you?" She was completely covered by the quilts and blankets, except for her face.

He smiled. "I think I can handle it."

Danny followed Nana who held the front door open.

"If it's a coyote, take a shot at him, even if you can't hit him. That'll keep him scared off for a spell." Nana closed the door behind him.

"Sure." Danny headed toward the barn cautiously. The long bellowing sounds from the cattle confirmed that something was not right at the barn. Nana hadn't lost any calves to coyotes yet, but other farmers in the area had. Losing a cow was bad enough when it was a source of extra income, but since the EMP the loss would be a much more serious hit. That thought motivated Danny to find and destroy the predator.

When he reached the barn door, he leaned the

shotgun against the wall so he could raise the wooden latch. Once inside, he hung the lantern on a high nail and picked up the gun to hold at a low-ready position. The cattle had an opening which allowed them to come in and out of the barn at will. Most of them were inside, huddled together to conserve body heat.

Danny looked around. "If there was a coyote in here, I think the cows would have run."

He continued examining all the areas that could provide visual cover for a coyote or any other harassing animal. He saw nothing. As he peered around the next stall, he noticed that the light coming from the lantern behind him was much brighter than it should have been.

His heart stopped. "Fire!"

Danny turned around and saw flames shooting up the post where the lantern had been hanging. "Oh, no!"

He looked quickly to locate a bucket. Once he found it, he ran to the cattle trough to get some water. The water level in the trough was much too shallow and he would never get back to the pump at the house in time to quench the blaze. He looked for a blanket to smother the flames. He turned back toward the flames which had now engulfed the entire side of the barn. "It's no use. How did it spread so quickly?"

He grabbed the shotgun and began herding the cattle out the doorway. "Get! Hya! Go on! Get! Hya!"

Suddenly, with a light creak, then a loud crash, the wall collapsed and the roof above the exit gave way. Most of the cattle were out by the time the doorway was blocked, but Danny was trapped inside.

Smoke and ash began to swirl around him. He frantically looked for another way out, but it was a hopeless endeavor. The ash burned his eyes and his throat. He coughed and knelt low to the ground pulling off his toboggan to use as a filter to breathe through.

He closed his eyes and strained to keep from panicking and the painful lowing of a cow trapped in the inferno did nothing to calm his nerves. "God, help me, please. I don't want to die."

He opened his eyes and the flames flickered softly, gently, as if in slow motion. He looked around as the floating embers and bits of soot hung suspended in the air above him. He dropped the hat and took a deep breath of clean, fresh air. Danny stood to his feet and stared at the blazing beams and siding from the collapsed wall. The trapped cow fell silent and slowly turned to face him.

Every hair on his arm stood up and a chill raced up his spine, through his neck and down both legs. Those familiar hollow eyes, the protruding ribs, skinny legs, thin skin and lifeless stare. But this cow looked right at him. It wasn't blind, it wasn't grazing on money, it was furious and it was blood red. Red! The cow standing in the midst of the flames was bright red, like a stop sign or a fire truck.

Horror and fear overtook Danny. "Another dream." He knew it wasn't real, which meant he wasn't going to die, but the evil beast standing before him was more frightening than death itself.

Then it spoke in a low angry tone, pouring over each syllable without hurrying. "Ichabod."

Danny tried to look away, but couldn't. Had the hideous creature actually spoken to him? He wasn't sure. As crazy as it seemed, he looked the animal in the eye and asked, "What?"

Again, the lips of the blighted bovine moved as if it were chewing its cud, and again, it repeated the singular utterance. "Ichabod."

Danny's heart felt sorrow and fear as he heard the pronouncement once more. His stomach felt sour and unsettled. Misery was overtaking him and he felt as if he might actually die. The smoke and ash continued to swirl about his head in a fantastic display. "Ichabod?" Despite the fire, he felt cold, freezing inside immediately after he had said the word, as if he'd been banished to the dark side of the moon which had never felt the warmth of the sun. He could feel cold sweat breaking out and it sent shivers all through his body.

"Danny! Danny, wake up!" Alisa's voice grew sharper and clearer. "Danny, are you awake? Danny!"

He felt her shaking him and opened his eyes. His heart was pounding, and he could taste the salt from the sweat running off his head and into his mouth. He sat up and clamored for his flashlight on the night stand, knocking his watch onto the floor. He clicked on the flashlight, took a deep breath and let it back out. "I'm awake."

The flashlight showed that her face was full of

fear as she clasped his free hand in hers. "Another dream?"

He took off his damp tee-shirt and wiped the perspiration from his face. "Yeah.

CHAPTER 2

When thou passest through the waters, I will be with thee; and through the rivers, they shall not overflow thee: when thou walkest through the fire, thou shalt not be burned; neither shall the flame kindle upon thee.

Isaiah 43:2

Danny's heart rate regulated and he took a deep breath.

"Do you want me to get you some water?" Alisa asked.

"I do, but we'll wake up Nana."

Alisa smirked. "It might be your only chance to do that. What time is it? She's probably up anyway."

Danny shined the flashlight at the floor, reached

down and retrieved his watch. "Five. You're right, there's a good chance she's already up."

Alisa got out of bed and quickly put on her hooded sweatshirt. She took the flashlight from Danny's hand. "Wait here, I'll be right back."

Danny lay motionless in the bed as he waited for her to return. He couldn't help replaying the dream in his head and wondering what it foretold.

Minutes later, Alisa returned with a glass of water. "Here. I'm going to put on another pair of socks. It's freezing!"

Danny took the water and laid the flashlight on the night stand so the light still illuminated the room. "Thanks." He took a sip. "The water tastes like it just came out of the fridge."

Alisa put on her extra socks. "No. If it were in the fridge, it would be much warmer than that."

Danny took another sip. "I meant a fridge from the time before the lights went out."

"So did I." Alisa got back under the covers. "Think you'll be able to go back to sleep?"

"Not a chance. The one day Nana was going to let us sleep in—wasted."

"Then you might as well tell me about the dream. It's fresh in your mind right now. You won't forget any details."

"I never forget the details. I wish I could, sometimes." Danny proceeded to tell Alisa everything he remembered about the dream.

Right away, Alisa began explaining what she thought the dream meant. "The fire, the collapse of the barn, that represents the destruction and the collapse of America. The fact that you were trapped and the smoke and ash were all around, suffocating you, means that the destruction is going to directly affect you. Then, you prayed and you were miraculously able to breathe fresh air from an unknown source. That means God is going to walk you through it and protect you. That's all obvious, right?"

"It wasn't obvious to me, but it sounds like a sensible interpretation. What about the cow? What do you think that means? And what about the word Ichabod?" Danny looked at her curiously.

Alisa wiggled deeper under the covers. Her muffled voice came back. "I don't know."

"I thought you were supposed to have the gift of interpretation."

"That was Pastor Earl, I never said that." She stuck her head out from beneath the covers. "I hope he's okay."

"He had a plan. I'm sure he'll be fine."

"We had a plan, and we barely made it."

"But God brought us home. He'll take care of Pastor Earl."

"What about Cami and Nick? Are you worried?"

"A little. Nick had a good plan and knew how to execute it, but they should have been here by now. If anyone can adapt and overcome, it's Nick, but we'll keep praying for them."

"A lot of people had no plan. They're definitely not going to be okay." Alisa hid her head back under the covers.

Danny figured she was referring to her parents, but it wouldn't do any good to make her articulate it. Of course, it was a broad statement and most likely included everyone from work, all of her friends from school, and the larger percentage of the country. "So, are you going back to sleep?"

"No, but this is the warmest place in the house."

"I think I hear Nana. Maybe I'll get up and stoke the fire."

"Okay, come get me when spring arrives."

Danny got out of the bed, put on a dry tee-shirt, and grabbed a sweater. He lit the candle on the night stand and clicked off the flashlight. He could see his breath in the cold air, just like in the dream. Danny made his way down the stairs, being careful not to make them creak, but there was only so much he could do about the creaking in such an old house.

He slowly opened the door of the potbelly stove. The fire was out and only a few small embers were glowing. "No wonder it's so cold," he said, below a whisper. Danny selected the smallest of the logs that he'd brought in the house the night before, and placed it in the stove. Next, he closed the door and opened the vent, hoping the flow of air against the embers would ignite the log.

Steven turned over on the couch behind Danny.

Danny looked back to see Steven's eyes open. "Did I wake you?"

"No. Every time I roll over, my leg hurts like heck. The pain has done a pretty good job of waking me."

"So, you didn't sleep at all?"

"Some; off and on. More off than on, since the whiskey started to wear off. I can't believe Nana got me drunk. I hope I didn't say anything stupid."

"Your leg looked like a pound of ground chuck.

You needed the whiskey. And no, you didn't say anything that was more stupid than usual." Danny looked in the vent of the stove. The log was catching fire, but he would give it some time before adding a larger log.

"Why are you up so early? I figured you'd be out till at least noon."

"Bad dream." Danny held his hands close to the stove.

"I don't think I can survive another one of your bad dreams. Do I even want to hear about it?"

"Probably not."

"I don't want to hear it, or you don't want to tell it?"

"Both."

Steven was silent for a while, then said, "You know the suspense is killing me. Come on, what was it about?"

Danny looked at the flames flickering through the vent of the stove and thought about the awful barn fire that had trapped him in the vision. Reluctantly, he relived the horror through words, as he described the dreadful nightmare to Steven. Once he'd relayed the dream, he added Alisa's interpretation. He then asked, "What do you think the red cow could be?"

Steven scratched his head. "I'm not sure. Can you drag my bug-out bag over here?"

"Sure." Danny complied.

Steven retrieved his Bible from his bag and turned to Revelation 6. "One of the four horsemen is riding a red horse. He represents war. Your red cow could mean war is coming. Five down, two to go."

Danny took the Bible from Steven to read the chapter. "What do you mean?"

"If it's going to be seven cows, you've dreamed about five, which means we've got two to go."

Danny read the section of scripture. "There's no guarantee. This could be the last cow or there could be ten more. No one said it has to be seven. Look right here; it's four horses."

"Good argument if you're dreaming about horses." Steven winked. "But since it's cows, I'm banking on seven."

Nana slipped into the room without announcing her presence. "Steven, did you live through the night?" Her voice was loud and a major contrast to the soft spoken tones the two young men had been using. Both were startled.

Danny regained his composure quickly. He was used to such surprises from her. "Good morning, Nana. Did we wake you?"

"No, I was awake before Lisa got up to get a drink of water. If you run out there and grab a bucket of water from the pump, I'll get some coffee and biscuits going."

"Sure thing." Danny went back upstairs to get his coat and hat.

Alisa was awake, reading her Bible by candlelight. "Listen to this, Revelation 6."

"The red horse? It means war. The red cow probably means a war is coming," Danny said as he put on his jacket and hat, and then grabbed his shoes.

"When did you figure that out?"

"Steven figured it out. Is that what you think it means?"

"Yeah." She looked surprised that Danny already knew. "I guess the fact that Steven thought the same thing is confirmation."

Danny smiled. "I've got to go get some water so Nana can make breakfast. We'll get ready for the war after we've had a cup of coffee."

CHAPTER 3

I have seen also in the prophets of Jerusalem an horrible thing: they commit adultery, and walk in lies: they strengthen also the hands of evildoers, that none doth return from his wickedness: they are all of them unto me as Sodom, and the inhabitants thereof as Gomorrah.

Jeremiah 23:14

For the first time in a week, Danny enjoyed eating breakfast at a table like civilized folk. He sat at the large solid oak table with Alisa, Steven, Dana, and Nana, when she wasn't scurrying back and forth from the kitchen to bring coffee, eggs or biscuits.

The conversation flowed steadily as they ate. The first order of business was to fill Nana in on the gruesome details of the trip. Danny wished he could avoid the topic all together. It made his heart race to relive the violent accounts of the two attacks in which he'd had to take human life to survive.

Once that unpleasantness was out of the way, the discussion moved directly to his latest dream. While not quite as upsetting as recounting the journey, he did not relish telling the ugly vision.

Steven put a hand in the air. "Wait! You didn't tell me about the cow speaking earlier this morning."

Danny shook his head. "I had to go get water for coffee. I didn't get to finish."

Steven crossed his arms. "But you can't just leave in the middle of a story like that without telling me about the talking cow."

Danny rolled his eyes. "Well, now you have the rest of the story. Any idea what Ichabod means?"

Dana spoke excitedly. "Ichabod. Ichabod Crane. The Legend of Sleepy Hollow. He was the school teacher who has to run from the headless horseman."

Steven shook his head. "I don't think the cow was talking about Ichabod Crane. Let me grab my Bible, I'll be right back."

"Rest your leg. I'll get it for you." Alisa got up and retrieved Steven's Bible.

Steven took the book from Alisa when she returned and flipped through the pages. "In First Samuel, chapter 4, the Israelites are facing a battle with the Philistines. The two sons of Eli the priest bring the ark of God into the camp, which represents the very presence and glory of God. The Israelites are sure that they will defeat their enemies, since the ark of God is in the camp, but instead, they are defeated and the ark is captured by the Philistines; and the two sons of Eli are killed in the battle. When the pregnant widow of Phineas, one of Eli's sons, hears that her husband is dead and the ark has been taken, with her dying breath, she names her son Ichabod. She says, 'The glory is departed from Israel: for the ark of God is taken.'"

"Ichabod is Hebrew for no glory. It comes from the root word, *kabod*, which means glory, abundance and riches. So, Ichabod is basically the absence of all of that."

Alisa raised her eyebrows. "That's a pretty accurate description of America."

Steven pursed his lips. "Yeah, but it's not good. It also represents the presence of God leaving the country as a whole. It would be one thing if all of our tribulation was simply God's discipline to bring us back to himself, but this sounds like his complete abandonment."

Danny asked, "Didn't the ark eventually come back to Israel?"

Steven nodded. "Seven months later. It had brought plagues on the Philistines, so they built a cart and sent it back to Israel. Of course, the Israelites didn't follow the prescription of the law for handling the ark and many of them were killed. This whole episode of the ark being taken and Israel being defeated is a rebuke against the priest class. Eli never disciplined his sons who were desecrating the temple sacrifices by taking the best cuts of meat for themselves before it had been sacrificed. So God took the priesthood from Eli and his sons and handed it over to Samuel."

Alisa said, "Pastor Earl told us that he thought what was happening to America was largely because church leaders were being too tolerant of sin. Do you think the same thing that happened to Israel is happening to America, like on a spiritual leadership level?"

Steven paused for a second. "Yeah, that make sense. Like Eli, they didn't want to confront sin, so now, all of the guys with the mega churches who were focused on entertaining folks, have had the proverbial priesthood ripped from their hands."

Dana looked sad. "But God eventually came back, right? Samuel was a good priest?"

Steven smiled. "Samuel was a good priest. Israel went through some tough times, being oppressed by the Philistines, but Samuel eventually anointed King David, who ushered in Israel's golden age."

"Then there's hope for us? For America?" Dana asked.

Steven nodded. "Eventually, after we've repented, there's hope."

Nana pointed to Dana. "But Dena might have a point. A colonel in the War of 1812, was named Ichabod Crane. A lot of miracles happened during that war. We just about lost this country, but the hand of God intervened in several battles.

"Even if Steven is right about the red cow bein' an omen of war, God can still work divine wonders to deliver his chosen ones."

Nana turned toward Danny. "You sure the cow wasn't like these on the farm? They're red. Most of 'em has that white face, but once in a while, we'll get one that's solid red."

Danny shook his head. "No, Nana. It wasn't like a Hereford. It was fire-engine red."

"I reckon that sounds about right then. I suppose a war is a comin'. Nick will know what to do when he gets here."

"How do you know he'll make it?" Alisa asked.

"I just know. I can't tell you how, I just do. Faith, I guess." Nana smiled.

Danny spun his coffee cup on the saucer as he thought. "Nick thinks the Russians or the Chinese might invade after enough time has passed for most of the American population to die off."

Steven's voice was nervous. "How could we possibly stand against the Russians or the Chinese?"

Danny shrugged. "The Afghan guerrillas did it. They fought the Russians for years and finally drove them out of the country."

"Yeah, with help from the CIA." Steven tittered. "If we can get a shipment of shoulder-fired rockets like the Mujahideen, we might have a chance. Unfortunately, the CIA is out of commission."

Alisa faked a smile. "On the bright side, we have to survive the winter before an invasion can even become a problem."

Danny took her hand. "We'll make it."

Dana held Puddin' in her lap and stroked the cat gently. "I have an announcement to make."

Nana shook her head. "You best not be fixin' to tell me that animal is pregnant. There's a limit to my hospitality."

"No, Nana. Puddin' is spayed." Dana giggled. "Last night, I prayed to ask Jesus into my heart. God kept his end of the bargain and gave us a miracle to save Steven, so I kept my end of the deal."

"Praise Jesus!" Nana threw her arms in the air.

"Congratulations!" Alisa got up from her chair and hugged Dana.

Steven pursed his lips. "You know, it's not a trade-off. God isn't a magic genie in a bottle. And I hope this is something you genuinely want to do . . ."

"What do you mean?" Dana furrowed her brow.

"I'm saying, I hope you aren't just doing this for me."

"Don't flatter yourself, Steven!" Dana got up from the table and stormed off to the other room with Puddin' in her arms.

"Good job, Steven. Couldn't you just be happy for her? Everything isn't about you." Alisa patted Steven on the shoulder and followed Dana out of the dining room.

Nana passed the biscuits to Danny. "Eat another biscuit, Daniel."

Danny took a biscuit and did as he was told.

Steven slumped down in his chair. "I goofed that up."

Danny just nodded as he put some jelly on his biscuit.

Nana said, "At some point in my marriage to Howard, I figured out when it was best to keep my mouth shut."

Steven sat with his arms crossed. "Thanks, Nana. But I doubt Dana and I will ever be married."

"Keep talking to her like that and you sure won't." Nana got up from the table and cleared the dishes.

Danny cleared the rest of the dishes and followed her to the kitchen. Nana used water from the bucket Danny had filled earlier to fill a wash pan in the sink. She washed the dishes and Danny dried them.

"We'll commence meetin' here on Sundays." Nana handed a plate to Danny to dry. "Why don't you ask Steven if he'll put together a sermon?"

Danny dried the plate and put it in the cupboard. "Steven knows the Bible. He's certainly been a believer longer than me, but do you think he's qualified to be a preacher? You can see that he sort of drops the ball from time to time."

"That don't matter none. The Lord knows what he's doin'. If we didn't let nobody lead a meetin' lest they was perfect, we'd a been waitin' more than two thousand years without no preachers on this earth."

Danny laughed. "I guess you're right."

"Besides, it's his callin'. And it might be the thing that gets him to behave like a man and quit actin' like a child."

"How many people will it be?" Danny asked.

"There was about eight or ten of us meetin' here, regular for Bible study. I'd imagine they'll be here, plus a few more. Folks might have a little more time for the Lord now that they ain't got a mess of distractions."

"Might get tight if you have more than ten people

in the living room."

"Then we'll meet in the barn," Nana said matter-of-factly.

After the dishes were finished, Danny and Alisa walked down to the barn. Rusty, the farm dog, followed close behind. They needed to throw out some hay for the cattle, as the ground was still covered with ice and snow.

Alisa climbed the ladder into the loft. Danny took two biscuits out of his pocket for Rusty to eat while he waited, then ascended the ladder.

"You look a little preoccupied. Are you okay?"

Danny cut the string on the bale and began pulling the hay apart to toss to the cattle below. "Yeah. The barn, it looks just like it did in the dream. It's spooky. And then there's the impending war, I'm not looking forward to that."

Alisa helped him toss another clump of hay over the ledge. "Maybe it won't affect us."

"It will affect us. You interpreted the dream. You specifically said it will affect us."

"I know; I was just trying to make you feel better."

"Thanks." Danny couldn't help but smile at the quirkily honest statement. He was grateful for the pleasant distraction that his new wife provided.

"Did you ask Nana about these plastic bins up here?"

"Never got around to it. I'll ask her when we get back."

Once enough hay had been dispensed for all the cattle to have some, they descended the ladder.

Rusty seemed anxious for them to return and quickly led the way out the barn door.

Danny followed him around the back of the barn where the RV was parked. "I think he has the scent of some animal. Come on."

"We should have brought a gun. It might be something we can eat." Alisa scampered to catch up.

"It might be a groundhog. Would you eat groundhog?"

"Does it taste like regular hog?"

"I doubt it. Groundhog is closer to a rat than a pig."

"Eww! Rusty will probably eat it though."

"Look, behind the RV, a metal shed. Nick must have bought it. I knew they were bringing more stuff, but there's plenty of room in the barn. I wonder why he went through the trouble of buying this."

"We're not finding out today." Alisa checked the lock to make sure it wasn't just dummy locked. "Any chance it could be an EMP shield?"

"Maybe. They might have some electronics in here. It's way too small for a vehicle."

"I hope he's got a boatload of batteries in there. Electronics won't be much good otherwise."

"I guess we'll know soon enough. Let's head back to the house." Danny patted his leg for Rusty to follow.

"Are you as sure as Nana is about Nick and Cami making it back?"

Danny sighed. "I'm not going to let myself start worrying. That won't do any good at all. But to answer your question, probably not."

When they arrived at the house, they found Dana in the back by the chicken coop.

She held an old plastic whipped cream container. "Look! I found eleven eggs!"

"Good job!" Alisa said.

Danny looked at the selection of eggs in varying shades of white and brown. "The chickens did most of the heavy lifting on that one, but thanks for helping out."

"And, I fed the chickens." Dana gloated. "I also fed the rabbits and named them all."

Danny knuckled his forehead. "That might not be the best idea."

"And why not?" Dana was visibly incensed.

He couldn't believe she didn't know. "Because, we're going to eat them."

Dana handed the eggs to Alisa and covered her mouth. "No! Danny! Are you kidding me?"

"That's what they're here for. You're from the mountains, you never ate rabbit?"

"No! I've heard of people hunting them, but people don't eat pet rabbits!"

"We do." Danny led the way back in the house.

Dana followed close behind. "Well, I won't!"

Danny walked into the living room and placed two more logs in the potbelly stove. "What about pet cows? Do you plan on eating them? You're going to be awful skinny if you don't eat pet cows."

"That's different."

"Because they're not as cute?" Alisa asked.

"Cows are cute." Dana pouted. "But not as cute as rabbits."

Alisa winked at Danny. "You can't dispute the logic. It's rock solid."

Danny shook his head and plopped down on the easy chair to rest.

Nana brought a pot of soup into the living room to simmer on the potbelly stove. "We have to conserve the gas as long as we can. When it's gone, it's gone. And ain't nobody gonna want a fire in this stove, come summer."

Steven sat silently on the couch, studying his Bible with notebook in hand, trying to put together a message for the coming Sunday.

After a short rest, Danny and Alisa took advantage of the remaining daylight to go through the clothing and personal items they had brought out to Nana's over the previous weeks. They worked on getting everything organized and Alisa picked out some clothes to give to Dana, since she had next to nothing. Dana was very appreciative and put the donated clothes away in the second guestroom.

CHAPTER 4

That which the palmerworm hath left hath the locust eaten; and that which the locust hath left hath the cankerworm eaten; and that which the cankerworm hath left hath the caterpiller eaten.

Joel 1:4

Friday morning after breakfast, Danny helped Steven hobble back to the couch. "I'm going to construct some crutches for you to get around on."

"I appreciate it. Sorry I'm such a bother."

"Steven, you saved that kid's life. Letting us help you while you're on the mend allows us to share in the blessing, right?"

"I guess so."

"No, you know so." Danny winked and gave

Steven an encouraging smile. "Now let's get these bandages changed out."

Alisa and Dana walked into the living room zipping up their coats.

Alisa wrapped a scarf around her neck. "We're going to feed the cows, chickens and rabbits. Be right back."

"Don't forget to check for eggs." Danny was already unwrapping Steven's bandages so he didn't look up.

"I already thought of that." Dana held up the large plastic whipped cream container then followed Alisa out the door.

Nana walked in the room with a dish pan of warm water, a towel and a bottle of iodine. "How's that leg lookin'? Reckon we'll have to take it off?"

Danny looked at Steven who was not at all amused by the comment. He fought back a grin. "No, Nana. His leg actually looks like it's healing quite nicely."

Nana slid the ottoman over to sit on as she cleaned the wound. "Yeah, it does, doesn't it?"

Minutes later, Steven's leg had fresh bandages. "Thank you both. I really appreciate it."

"Glad to help." Nana collected the towels and iodine in the wash pan.

A scream shot out in the distance.

"That was Alisa!" Danny jumped up.

Steven pointed at his shotgun next to the couch. "Take my gun. It's loaded. Go!"

Danny grabbed the gun but didn't bother with a coat. He bolted out the door and toward the barn. Alisa, Dana and Rusty were running in his direction and they soon met up.

Danny put his hand on Alisa's shoulder. "What happened?"

"The cow, it's dead!" she replied.

Dana walked behind Danny and turned to face the barn. "It was awful. The cow's legs are gone."

Rusty barked as if to give his account of the scene as well.

Danny's first thought was that this was another dream. A cow with no legs, it sounded like some type of allegory, perhaps it spoke to the fact that no one had any mobility because most of the cars had been taken out by the EMP. But in every other vision, the second he realized he was dreaming, the nightmare would intensify. Not this time, he could tell this was really happening.

"Let's go check it out. I have to find out what's going on." Danny led the way with Rusty bravely at his side.

Alisa and Dana trailed behind reluctantly.

As he walked around the corner of the barn, he saw it. The poor beast lying there with no front nor hind legs. The back legs had been taken off at the hip joints. The front legs were removed just below the joints. The strangeness of the abhorrent image before him was certainly on par with the grisly appearances of his dreams of late, but he knew this was real life.

Danny looked, but saw no bullet wounds. "I doubt it would have died if it had been shot in one of the missing legs. But somehow, I suspect poachers are responsible for this."

"Could the bullet hole be on the other side?"

Dana asked.

"Maybe, but I would guess most guns large enough to take down a cow would go straight through." Danny walked around, inspecting the deceased bovine from every angle.

Alisa stepped a little closer. "What if it were a hollow point bullet? Didn't Nick tell us something about that preventing over penetration?"

Danny shrugged. "Perhaps."

"Or, it could have been a bow and arrow. That would explain why we never heard a gunshot." Dana stood back with her arms crossed and a look of disgust on her face.

"Maybe, but why would they have turned it over?" Alisa asked.

"The poachers could have shot the cow with an arrow, took out the arrow, cut the leg off the side they shot it, then flipped it to cut the legs off the other side. That would explain it." Dana walked up to stand right behind Alisa.

"That fits. Want to help me flip it over to find out if your theory holds?" Danny asked.

"No way!" Dana turned and began walking back to the house.

"I guess I better tell Nana and see what she wants to do about it." Danny left the butchered animal as he'd found it.

"Can we still eat it?" Alisa asked.

"I don't know, but I'm sure Nana will."

Danny and the others arrived back at the house. Nana met them on the porch. "What was all the fuss about?"

Danny motioned toward the barn. "Poachers

killed a cow last night. I guess they were in a rush. They took the legs and left the rest of the carcass."

"You best go fetch Rocky up the hill. Tell him what happened. He'll help you skin it and figure out what's worth savin'."

"Yes ma'am. I'm going to grab a coat." Danny wiped his feet on the welcome mat. "Do you girls want to come with me?"

"Sure." Dana said.

Alisa nodded.

Danny put his coat and toboggan on. He then led the girls across the bridge, which went over the creek, and up the hill toward Rocky's. Danny walked to the door and knocked.

"Who is it?" a woman's voice called from the other side.

"It's Danny Walker, ma'am. I'm looking for Rocky."

"Oh, Miss Jennie's grandson. Hold on one minute." The clamor of the deadlock being unbolted was followed by the sound of the door chain being removed.

A woman who had aged gracefully opened the door. She was clean, as was her house. She wasn't skinny, but neither was she overweight. She had the gently lined face of someone who had worked hard all of her life and enjoyed it. "Come in, I'm Pauline Cook, Rocky's wife. Sorry about the door, but you can't be too careful these days."

Danny introduced Alisa and Dana.

"Rocky is down at the barn. He should be back in half an hour or so. Will you have some coffee?"

"That would be great if it's not too much

trouble." Danny smiled.

Mrs. Cook led the way into the kitchen. "I just made it, no trouble at all. Miss Jennie told us about your dream. Otherwise we probably wouldn't have any coffee at all. So, I suppose we have you to thank for it."

Danny dropped his head. "I had very little to do with it. I'm afraid I can't take the credit."

She took three cups from the cabinet. "You were faithful to warn folks, so you did your part. A lot of people would have worried that people would think they were crazy and not have said anything."

Alisa joined the conversation. "Our pastor in Savannah told us the story of Jonah. He ended up doing what he was told to do anyway. It's easier to just follow God's instructions in the first place."

Mrs. Cook poured the coffee. "Yes, but most folks choose to do it the hard way. What did you want to talk to Rocky about? Is Miss Jennie doing alright?"

"Yes, she's fine. Someone killed one of our cows last night. Nana thought Rocky might be able to salvage some of the meat." Danny sipped his coffee.

"Oh dear, that's dreadful. I suppose we knew folks would start getting desperate sooner or later; I had hoped it would take longer than this." Mrs. Cook looked distressed. "It took you a while to get here from Savannah. Did you run into trouble?"

Danny nodded. "We did. It was a rough journey."

"But God brought us here alive," Dana added.

Rocky came in the back door wearing slightly soiled overalls and work boots. He removed his ball cap, revealing his short, thin, grey hair. "Hey, Danny! You made it. When did you get in?"

"The day before yesterday." Danny shook Rocky's hand, introduced him to the girls and explained why they were there.

Rocky rubbed his chin. "That's terrible. Let me get my things and we'll see what we can save. Normally, a cow should be gutted right after it's killed. Maybe since it's so cold outside, it will have bought us a little time. Otherwise, Rusty and my dogs are going to have the feast of a lifetime."

Danny and the girls thanked Mrs. Cook for the coffee and walked outside to wait for Rocky.

Rocky came from around back with a selection of knives, some buckets, trash bags, and a bone saw. "I've got a plastic barrel behind that shed. If two of you want to grab it, and bring it with us, I'd appreciate it. It's not heavy, just cumbersome for one person to carry."

"Want to give me a hand?" Danny looked at Alisa.

"Sure." She followed him to retrieve the 55-gallon barrel.

Dana walked next to Rusty as the group followed Rocky back to Nana's barn.

Rocky turned to look at Danny as they walked. "Do you know if Miss Jennie picked up the extra vinegar she was planning to buy?"

"Yep. She loves to make her pickles, relishes and ketchup. She bought several gallons."

"Good. We're going to need some of it. Since the cow went so long without being gutted or bled, it's going to have blood in the meat. Soaking it in vinegar and salt water will pull that out and stop any bacteria that might be setting up. Dana, do you think you could run back to the house, ask Miss Jennie for a gallon of vinegar and bring it over to the barn?"

"Sure. I'll meet you there." Dana sprinted ahead with Rusty tagging along behind her.

"Do you need salt?" Alisa asked.

"Nope. I've got a box in my bucket."

When they arrived at the carcass of the cow, Rocky separated his buckets and turned one upside down to use as a stool. He lifted the animal's head to look underneath. "Looks like they took it down with a bow and arrow." He made quick work of gutting the animal.

Alisa said, "I don't think I can watch this."

"Would you mind filling my other two buckets with water and pouring them into the barrel?" Rocky continued his task.

"Sure." Alisa grabbed the buckets.

Dana was approaching about that time with the vinegar.

Alisa caught her arm. "Come on, help me get water. Trust me, you don't want to see what's happening over here."

Dana didn't protest. She set the vinegar next to Danny, then took one of the buckets as Alisa handed it to her.

"Looks like you've done this before." Danny forced himself to watch in case he had to duplicate the job at a later date.

"I butcher two or three deer every year. This is my first cow, but the skill set seems to be transferring over pretty well."

"Do you think it's going to be edible?" Danny asked.

"Yep. It still looks fairly fresh. After a good soak in the salt and vinegar, it'll be just fine." Rocky went through the gut pile and pulled out the kidneys, heart, lungs and liver. "I'm going to use all of this for dog food, unless any of you eat liver. I know Miss Jennie doesn't care for it."

Danny felt queasy but forced himself to keep watching. "I think I speak for everyone; the dogs can have it."

"Once I'm done here, you should bury the head, the rest of this gut pile and any other waste left over. Otherwise, it will attract coyotes and they'll start associating your cattle with a free meal."

"Thanks. Any idea how we can keep the two legged coyotes away?"

Rocky looked up with a quick smile. "Yep, they're gonna be a problem, ain't they." He continued skinning the cow. "I suppose someone will have to watch them around the clock, like a shepherd. It's going to be a big task. Not a lot of work, but very time consuming."

"Any chance we could put our cows in with your cows and take turns watching them?" Danny asked.

"That's a good idea, but we wouldn't have enough grazing land on either property."

"Couldn't we herd them back and forth?"

"Yep. I suppose we could. Then we'd have to figure out how to know which cattle belong to who. I guess we could brand them. It wouldn't have to be a complicated brand, just something simple."

Rocky chuckled as he finished peeling back the skin off the cow. "You know, these idiots took the cheapest cuts and left the best parts. We've still got the ribeye, the filet, and the T-bone. But I guess they were in a hurry to not get caught.

"When the girls get back with the water, you can mix that box of salt in one of the buckets of water before you dump it into the barrel."

"Sure thing." Danny saw Alisa walking toward him with the water bucket, struggling to carry it, so he went to help her with it.

It took a couple of hours for Rocky to get the meat cut up into small enough pieces to fit into the barrel, but he eventually completed the mission. "We'll let that soak overnight and all day tomorrow. (The thermometer on my back porch said 34, so hopefully it won't freeze solid. If it does, we'll just cover it up and leave it till it warms up.) I'll herd my cattle down here before dark tonight. You watch em' tonight and I'll stand guard tomorrow night."

"Okay, sounds good. And thanks for all of your help." Danny waved as Rocky walked away with his tools and buckets. He then retrieved a spade shovel from the barn to begin digging a hole for the gut pile. As he started excavating the dirt next to the waste, he realized that surviving this new way of life was going to require more than simply learning to get by without a cell phone.

CHAPTER 5

Give us this day our daily bread. And forgive us our debts, as we forgive our debtors.

Matthew 5:11-12

Danny awoke to Alisa's gentle nudge and soft voice Saturday morning. "Danny, wake up. I brought you some coffee."

He opened his eyes and saw bales of hay. Danny quickly realized that he'd fallen asleep in the loft of the barn while on watch. His heart jumped. "Oh no! I fell asleep?"

"Relax. All the cows are fine."

"Yeah, but what if they weren't? It would be my fault!" Danny jumped up and looked out the ventilation window he'd been using for a gun port.

He surveyed the cattle to make sure there were no half-harvested carcasses.

"It was your first night and you were exhausted from skinning a cow, herding cattle, burying guts, and making crutches for Steven yesterday. You're being harder on yourself than anyone else would be. If anything would have happened, you would have woken up." She placed her hand on his shoulder and looked out over the cattle which were searching for grass beneath the melting snow.

Danny sighed. "I doubt someone shooting an arrow into a cow would have roused me. I was out cold."

"You'll be rested up and prepared next time. No harm, no foul. Drink your coffee." Alisa handed him an old metal thermos.

He removed the cap and took a small sip. "Thanks."

She hugged him tightly. "I missed you last night. All I could think about was you being out here in the barn, freezing."

"I missed you, too. I was bundled up. It wasn't that cold."

"Well, you'll be back in your own bed tonight."

"Hey!" Steven's voice came from outside.

Danny walked over to the loft door where the hay was loaded in via a pulley suspended from an overhanging bracket. He lifted the latch, opened the door, and looked out to see Steven standing with his homemade crutches. "Wow! Look at you. You're getting around pretty good."

Steven shielded his eyes from the light as he looked up. "Yeah, these crutches aren't bad considering you threw them together with saplings and duct tape. Nana said to get to the table. Breakfast is almost ready."

"Okay, we'll be right down." Danny closed the door, gathered the blanket he'd brought to keep warm, and slung the AK across his back. He and Alisa climbed down the ladder and made their way back to the house.

After breakfast, Rocky and Pauline Cook stopped by with two boxes of canning jars. The rest of the day would be spent processing the beef from the day before. The freezing temperatures were gone and it was unlikely that they would return any time soon. This meant that any meat they couldn't eat in the next few days would have to be made into jerky or canned.

The better cuts of meat were cubed up and canned. The scraps and the tougher cuts were ground into hamburger which was also canned.

"You make the cutest little butcher," Danny said to Alisa as she worked diligently to remove as much meat as possible from the rib bones.

"Stop it!" She blushed as she handed a pile of scraps to Dana who was operating the hand grinder.

Danny smiled and kissed her. "Having spent so much time in the restaurant business, I hate to see such beautiful cuts of T-bone and ribeye cubed up and canned for what amounts to stew meat."

She smiled. "Me, too, but I'm thankful that we have food, a means to preserve it, and that we're in a safe place with friends and family."

Danny nodded. He was happy that they were safe as well, but he wished his sister were there also. As each day passed without Cami and Nick showing up, he couldn't help but think that the chances of them making it home grew slimmer and slimmer.

Nana and Pauline ran the canning operations, delegating various tasks to the rest of the group. Additionally, Nana prepared the tenderloin along with instant mashed potatoes for the day's lunch. Except for breaks to eat or rest for a few minutes, the task of preserving the meat occupied the entire day.

The next morning was Sunday, and as Nana had anticipated, there was a large turnout and had to be moved to the open side of the barn. Pauline Cook was the first to arrive. Rocky didn't come as he'd been up all night standing guard over the cattle.

Catfish pulled up in one of the few working vehicles around and was dressed as though he was accustomed to attending church in a barn.

Next to show up was the Reese family -- Korey, Tracey, and their three children; Jason, who was ten, Kalie, seven, and Emma, three.

Danny, Dana, and Alisa carried the lawn furniture down to the barn and found whatever they could to provide seating. Hay bales made up the majority of the seating and proved to be quite comfortable.

The Castells came last. Nana introduced everyone: JC and Melissa and the two children who were with them; Jack, aged sixteen; and Annie, who was two.

Danny shook JC's hand. "Nice to meet you."

JC looked like a South Carolina native. He wore cowboy boots, jeans, a big belt buckle, and a John

Deere hat, but when he spoke with a thick New York accent, it was quite obvious that he had not grown up around these parts. "Yeah, you too."

Danny's surprise must have been obvious to Nana, who said, "He don't look it, but he's a Yankee. If you don't understand him, get Lisa to translate for ya."

"I think I can manage, Nana," Danny chuckled. "So, how long have you been in South Carolina?"

"Two years. I retired from the NYPD after twenty years on the job. I had to get my wife and kids out of there; place is turnin' into a zoo."

"You look like you've assimilated to the new environment fairly well." Danny didn't quite know what to say, and he hoped that didn't sound offensive.

JC didn't seem to take it wrong. He laughed. "Yeah, I guess I've really embraced it. I was ready to leave that place behind."

"I'm sure you're happy to have got out of there before the lights went out. You must have retired young."

"If you make it twenty years doing what I did, you cash in your chips and get out of the casino. Know what I mean? And I ain't that young anymore neither. I've got a son about your age."

"Oh?"

"Yeah, Chris. He's in the Air Force. Been in about a year. I pray every morning and every night that God will bring him home safe. He's a smart kid, top of his class in everything he's done in the military. If anyone can make it home, he will."

"Sorry to hear that. I'm sure it's different when

it's your kid, but I know the feeling. My sister, Cami, she's still out there too."

"Yeah, I stopped by to check on Miss Jennie before you got here. She told me about the both of you. I'm glad you made it. She says Cami's husband is a pretty resourceful guy. I think they'll make it."

Danny nodded. "I'm praying they do."

"Y'all need to find a seat. We're a-fixin' to start this meetin'." Nana spoke loud enough for everyone to hear. "Catfish is goin' to play the French harp. Everybody ought to know these songs, but I wrote the words out on three pieces of paper, just in case. If there's more than three of ya that don't know the words, why you'll just have to share."

Danny held one of the handwritten song sheets with Alisa on one side and Dana on the other, looking on. He looked around at the others, who were all struggling to see one of the few pieces of paper containing the lyrics. As was customary, Nana's assessment of the way things should be was greatly divergent from reality.

Steven sat on top of a bale of hay in front of everyone else as he was going to be teaching. Catfish took a harmonica out of the top pocket of his bib overalls and blew on it a few times as if he were warming up.

Alisa whispered to Danny, "Is that what she calls a French harp? I was expecting some elaborate instrument."

"Elaborate instrument? This is Catfish we're talking about."

She tittered. "Point taken."

Catfish found a melody and Nana began singing *Bringing in the Sheaves*.

It took a few moments for everyone to catch on, but soon the barn was filled with the voices of the small group in joyful worship. Next, they sang *All Creatures of Our God and King*, and finally, *Amazing Grace*.

Afterwards, Steven said a short prayer, thanking God for his blessings and provision and asking him to bring everyone else home. He then looked up and opened his Bible. "Nana asked me to prepare a Bible study for this morning. I didn't feel worthy of the task, but after some reading and prayer, I accepted the offer.

"Paul says in I Corinthians 15, for I am the least of the apostles, that am not meet to be called an apostle, because I persecuted the church of God. But by the grace of God I am what I am.

"Paul is abundantly aware of his shortcomings. And he could have used them to hide behind rather than fulfill his calling and preach the Gospel, but he didn't. He didn't find his qualifications to teach in his own righteousness; rather he found it in the grace of God. Some of you, especially Dana, Alisa, and Danny, have known me long enough to see me really mess up. And the rest of you who will hopefully get to know me will also see me drop the ball from time to time. So before I even start, let me ask for your forgiveness if I've wronged any of you and ask for mercy if I wrong you in the future."

Steven paused for a moment and took a deep breath. "Please bear with me while I get a little more specific. Dana, I've been judgmental, dismissive, and downright mean to you over the past week or so. And during the most traumatic period of US history, at a time when you most needed a friend to be gentle, caring, and kind. I'm very sorry. I'm not there yet and I need grace, but I am committed to trying.

"And it is with my own shortcomings in mind and the regret for having acted in such an obnoxious manner that I composed today's Bible study. If everyone will please turn to Ephesians 4:32."

Danny found the verse in his own Bible and then helped Dana as she struggled to locate the scripture in the Bible Nana had given her.

"Thanks," she whispered. Obviously touched by Steven's public apology, Dana's eyes were filled with tears.

Steven read the passage. "And be ye kind one to another, tenderhearted, forgiving one another, even as God for Christ's sake hath forgiven you.

"It's a little tough to ask all of you to adhere to this verse when I've fallen so miserably short myself, but like I said, I'm committed to doing better.

"In the coming days and weeks, times are going to get tough. Some of us are going to be in tight quarters. There's going to be a lot of tasks that we're not used to doing. We're going to be tired, cranky, and edgy. I think it would serve us all well to really dedicate ourselves to living according to this verse. A little kindness, forgiveness, and compassion will go a long way in making the end of the world as we know it a little easier to survive.

"And then there'll be times where the other

person is absolutely wrong. After all, we are all selfish by nature and prone to hurting others. Expect that to come out of the people around you, especially considering the added stress and close proximity to each other. In those times, even when they don't deserve forgiveness, remember the second half of today's verse. Forgiving one another, even as God for Christ's sake hath forgiven you.

"I know it's hard. Some may say it's downright impossible, but that's the standard that has been set by our King, and while we'll never be perfect, with his help, we can grow in grace."

Steven bowed his head and said a prayer to dismiss the service. Nana stood to make an announcement before anyone left. "I'm making fresh steaks at the house. We've got plenty for everybody. It might be a while before we kill another beef, so come on over and eat."

JC walked up to Danny as they left the barn. "You guys already slaughtering your cattle?"

"We didn't exactly have a say in the matter." Danny filled him in on what had happened.

"Wow. They didn't waste any time." JC rubbed his beard.

Danny continued to tell JC of how he and Rocky were pooling their herds.

JC nodded. "That's smart. I've got thirty head of cattle myself. My place is diagonally behind the Cooks' farm. I'd be willing to work with you guys if you want. It would make it easier for everybody by having me and my youngest son, Jack, worked into the security rotation."

"That sounds great. I'm sure Rocky would be

more than happy to have you on board."

"Okay then. We'll figure out a way to get them all marked or branded over lunch and start work on it tomorrow. I have a feeling we'll be working together a lot in the future. I doubt cattle rustlers will prove to be the worst we'll see out of all this."

Danny glanced at JC as they walked toward the house. "Sounds like you've thought about this."

"I've seen the darkest side of humanity and have a pretty good idea how deep the depravity can plummet. Part of what motivated me to bring my family down here from New York was an expectation of the economic collapse. The numbers just didn't add up. I can't believe it took so long for the financial system to fall apart. I have to hand it the bankers. They held it together with smoke and mirrors for an incredible amount of time. The financial collapse should have happened years ago. We'd been putting things away for the inevitable monetary disaster for a while.

"Just from reading up on preparedness for the economic turmoil, I knew what an EMP was and knew the potential devastation. I hoped it would never come to this. But, now it's here. I guess we're better prepared than most, but there's always other things you wished you'd done or bought."

Danny nodded. "But if you've been prepping for years, you must be in pretty good shape."

JC looked around as if he wanted to see who else could hear their conversation. "Better shape than most, I guess. I've been talking to the Bible study group that meets at Miss Jennie's for the past year or so about the risks to the economic system and the need to prepare. At first, they were a little reluctant, but as they saw things happening that I'd told them about, they took a little more interest.

"Then, Miss Jennie told the group, Rocky, Catfish, and the Reese family, about your dreams. That really kicked them into high gear. I'd say we have about as good a chance of survival as anyone, but we'll have to work together. Like I said, people can get pretty nasty."

Danny followed JC's eyes toward the road. It was the first time he'd thought about the entire rest of the world in a *them-and-us* paradigm. "Do you think we need a security force, besides watching the cows?"

"Yeah, and the sooner the better. But everyone has to understand the need or they won't be motivated to put the time and effort into training and working the shifts. Unfortunately, everyone recognizes the need after something bad happens. Like your cow for example; now you know someone has to fill the role of watchman. Before, it would have seemed like a waste of time."

Danny knew he was right. "Let me know when you're ready. I'll train or do whatever needs to be done."

"Okay. Let me see where everybody else is at and who else is ready to start training. Even if it's just you and Jack, we'll train up. Then you two can help me bring everyone else up to speed when the Boogie Man comes and wakes the rest of them up."

A chill shot down Danny's spine. "Who's the Boogie Man?"

"I wish I knew." JC snorted and looked back out

toward the road. "But he's out there, I guarantee it."

Danny, Alisa, and Dana chipped in to help Nana prepare and serve lunch. Afterwards, Danny made a point of getting to know the rest of JC's family as well as the Reese family.

CHAPTER 6

Say to them that are of a fearful heart, Be strong, fear not: behold, your God will come with vengeance, even God with a recompence; he will come and save you.

Isaiah 35:4

The days passed and Daniel began to find a rhythm in the day-to-day tasks that had to be done in order to keep the farm operating efficiently.

The weekly church service in the barn was quickly becoming the hub of community for the families who lived on the surrounding farms.

Steven had delivered the message every Sunday since they'd arrived. His leg was healing nicely. He'd been walking without his crutches but was still taking it easy. During his period of impairment,

Steven had taken Danny's shifts watching over the cattle at night. It gave Steven something productive to do while he was on the mend, and it allowed Danny to pull some of Steven's weight with gardening, fetching water, and cutting firewood. Due to the heavy workload, Danny hadn't gotten around to training with JC as much as he'd planned.

March arrived and the seedlings that Danny and the others had started indoors were moved outside. They used a wide array of household items as seed-starting containers. Pudding cups, yogurt containers, and egg cartons were among the most commonly used articles.

Danny headed out to the garden plot by himself early Thursday morning after breakfast.

Dana was tending to the chickens and the rabbits as usual. Alisa had gone to toss some hay from the loft down to the cattle and would be meeting up with Danny to help him in the garden. The grass was beginning to grow, but with three herds combined, they wouldn't leave anything to grow back if their diet wasn't augmented with a bit of hay. All of the cattle would be moved to Rocky's in April, and JC's grazing land would be used to grow hay for the following winter. Letting the grass grow long and tall would make it easier to cut with scythes and maneuver with pitchforks.

Danny sighed as he looked out toward the road. He diligently dug a hole and planted another one of the small tomato plants. He hoped against hope that he'd see Nick and Cami walking down the gravel path to the house.

He mumbled to himself, "Today's the fourteenth.

It's been one month exactly, since the EMP. Every day that passes reduces the chance that I'll ever see my sister again." The worry of whether Cami was alive or dead ate at Danny's soul. It had grown from a slight feeling of uneasiness when he'd arrived at Nana's three weeks earlier to a nagging sense of dread that hung over him like a cloud of darkness.

Danny looked up. His eyes scanned the clouds as if he were looking for God. Despite reading his Bible and praying every day, he simply didn't feel like God was around. "I know I should have faith, but the reality is that she may never make it back. Lord, if you're listening, please bring my sister home."

Danny continued to plant seedling after seedling. He was glad he had something to keep his hands and his mind occupied. Otherwise, the unknown may have driven him mad. Once all of the tomato plants were in the ground, Danny stood to brush the dirt off his jeans. He looked across the field between the barn and himself, but didn't see Alisa. "She's probably in the house yakking with Nana and Dana. I'll get the green bean seeds and get her to help me with those."

Normally, Nana would hold back half of her seeds in case any particular crop had a bad year. This time, they were using three-quarters of all the seeds so they could build up a larger seed bank for the coming years (and be sure to have enough canned vegetables to get them through the winter.)

They were very fortunate to be in a part of the country that had a robust growing season. With Nana's experience, they'd have fresh seasonal vegetables of some sort from late March until early December. Even now, the mixed field greens were coming in; however, they'd give them another week so the leaves could fully mature.

Danny arrived at the house and kicked the dirt off his shoes before walking into the closed-in back porch. "Hey, Nana. Is Alisa in the house?"

"I thought she was out in the garden with you." Nana was starting lunch already.

Danny shrugged. "She was supposed to be."

Dana came into the kitchen. "Do you guys need some help in the garden? I'm finished cleaning out the coops and feeding the chickens and rabbits."

"You haven't seen Alisa?" Danny asked.

"Not since breakfast. She's not in the garden?" Dana looked more curious than concerned.

"She might've fallen! You best get on down to the barn." Nana's voice was imperative.

Danny turned around and briskly began walking toward the barn.

"I'll come with you." Dana followed close behind.

He reached the barn and found the door hanging open. "Alisa!"

"Alisa, hey, are you all right?" Dana walked in and began looking around.

"Alisa, where are you?" Danny walked to the ladder, which led to the loft. He found a piece of paper stuck to one of the rungs with a steak knife. "Oh no!"

Dana walked over. "What's that?"

Danny pulled the knife and unfolded the paper. His heart sank to his stomach. "Ransom note."

"Ahhgh! No!" Dana screamed and covered her mouth.

Danny's voice cracked, and his mouth went dry as he began reading. "If you want to see the girl alive, we need food, and lots of it."

His knees shook, and his head began to swim. He knew he was going to pass out if he didn't get a hold of himself. He sat down on the dirt floor of the barn and let the note lie at his side while he focused on his breathing.

Dana was crying. "What else, Danny? What else does it say?"

He took a deep breath and let it out slowly. His hands were shaking so badly the paper rattled as he tried to read. "We will be back tonight. Make sure there is no one guarding the cattle. Load dry goods and ammunition on the backs of two cows and have rope tied around their necks. If you do it right, we'll bring the girl back tonight. Don't be stingy! We want coffee, flour, sugar, canned goods, and shotgun ammo."

Despair overtook Danny, and he let his hand fall to the ground as he stared at the ladder.

Dana sniffed in between sobs. "Danny, what are we going to do?"

"Exactly what they want. We'll give them everything we have if that's what it takes to get her back."

"Okay. Should we go tell Nana?"

Danny took another deep breath and let it out slowly. "Yeah."

As they walked back to the house, Danny's panic began to morph into worry. What if they were treating her badly? What if they killed her? Then the worry became anger. He thought about who could have done such a thing to the person he loved more than anyone else in the world. Then the anger melted back into panic, then sorrow. His mind and his heart were torn to pieces. This was more than he could bear.

Dana went in first. "Nana, someone took Alisa!"

"What?" She turned the stove off and looked at the note Danny handed to her.

"Lord Jesus! Please, protect that little girl, Lord, help!" Nana covered her mouth as she read the paper. "Daniel, you run and get JC. Make sure he knows it's you comin' or he's liable to shoot you. Show him this." She handed the paper back to Danny.

He crumpled it and stuffed it into his pants pocket as he ran out the door.

"I'll come too." Dana followed Danny again.

The two of them ran full speed down the hill to the bridge that crossed the creek. They moved quickly back through the woods and over the fence that separated Nana's farm from Rocky Cooper's place. JC's farm was diagonally behind Rocky's so they had to maintain the pace across the Coopers' farm and all the way across JC's property. It took nearly fifteen minutes to reach JC's house.

Jack was walking around the yard with an AR-15 when they arrived. "Hey, Danny. What's up?"

"Where's your dad? Someone grabbed Alisa!" Danny fought to catch his breath.

"Dad!" Jack called out and began walking to the house.

Dana was also winded. "What was Jack doing in the yard with a gun?''

"Standing guard. JC said he wasn't going to wait for something bad to happen before he stepped up his security. I guess I should have done the same thing."

JC came running out of the house, buckling his gun belt and fastening the leg rig around his thigh. "What happened?"

Danny gave him a quick analysis of the situation.

"Got the note with you?" JC didn't look the least bit shaken. It was almost as if he'd expected such news.

Danny pulled the wadded note from his pocket.

JC took the glasses from his shirt pocket and began reading. "See what I mean about the Boogie Man?"

"You were right. We should have been more proactive." Danny hated that he could have prevented this situation.

JC looked up over the top of his glasses at Danny. He seemed to know the pain Danny was in. "I didn't mean it like that. I used to see this stuff all the time." He continued reading the note. "If you're not familiar with it, it's hard to believe people can be this nasty."

Danny waited for him to finish reading. "What do you think?"

"I think she got kidnapped." He handed the note back to Danny.

"What are they going to do? Will they give her back if we give them what they want?"

JC looked toward the base of the tree in front of

him. "I don't know, Danny. Maybe they will, maybe they won't. You pretty much have to go along with them. It's the only shot you have."

"Can you help me?"

JC looked over at Jack. "Keep an eye on things here. Tell Melissa and Annie to stay in the house. I'm gonna take a walk over to Miss Jennie's."

"10-4." Jack seemed to understand the gravity of the situation.

JC quickly led the way. "Tell me everything that happened today. Start with, you got up, ate breakfast, whatever. Tell me every detail that you can think of."

Danny did so. He told JC all the details that he could remember about the day.

They soon arrived at the barn where Danny showed JC the spot where he'd found the note and the knife.

JC looked around. "And it was becoming a habit? Alisa coming down here to feed the cows by herself?"

"Yeah, we have so many chores. Everyone has to be doing something different." Danny waited for JC to speak.

JC took his time looking around the barn, observing the distance to the house, to the road, to the tree line. "I'd say these guys are ex-military. They've probably had the farm under observation for a while. They seem to know what types of supplies you have. They knew when the cattle were being guarded, when they weren't, when Alisa would be alone. They watched your patterns and exploited them."

"So the fact that they're ex-military, is that bad?" Danny stuck his hands in his pockets.

JC raised his eyebrows. "Depends on how you look at it. On one side, if they know what they're doing, it will be hard to get the drop on them. On the other side, if they're all ex-military, or even just the top guy, they might have a higher level of honor about how they treat Alisa while she's a prisoner. Even if they've gotten desperate enough to pull off something like this, most guys who were in the service wouldn't rape or stand by while anyone else mistreats a girl. I don't want to scare you, but I'm sure I'm not saying anything that hasn't already crossed your mind."

Danny had tried to avoid thinking about that subject, but he was inevitably going to have to deal with it. "Yeah. Well, I pray they're not complete scumbags."

Dana looked away in horror. She said nothing as she crossed her arms and shivered.

"Have you thought about how you're going to get two cows to let you tie a rope on their necks or load stuff on their backs?" JC handed the note back to Danny.

"Pop used to have a few dairy cows. I could put feed in two of the milking bays. Each of the bays has a clamp that locks the cow's head in place while someone milks them. I could at least get a rope around their neck. I don't think any cow is going to let you load saddlebags on their back if they haven't been broken."

"Yeah, me neither. Obviously, these clowns don't know too much about cattle," JC snorted. "We could use that to our advantage."

"How?"

"Give these guys everything they've asked for. Load 'em up with tons of heavy supplies, then let them deal with getting it back to their base of operations. If they actually bring Alisa back, somebody could tail them back, since they'll be easy to follow with all of that weight. Then we can see what size force we are dealing with, draw up a plan, and hit them at a later date.

"If they are messing with us and don't bring Alisa back, we can take them while they are bumbling around with the loot and the cows."

Danny was already starting to breathe a little easier. Just having someone who could even think through this situation gave him hope. "And you think we could take them?"

"If they don't bring her back, we've gotta try."

"How many guys do you think it is?"

"I don't have a clue. They're asking for two cows with ropes, so you might have two guys planning to lead the cattle back plus a security team. Maybe two guys working security for the two leading the cattle back, and two more working overwatch security from a distance. But it could be way more. I'm just guessing here." JC shook his head.

"Do you have a plan? What can we do?"

JC drug his foot through the dirt on the barn floor. "How good of a shot is your buddy, Steven?"

"I don't know. He hasn't really trained a lot."

"Yeah. Nobody has. This is not the best-case scenario. Rocky can shoot distance. He's been hunting these woods since he was a kid. So has Catfish. Korey Reese looks like he could shoot and move. That leaves me, you, Korey . . ." JC paused. He obviously didn't want to finish his sentence. "And Jack for the fire team. We need Steven, but he's got that bum leg. He won't be able to move fast if we get in trouble."

"I'll fight. I'll do whatever I can." Dana had quit crying. Now she looked mad.

JC sighed. "You know how to shoot a shotgun?"

"Yes." She looked determined to do her part.

"We might have to use you. We need about four times the amount of people we have to even consider an operation like this." JC bent down and began making marks in the dirt floor with a stick.

"We'll give them a bunch of cumbersome stuff so they have to figure out how they're going to carry it back. We'll put Rocky and Catfish up along these two hedgerows looking down on the barn. Steven will be up in this clump of trees, a little closer so he won't have such a long shot. If they don't bring Alisa, the fire team will walk in from the back woods and try to locate and capture their overwatch support. Then, we'll capture the people planning to make off with the goods."

"Then what?" Dana asked.

"Then we'll make them talk. Make them tell us where Alisa is."

"What if they won't tell us?" Danny asked.

JC didn't flinch. "If I can catch two of 'em alive, one of them will tell me everything I want to know."

Danny furrowed his brow. He didn't know

exactly what JC meant, and he didn't want any clarification.

JC stood up. "For now, we need to get everybody rounded up. Dana, you go tell Nana what we're doing. Explain that everyone is going to need to eat. Next, wake up Steven and tell him what's going on. Then run over to Rocky's and have him go get Korey. Tell everyone it's urgent and to meet up at Nana's as quick as possible, and tell them to bring guns."

JC looked at Danny. "Where's your gun?"

"I don't have it."

JC shook his head. "Never leave the house without it again. Run and get it. Meet me back here. We need to sweep the property and make sure they don't have somebody watching us right now."

"Okay." Danny ran to the house, grabbed his AK, two extra magazines, and came right back.

JC was waiting when Danny arrived. "Let me see your rifle."

Danny handed it to him. JC pulled the ejection port lever just enough to verify that there was a shell in the chamber. JC switched off the safety and handed it back to Danny. "You got extra magazines?"

"Two, in my jacket pocket."

"Let me see you do a magazine change."

Danny fumbled to hold the rifle in one hand and retrieve one of his other magazines from his jacket pocket. It took him nearly twenty seconds to switch out the magazine.

JC shook his head. "What if someone were shooting at you while you had to do all of that? Let me see your rifle again."

Danny handed the rifle back to JC.

JC held out his other hand. "And let me see one of those extra magazines."

Danny complied.

JC stuck the magazine in his back pocket. "I've got an extra vest for you at the house. Practice with it before we go out tonight. For now, if you have to change magazines, keep your mag in your back left pocket. Hold your rifle up against your chest like this with your right hand wrapped around the trigger guard and hit the release lever. Keep your right hand like this while you extract the spent mag with your left. Drop your spent mag in your jacket and quickly grab the other. Make sure the bullets are facing out so it will naturally go directly in the mag well."

JC demonstrated the instructions then handed it to Danny. "You try."

Danny took the weapon and performed the exercise in about five seconds. "That's much faster. Thanks."

"Improvement is all we're looking for. Let's roll out. Stay about ten feet behind me so they can't kill us both with one bullet. If you see something, click your teeth twice. It sounds like a woodchuck."

Danny sucked his teeth in an attempt to make the desired sound effect. "That doesn't sound like a woodchuck."

"Yeah, not when you do it. But still, it blends in better with nature than yelling '*Hey, buddy*.'" JC drew his pistol and led the way.

They worked their way around the perimeter of

the fence that ran along the road, then circled around the back side of the property and into the woods. They walked cautiously, picking a methodical path through each section of forest.

Once they'd covered all the areas from where they could be watched, JC motioned for Danny to come up closer to him. "What does your brother in-law have in that RV?"

"I don't know. He has a really good lock on it."

"Yeah, I saw that. Think he has any hardware in there? I'm sure if he knew our circumstances, he wouldn't mind us getting into it."

Danny shrugged. "If we do get into it, we wouldn't be able to lock it back. Then it would be wide open for looters."

JC nodded. "You're right. We've probably got most everything we need for this in the way of guns. Me and Jack both have ARs. You've got an AK. Everybody has shotguns, and we've got plenty of deer rifles for our long-distance shooters. I've got two night vision scopes. It would be nice to have a few more of those. Do you remember Nick saying anything about having night vision?"

"No. Wow! That's awesome that you have some." Danny followed JC as they continued back toward his house.

"Yeah, they're Gen 1, which isn't the best, but in the land of the blind, the one-eyed man is king. And that's exactly what working at night is, the land of the blind. If we have night vision and they don't, we'll eat them alive."

Danny was starting to feel better about the situation. "If we had silencers, we'd be like ninjas."

"I thought of that after your Nana told me about your dreams. I was going to splurge and get one, but there was no way I could get through all of the paperwork in time. We do have bows, and Jack has a .357 Benjamin air rifle. Those weapons systems might work if we can locate and sneak up on the overwatch team."

Danny glanced over at JC. "An air rifle? That will kill someone."

"A head shot with a .357 Benjamin will. People hunt deer, hogs, coyotes, you name it, with that gun." JC held down the top wire of the fence for Danny as they crossed over onto his property.

Danny's mind was racing, thinking about the fight that was coming in a few short hours. He had to focus on the task at hand, gearing up, training on the fly, and being mentally ready for whatever was ahead. As stressful as it was, the intensity of the circumstances was a welcome distraction from worrying about his young wife. Each time he caught himself drifting into the territory of speculating on her condition or how she was being treated, he forced himself to refocus on the mission before him.

When they arrived back at JC's house, he called out to his son. "Jack."

"What's up?" Jack hurried off of the porch.

JC shook his head. "It ain't good. They grabbed Alisa. We're going to try to get her back. Hopefully, they'll play nice and it will be an easy exchange, but we can't count on that. We gotta be ready for anything. Gear up. We've got a bunch of guys to get trained in the next couple hours."

Jack snorted. "Two hours? You can't train

anybody in two hours."

"I know, but we're gonna do it anyway." JC headed toward the house. "Danny, come on in here. Let's get you in a good vest to carry your magazines. I'm going to have Melissa and Annie head on over to Nana's also. If things get rough, it would be best to have all the ladies in one place. Melissa can hold her own with a gun, so she can defend the house as long as Nana or Rocky's wife can watch Annie."

JC led Danny to his bedroom and went into his walk-in closet. He came back out carrying an olive drab tactical vest. "See how this works for you."

"Thanks." Danny put on the vest and zipped it up. He placed his two spare magazines in the pouches.

"How are you feeling?"

"I'm worried. I just can't let myself start thinking about what they're doing to her."

JC looked at the floor. "Yeah. I'm sorry for your situation. What I really meant was, how are you feeling about a potential gunfight?"

"I don't know. I'll just do what I have to do, I guess. I felt sort of sick after I shot those people when we first left Savannah. And pretty much the same way when I had to kill that kid's dad, maybe a little worse because of the kid."

JC looked back up at Danny. "You've been through it. It ain't ever fun, but at least you know you ain't gonna freeze up. That's all I need to know. I wouldn't wish that sick feeling on anybody, but I do wish everybody else on our team had been tested in the fire, so we'd know for sure that they're good when it comes to pulling the trigger."

Jack walked into the room. He had a similar green tactical vest with a Glock in the pistol holster and several magazines for his AR-15. "Ready."

JC looked up at his son and sighed. Danny could see the tears welling up in his eyes. He felt bad for JC. His oldest son, like Cami, was still out there, somewhere. Now, he had to deal with putting his youngest son into harm's way. Danny watched as the man took hold of his emotions and pushed back the tears.

JC nodded and smiled at Jack. "Good. Grab your bow and your Benjamin. We need to have plenty of options."

"Okay, be right back." Jack leaned his rifle against the door jam and left to retrieve the other items.

JC went back in the closet and retrieved his vest, magazines, rifle, and two small cases. He opened one of the cases and took out the night vision scope. He removed the reflex sight from his AR-15, and replaced it with the scope. He placed a forty-five-degree offset rail on the back of the rifle and placed the reflex sight on that. Next, he repeated the process for Jack's rifle. "We won't be able to sight these scopes in until the sun goes down."

"Won't they hear us shooting when you sight them in?"

"No, I have a chamber boresighter. It's the same size as a 5.56 round. Basically, a laser pointer that shows you right where the round will go."

"And the EMP didn't affect it?"

"No circuitry in it. It's just a flashlight."

"And what about your night vision?"

"I don't know if they're not susceptible to EMP or if the gun safe protected it, but they both still work."

"That's all that matters." Danny watched as JC double-checked all the changes he'd made to the configuration of the rifles.

"I've got everything, Dad." Jack stood at the door with his bow and the Benjamin rifle.

"Wow. That's a cool-looking air gun." Danny inspected the rifle.

"It's called a bullpup. Here, take a look." Jack handed him the weapon.

"Thanks, I can carry it back to Nana's if you like. It looks like you've got your hands full."

Jack accepted his offer. "That would be great."

The three men packed up all of their gear, waited for Melissa and Annie to get ready, then the group headed back to Nana's to meet up with the rest of the posse.

When Danny and JC's family made it back to Nana's, Catfish had just arrived. "Sorry to hear about Alisa, but we'll get her back." His sympathy for Danny showed through his unkempt beard and bushy eyebrows.

Danny forced a smile. "Thanks for coming. I appreciate your help."

Steven was sitting on the couch and loading the shotgun with buckshot. "JC, do you have a plan?"

"I'm working on one. As soon as everybody shows up, I'll go over it."

Dana had returned from Rocky's and was sitting

next to Steven. "I'm still on the team, right?"

"Yeah. We need everyone who's willing. But when it comes time to pull the trigger, you can't hesitate. You'll get yourself and everybody else killed if you do. If you think you're going to have a problem with it, it's much better to tell me now. No one will think any less of you. Catfish, Steven, that goes for you guys, too."

Catfish scowled. "Them filthy vermin, grabbin' that little girl. Boy howdy, I'd skin 'em all alive. They'll be fortunate if all I do is shoot 'em!"

Nana was cooking a large pot of chili for everyone. "Hush up talkin' like that, you old coot! Y'all get in here and get cha somethin' ta eat."

"I ain't just talkin', Miss Jennie. I'll send ever one of 'em straight to hell. Let the devil contend with 'em." Catfish made no argument about being told to eat as he made his way to the dining room table.

JC looked at Steven as the rest of the group meandered toward the table. "What about you? Think you can do it when the time comes?"

Steven pursed his lips. "Yeah. Getting shot sort of changed the way I feel about people pointing guns at me or the people I care about."

Dana did not look happy about any of this business. She looked at JC. "I can do it . . . if I have to. Alisa saved my life by getting me out of Savannah. I owe it to her to do whatever I can to save her life. I'll do what you tell me. Please, just help us get her back."

"I'll do my best." JC put his hand on her shoulder.

Rocky, Pauline, and the Reese family came in shortly after the others had begun eating.

Danny stood up to give his seat to Pauline. "I can eat chili standing up. You sit here."

JC, Jack, and Catfish all stood to offer their seats to the ladies as well.

Steven started to get up, but Danny stopped him. "There's plenty of chairs. You stay seated. Save your leg for tonight."

"Okay." Steven nodded.

Everyone talked about how horrible it was that Alisa had been taken. Danny tried to block the conversation out. It was all he could do to eat. His stomach was queasy and shaky, and he had no appetite whatsoever, but he knew he needed his strength, so he forced himself to finish the bowl of chili.

Once they'd finished eating, JC addressed the ladies and the children. "Melissa is your tactical commander for the house. It's very important that everyone follows her directions tonight. If you hear gunfire, stay low to the ground and away from windows. Pauline, you, Tracey, and Nana all know how to handle a weapon, so you'll be Melissa's backup. She knows how to make sure none of you get caught in a crossfire and end up shooting each other, so you have to follow her lead."

JC tussled the hair of ten-year-old Jason Reese. "Think you can handle the kids tonight?"

Jason looked offended. "I can shoot. Let one of these women watch the children."

It was obvious that the response had caught JC off guard as he fought back a laugh. JC turned to

Korey.

Korey gave a reluctant nod. "He's pretty good with a .22."

"Did you bring it?" JC asked.

"Yep," Korey replied.

JC looked back at Jason. "Then how about you stand guard with your .22, in the room with the kids?"

Jason stood tall and proud. "I'll protect them."

Seven-year-old Kalie Reese stood next to her older brother. "I can watch Emma, and Annie, too, if you want. I watch Emma all the time at our house."

"That will be fine. Thank you for your help." JC bit his lip. "Miss Jennie, we're going into a less-than-ideal situation. I'm going to do everything I can to go over the basics and get everyone up to speed for this mission. But, there's a limit to what we can accomplish with the amount of time we have to work with. Besides that, I'm just a man. If we're going to bring Alisa home safely, we're going to need some help from the Lord. Would you be in charge of a prayer vigil? If you could dedicate a room to prayer and have someone manning that position constantly until we return, I'm sure God will honor your petitions."

"We'll be intercedin' for y'all. Don't you worry about that," Nana said.

"Thanks. And Kalie, I need you and Jason to take care of Rusty. Bring him in the house and keep him inside until we get back. If he starts barking at the bad guys, it will give away our position. Besides that, he'll add an extra layer of protection for the house." JC grabbed his rifle and the duffel bag he'd brought with him and stood by the door. "Gentlemen."

"Ahem." Dana cleared her throat.

"And Dana," JC said, "let's head on down to the barn. We've got a few things to go over."

Once at the barn, JC took out a small box of plastic army men.

"Are those mine?" Jack inquired.

"Yeah, you haven't touched them since you were ten. Video games and cell phones took all of your attention." JC separated out the taupe-colored soldiers from the green ones.

"Cell phones and video games are a thing of the past," Jack said.

JC began arranging them. "What, do you want 'em back?"

"I don't know. I might." Jack seemed to be toying with JC more than anything.

"Ahhy." JC shook his head. "This box is the barn, where we are now. Here's the road to the right, and the woods behind us.

"The enemy has to be coming in through the pasture. This hill is giving them cover for their approach. I'd guess they're taking the road in from Anderson and cutting across the field next to the school. Danny and I walked the perimeter. We didn't see any cut wire on the fence separating the Walker place and that back pasture, but if I was running their op, I wouldn't cut the fence until I had to, for the cattle.

"Rocky, you'll be up here in this hedgerow along the road. You should be able to spot them coming over the hill. Just sit back and wait until the fireworks start. Hopefully, they'll bring Alisa, take the goods, and leave in peace.

"If so, Danny and I will follow them back to their AO and recon the location. Then, we'll decide if we have the strength to go take our stuff back.

"If they don't bring her back, Rocky, you'll have to cut down anyone trying to leave the property. If anyone gets away and gets back to their operating base to tell them what's going on, they'll probably kill Alisa."

Rocky crossed his arms. "What if it's a kid that they're using for a runner? What do we do then?"

JC shrugged. "Listen, folks, we are all risking our lives to try to get Alisa back. We have to decide if we're willing to do whatever it takes to get her back or not."

Rocky shook his head. "I don't mind dying, but I don't want to be in the position to have to shoot some kid that's running away."

Catfish spoke up. "Put me up on that hill, boss."

JC nodded. "Rocky, we'll move you down to the cover position, overlooking the ambush. Our genius assailants have requested lots of heavy items and two cows that they'll have to figure out how to retreat with. We plan on giving them the two orneriest cows in the herd and plenty of rope to hang themselves with. While they're fumbling with the goods, the fire team -- me, Jack, Danny, Korey, and Dana -- will come in and take them; we need them alive, if at all possible.

"Dana and Korey, you two are going to be the restraint team. As soon as we get them face down on the ground, you'll zip-tie them." JC handed several sets of plastic zip restraints to Dana and Korey.

"Keep them out of the way of the rest of your gear, on your back belt loop with these." He handed them both a small carabiner clip.

"Steven, you'll be along the back tree line, about halfway between the house and the barn. You'll be responsible for making sure no one slips up on us from that side, taking out hostiles if the fire team has to engage, and providing a barrier between the barn and the house. I don't have to tell you how important the last part of that mission is. If hostiles get to the house and overtake it with our wives and children inside, it's game over. We all might as well shoot ourselves in the head right then and there."

Steven nodded. "Got it."

Danny had gotten to know JC fairly well over the past three weeks, but he was never sure when he was serious and when he was making a statement for effect. Nevertheless, he'd made his point clear to Steven and everyone else in the group.

JC pointed at Steven. "And always be conscious of where the rest of your team is. Remember, we'll be approaching from this back wooded area, Rocky is right across from you here, and Catfish is up in this area of the hedgerow. And obviously, all the ladies are in the house. You can't take a shot if any of us are behind your target."

JC pulled some chemical lights, mousetraps, and fishing line out of his duffel bag. "Unfortunately, no one has any functioning radios. If I had it to do over, that would have been the one thing I'd change. I would have built a Faraday cage and put some radios in it. That would have been an absolute game changer. No point crying over should've, would've, could've. We just make do with what we have.

"We'll rig up a chem light on a tree nearby each of the sniper hides. It'll be far enough away from each one of them to not give away the nest, but close enough to be able to trigger the light with a length of fishing line, about forty or fifty yards away from each sniper. As soon as any one of you see the hostiles approaching, trigger your light. You'll all be able to see one another's lights, so only the first spotter triggers his light. That will also give the fire team a clue on the direction that they're coming from." JC looked around at the group. "Any questions? Ask 'em now."

CHEM LIGHTS

Danny wasn't super clear about how all the parts of this plan were going to fit together, but he couldn't formulate his present confusion into a cohesive question so he remained silent.

JC pulled a tube of green face paint out of his duffel bag. "Snipers, go change out into your best camos. Meet back here in one hour. We'll get you positioned and covered up with brush as best as possible."

Catfish said, "I don't reckon I never seen no need fer camouflage. I've always hunted in my overalls."

Rocky patted him on the back. "Come with me to the house. I've got a jacket for you at least. I might have some pants that would fit you as well."

Catfish nodded and followed Rocky out the barn

door.

Steven walked up to JC. "I'm not really the outdoorsy type. At least I wasn't before all of this. I don't have any camouflage either."

"Jack's stuff will fit you. It might be a little loose, but with a belt, you'll be okay." JC looked over at his son. "Jack, take Steven back to the house and get him in some camos. Your old woodland stuff will work. I'm going to be going over the basics of small unit troop movement with these guys, stuff you already know, so you won't be missing much. But get back quick, so we can practice the specifics of our mission. Daylight is burning."

"Yes, sir." Jack motioned for Steven to follow him.

JC stopped them. "On second thought, Jack, you run and grab it for him. I don't want him wearing out that bum leg. He might need it tonight if things get dicey."

"Okay." Jack shut the barn door behind him.

"Steven, even though you're not on the fire team tonight, pay attention to all of this. Your day to put the training to use may come." Right away, JC began drilling Danny, Korey, and Dana on hand signals, distances to keep between one another, and various formations. He instructed them as to what sector each one would be responsible for guarding, depending on their position in the formation. He had them all drill with reloading weapons and discussed how they would handle the situation if one of them were to be shot.

When Jack returned, they set up a practice

ambush site with the actual buckets of provisions that would be left out for the kidnappers. JC instructed them on how they would approach the hostiles and the method that Korey and Dana would use to place the restraints on the ones who could be captured.

After about an hour of training, Catfish and Rocky returned.

JC said, "Fire team, take a break. I'm going to get these guys painted up and set up in their nests. While I'm gone, try to think of some soft-sabotage methods for the ransom goods. Nothing that looks like we are obviously trying to make it more difficult, but dumb stuff that could slow them down. I'll be back in a while. After that, we'll do a quick sweep to make sure we're still not under observation, then get into position. Everybody clear?"

"Clear," Danny said.

Korey, Dana, and Jack all nodded that they understood as well.

"Good. Be right back." JC headed out with the snipers.

Jack looked at the buckets containing rice and other dried goods. "I guess they are planning to lay these across the back of the cows."

Danny snorted. "Good luck with that, especially with the cows we're planning to give them. If I can get Old Red-Eye over there with the patch of red fur around one eye, they'll have the time of their life trying to get her to do anything."

"How will you catch her?" Korey asked.

"She always bullies her way to the trough first. If

I only put feed in two of the milking stalls, I can almost guarantee she'll be in one of them," Danny answered.

"Too bad you don't have two cows that difficult." Dana crossed her arms.

Jack put a finger in the air. "We might be able to give the second cow a slightly less-sunny disposition. What if we can wedge a rock in between its hoof? It won't permanently injure the animal, but it will be uncomfortable, and it will slow down the retreat of the hostiles if they do get out with the cattle."

"Really good idea, Jack." Danny smiled.

Korey looked at the buckets. "What if we give them feed sacks instead of buckets? We could get a small starter hole in the bottom of the bag that might eventually tear out before they get back to camp."

Danny put a finger on his chin. "Especially if we put something small right near the opening of the hole and heavier items on top."

Jack looked at the rope that was to be used for the cows. "If you cut this rope and rejoin the two pieces with a square knot, there's a good chance it will slip loose, particularly if you have an unhappy animal on the other end of it. Unless they are really up on their knots, they'd probably never notice. You should always use some type of bend knot to join rope that will be load-bearing."

Dana looked at the rope. "And I'm sure we could tie it in such a way that would encourage it to slip loose. Right?"

"Exactly," Jack said.

Shortly thereafter, JC returned to the barn. Danny and the others filled him in on the proposed soft-sabotage techniques.

JC smiled. "Good work, guys. Let's get those two cows in the stalls and roped up. Get them outside to the overhang by the cattle entrance to the barn. Then, implement your sabotage ideas as quickly as possible so we can do our perimeter sweep. I want to be in position well before sunset."

CHAPTER 7

And when Abram heard that his brother was taken captive, he armed his trained servants, born in his own house, three hundred and eighteen, and pursued them unto Dan. And he divided himself against them, he and his servants, by night, and smote them, and pursued them unto Hobah, which is on the left hand of Damascus.

Genesis 14:14-15

Danny sat silently just inside the tree line. He'd been in the same position for more than three hours. The deep anticipation of rescuing Alisa made it seem like a much longer period of time. The nagging questions persistently assaulted his mind.

Was Alisa okay? Was she even alive? Would they bring her back and keep their word to exchange her for the goods requested? In the duration of monotonous waiting, he had to stay ever vigilant to not let worry and anxiety completely overtake his thoughts.

The moon was more than half full, but the sporadic clouds made it unreliable as a light source. It was after ten o'clock and still no sign of the kidnappers.

"I have to go find a tree," Korey whispered.

"Hurry, and be as quiet as possible," JC replied in a low, agitated mutter.

Danny knew JC wouldn't like it, but he was also going to need a tree soon. He decided he would go right after Korey returned. As bad as it was to be moving around at this time, it was much better than having to go after the kidnappers had been spotted on the property to retrieve the ransom. And, he definitely did not want to go into a firefight with a full bladder.

Korey soon returned. Danny looked over at JC. "Be right back."

JC pursed his lips, tapped his watch with his index finger, then put that same finger over his lips. Finally, he pointed with the same finger into the direction he wanted Danny to go.

Danny hurried, moving as silently as possible, deeper into the woods. Once finished, he returned to his position in the same manner.

JC looked at Dana and Jack. "If you guys need to go, do it now."

They both nodded and went in turn. Jack went

first, then Dana. While Dana was still back in the woods, JC waved his hand and pointed toward Catfish's position up on the hill. "Chem light. We've got company. Jack, you stay put with Korey and Dana. Danny and I will sweep for an overwatch team, then rally back here with you. Keep watch with your night vision. If you see us moving toward the barn, break cover and move your team, ranger file, to meet up with us."

Jack nodded that he understood. JC put the bow over his shoulder via a sling and led the way, watching through his night vision scope as they walked. Danny slung his AK over his back and held the Benjamin .357 air rifle for the initial sweep as he followed JC.

Dana was returning to the position just as JC and Danny were walking away. JC pointed at Jack. "Go back over the plan with her."

Jack nodded and gave his father a thumbs-up as he and Danny departed.

It had been discussed during training that if Danny had to take a shot at a hostile in the woods, he would do so with the air rifle in hopes of not alerting the other enemy teams. The advantage of the Benjamin bullpup rifle was that it was a silenced, large-caliber rifle, capable of taking out a hostile with minimal noise. The disadvantage was that each round had to be loaded by way of a side lever, so that the Benjamin functioned similar to a bolt-action weapon. The pre-charged rifle could shoot up to ten rounds per charge, and the magazine held five rounds plus one in the pipe, but the precious seconds involved in working the side lever made it a poor choice for close-quarters combat. If the hostiles weren't taken out by Danny's first shot with the Benjamin or JC's initial arrow, via the bow, they'd be forced to switch to their primary battle rifles which would make a lot more noise.

JC picked his way through the exact same path they'd used in their earlier sweeps. This helped Danny to be quieter, since he had some familiarity with the trail and the obstacles therein.

When they reached the point where they could observe the individuals who had come to collect the ransom, JC halted. He whispered to Danny, "Six guys. No sign of Alisa."

Danny's heart dropped, and nausea filled his gut. He felt dizzy for a second but gritted his teeth to force himself to stay focused. He sucked back a wave of sorrow and swallowed the knot forming in his throat.

As they reached the first likely position of an overwatch sniper, JC slowed to a crawl, and Danny followed his lead. No one was there, so they proceeded to the next possible position. Sure enough, Danny spotted a lone figure holding a long rifle with a scope. JC had spotted him too, evidenced by his distinct motion of putting one fist in the air signaling Danny to halt. JC continued to put one foot in front of the other with extreme caution at a glacial pace. He moved less than three feet in the course of the next two minutes as he found a position. JC silently surveyed their immediate area with the night vision scope mounted on his rifle for the next few seconds. He then slowly turned to make eye contact with Danny. He held up one finger indicating to Danny that he saw only one sniper. Danny nodded and moved into position.

They had discussed that in the event there was only one enemy shooter, JC would shoot first with the bow, and Danny would shoot as soon as he heard the release of the arrow.

Danny could see the dark silhouette of the sniper just ahead of him. He could see that the shooter's attention was focused on his team moving toward the barn.

Once in place to have a clear shot of the sniper, Danny nodded to JC, who drew his bow. Danny took aim at the man's head and held his breath.

JC released the arrow, which made a muffled bump; the arrow hit the man, creating an even thud, followed by the low pop of Danny firing the air rifle. Half a second later, the dark figure in the brush ahead dropped his weapon and fell on top of it. JC dropped the bow and pulled up his rifle by the single point sling. He picked his way through the brush to the sniper with Danny five feet behind. When he reached the sniper, JC kicked him over so he could see his face. Next he kicked the rifle away, let his rifle hang by the sling, and pulled his knife from the sheath. Danny looked away as JC bent down and slit the throat of the fallen man.

"You can never be too careful. You have to be sure they're dead. If they're not, it could ruin your whole day," JC whispered, then led the way to the next possible overwatch position along the tree line.

Danny didn't need JC to explain the logic, but neither did he want to watch the gruesome deed.

The two men soon completed the sweep of the

tree line and potential enemy sniper positions without locating any others. Rather than return to the original position, JC slid out from behind cover and stuck his hand in the air making a circular motion. This signaled to Jack's team that they should rally to JC's position rather than wait for him and Danny to return.

Jack quickly moved from his position, with Korey and Dana close behind. Once they'd arrived, JC leaned up against the barn wall to listen. Danny and the others did the same.

The low voice of one of the hostiles said, "Joey, we need you guys to help with this stuff. We can't get the cow to stand still long enough to let us put the sack over its back."

Another voice replied. "Two of you stand on that side. Bret, you and Pat stand on the other side so the cow can't move."

Danny could hear the ruckus going on through the boards of the barn. The cow, Old Red-Eye most likely, began lowing, a loud, annoyed bawl. The noisy cries of the animal provided the perfect distraction.

JC motioned with his hand that it was time to engage. He led the way out and away from the barn wall with Jack right on his tail. Danny came around the wall and stood with his rifle leveled at the nearest enemy assailant. Korey and Dana stood side by side, between Danny and the wall. The formation created an L-shaped perimeter around the kidnappers. With the wall of the barn on the opposite side of JC and Jack, the enemy had only one path of retreat.

JC screamed, "On the ground! Face down! On the ground now!"

The four men who had been fumbling about with the cow and the supplies put their hands in the air and quickly complied; the two remaining men standing guard turned their rifles toward JC.

Several shots exploded from both sides. When the air had cleared of the ringing sounds of rifle cracks and shotgun blasts, JC, Jack, Dana, Korey, and Danny were still standing. The two men who'd fired on JC were dead. One of the kidnappers, who hadn't lain prone on the ground as instructed, also caught a stray bullet in the chest. He lay lifeless in a puddle of his own blood.

The other three lay motionless, with their hands on their heads. JC walked around shooting the three injured men twice in the head, then moved in quickly to the others. He pointed his rifle at one. Jack and Danny did the same, covering the other two as Dana and Korey moved in with the restraints.

Once they had the zip ties securely on their hands, Korey and Dana made a quick search for pistols or knives.

JC turned the first one over so he was lying face up on his back. "How many other people are with you on the farm?"

"None," the man answered.

"Bad answer." JC shot him twice in the head and moved to the next. "How many?"

"One, there's a sniper over in the tree line." The next man was shaking and quivering as he spoke.

JC moved to the next guy and flipped him over

with his foot. "This is kind of like a reality show where only one contestant gets to live. Lying to me is an automatic elimination and you have to leave the island immediately, if you know what I mean. How many other people are with you guys and what type of weapons do they have?"

This man was also shaken up very badly. "Like he said, just one, in the tree line. He has a deer rifle with a scope."

JC kept the rifle pointed at him. "Now, where's the girl?"

The other man cried out. "Don't say anything, Bret. Make him promise to let us both go."

JC glanced over at the man, then back at Bret. "That's right, Bret. Don't say anything." JC walked over to the other man. "First, I'm going to demonstrate on, what's your name?"

"Travis."

JC smiled. "Travis. I'm going to demonstrate on Travis here, exactly what I'm going to do to you if you don't draw me a map and tell me everything about who's watching the girl. And I mean I want every detail, right down to what type of flooring and paint color you guys have at your place.

"Jack, you and Danny get a rope over that rafter and string Travis up by his hands. Korey, you and Dana go keep watch behind the barn and make sure nobody slips up on us."

Korey and Dana looked happy to get out of the barn before Travis was placed in suspended interrogation.

Jack and Danny did as they were instructed, and JC pulled his knife from its sheath. "Jack, run and get Catfish. Tell him to get his truck and pull it up to the barn. Then go get Rocky and Steven and bring them back here."

Jack immediately followed the directive.

Danny again turned away while JC worked his craft. The shrill cries from the tortured man made Danny's blood curdle, but he felt no sympathy for him. If he'd known that it would get Alisa back, he would have done it himself, although he was content to have JC doing it instead.

He walked over to Old Red-Eye and the other cow and untied them. At least they could escape being in the vicinity of the carnage. As the two cows ran away, he recalled the image of the blood red cow in his latest dream. He wondered whether the event he was now in the midst of might be the war and violence that the vision had foretold, or if the worst was still yet to come.

Four minutes later, Travis' agonizing screams faded into incoherent moans, and then into silence. His eviscerated body dangled lifelessly from the rafter beam above.

JC walked back over to Bret and bent down. He wiped the blood from his knife in Bret's shoulder-length brown hair. "I'm a little pressed for time, so I had to work kind of quick with Travis over here. But let me make you a promise." JC stuck the point of the knife firmly to Bret's sternum. "If you screw with me, if we don't get the girl back alive, or if you pull any funny business whatsoever, I'll spend weeks on you getting in touch with my creative side. You'll be like my Sistine chapel.

"Now, you ready to tell me where we're going

and who we're going to find there?"

Bret's face was as white as a ghost, and he shook like a leaf. "Ye-ye-yes, sir."

"Good boy!" JC stood and kicked dirt in Bret's face. "How many people are there?"

"Two. Gwen and Jena. They have a revolver and a shotgun. The girl is tied up in the bathroom of the master bedroom. It's about two and a half miles from here on McClain, up New Hope, left on Mar-Mac, right on McClain."

"Do you know where that is?" Danny asked JC.

"Yep, it's back in that neighborhood." JC turned back to Bret and pointed the knife at his eye. "If you're lying to me, I'm going to cut you up in little pieces. You know that, right?"

Bret nodded.

The others came in shortly thereafter. None were prepared to see Travis' mutilated body dangling from the rope.

And no one said anything, except for Catfish who walked up to Travis' cadaver and poked him with the barrel of his gun, causing the corpse to swing like a morbid pendulum. "Lucky I didn't get a hold of 'im. He'd a-been a mite messier 'n he is now."

JC looked over at Catfish. "If this one's lying, I'll let you show me a thing or two."

Catfish smiled a sinister grin at Bret. "Hmmm."

JC looked at Steven. "You hang out here and watch our new friend. If he moves, blow his feet off with your shotgun. Make sure he doesn't die. If Alisa isn't where he said, he's got Catfish to answer to."

Steven nodded but said nothing. He looked appalled by the grotesque scene of blood and corpses littering the barn.

JC pointed to the men as he called their names. "Danny, Jack, Korey, and Rocky, you guys ride in the bed of the truck. I'll sit up front with Catfish."

Dana asked, "JC, do you want me to go with you guys?"

"Yeah, it might help Alisa to see a friendly female face. She's had a tough day. You might have a more calming effect on her than all this testosterone. You can ride up front in the middle."

Danny patted Steven on the arm as he walked toward the truck. "You'll be okay till we get back?"

Steven nodded. "Just go get our girl."

"I will." Danny put his foot on the back bumper and hoisted himself into the back of the truck.

Catfish drove down the driveway and to the road. In less than five minutes they hit the subdivision. Catfish turned the lights off and used the intermittent moonlight to navigate slowly toward the house. He pulled off the road three houses down from where Alisa was supposedly being held.

JC surveyed the surrounding area. "If Bret is telling the truth, there should only be two girls guarding the house. Don't let your guard down because they're girls. A bullet from a girl's gun will kill you just as fast as one from a man's. If anyone thinks they'll have trouble defending themselves against a woman, speak now. Rocky?"

Rocky lowered his head. "You better put me in the back of the line."

"That's nothing to be ashamed of. It is what it is and you recognize it. Anybody else?" JC looked each of them in the eye.

Catfish looked away when JC's stare met his. JC put his hand on his shoulder. "Catfish, you've got a shotgun. I'm going to make you the key man. You'll shoot the door knob off when we breach, then fall in the back of the line when we enter. Do you have any deer slugs? That's the best round for a breach."

Catfish nodded and JC quickly showed him the angle that he would hold the shotgun for the breach.

JC looked his son in the eye, then moved to Danny.

Danny looked straight ahead. "They've got my wife. I'll kill anyone who gets between me and her."

JC nodded. "Okay. When we stack up, the order will be me, Danny, Jack, Dana, Rocky. Catfish will breach and follow the rest of us in. We'll penetrate as deep into the house as we can. If you hesitate to take a shot, and the hostile is able to get Alisa to use as a shield, your hesitation might be the thing that kills her. Sorry to be so direct, but this is life and death. I can't sugarcoat it, people."

Everyone nodded, and they approached the house. There were no sounds or light coming from inside and Danny wondered if this was the right place. But of course, with no power or electronic devices, a human voice was one of the few sounds one could expect to hear.

Catfish approached the door with the shotgun and held it up at a forty-five-degree angle from the door knob. He waited for JC's signal. JC looked behind him to ensure that the rest of the team was stacked up properly, then dropped his hand.

Catfish blew the lock and kicked the door. JC led the way through and cleared the living room.

Danny saw a shadow move across the candlelight in the kitchen. "Gun!" He turned to see a woman with blonde hair and a shotgun take aim at him.

He fired his weapon as did JC and Dana. The woman shot into the air as she fell limp.

JC had Danny, Jack, and Dana stacked up again outside of the bedroom door. He checked the knob; it was locked. JC took out his knife and used it like a screwdriver to turn the lock of the bedroom door. He sheathed his knife and turned the knob slowly. JC simultaneously kicked the door open and leveled his rifle as he entered the room.

A young woman sat screaming in the corner of the room with her hands on her head. "Don't shoot! Please! She's in the bathroom."

Danny rushed to the door and opened it. "Alisa!"

She looked up at him, her hands duct-taped. "Danny! You found me!"

JC came in next and cut the tape off of her hands. "How many people were in the house?"

"I don't know. Since the men left to get the ransom, I've only seen the two girls." Alisa looked rough.

JC patted Danny on the shoulder. "Take care of your wife." He turned to Dana and pointed at the girl crying in the corner. "Get restraints on that one. Jack, Rocky, help me clear the rest of the house."

JC, Jack, and Rocky left the room to ensure that no other hostiles were in the house. Dana zip-tied the crying girl, and Danny held his wife close.

He pulled his head back to look her over. "Are you okay?"

Tears were streaming down her face. She smiled and wiped her cheek with the sleeve of her shirt. "Yeah. I am now. I was so afraid, Danny. Afraid I wouldn't see you again. I love you so much."

"I love you, too. I'm sorry I let this happen." He pulled her close again. "Did they hurt you?"

"Not too bad. When they grabbed me, they were pretty rough. Someone grabbed me from behind, and another person stuck a sock in my mouth and duct-taped it in. Then, they held my hands and feet together and wrapped them with duct tape."

"But no one . . . bothered you?" Danny couldn't bring himself to say the word.

Alisa was still crying. "No, but I was afraid they might. One guy, I think his name was Bret, he kept bothering me, saying stuff, but Gwen, the girl over there in the corner, she stopped him. She brought me food, water, and cut my hands free so I could go to the bathroom. Take it easy on her."

Danny looked over at the prisoner. "But she didn't set you free either."

Alisa pleaded with Danny. "I know, but it would have been a much worse experience without her. If she hadn't protected me from Bret, it could have been a lot worse. The only reason she was even mixed up with these guys is because of her boyfriend, Travis. He tells her what to do, and if she steps out of line, he knocks her around. Regardless,

God used her to help me through this."

Danny pursed his lips. "But God could have used her to get you free. It was just her and the other girl here. There's a pistol on the nightstand. She could have got both of you out of here. We would have taken care of her."

"I told her that, but she was so scared of Travis."

"Well, whatever happens, she won't have to worry about him anymore." Danny thought about the butchered remains dangling from the rafter back in the barn. "Let's get you home. Nana will boil you some water for a hot bath; there's a big pot of chili waiting for you. You can eat, have a nice cup of tea, and go to bed."

Alisa squeezed his neck. "Thank you."

JC's voice rang out from the living room. "All clear! Let's move out!"

Dana stood in the door way. "I'm glad you're okay. We were all praying for you."

"Dana, you look like a commando," Alisa said.

"Anything for you." Dana pushed Alisa's hair out of her face with her fingers. "You did the same thing for me."

"Not exactly." Alisa held Danny's hand as they walked out of the bedroom.

Dana followed. "Close enough. You got me out of Savannah. Who knows what would have happened to me if I had stayed. I doubt I would still be alive. And if I were, I might be wishing I was dead."

Jack and Korey grabbed Gwen and escorted her to the truck.

Alisa instructed them. "Take it easy on her.

She's a good person. What are you going to do with her?"

Jack shrugged. "Dad wants her to see her friends."

"What does that mean?" Alisa asked.

"I don't know. I guess he wants her to see what we did to them. Maybe just to frighten her, so she'll think twice about getting mixed up in a crew like this again."

"What did you do to her friends?" Alisa asked.

"They're dead, all except for Bret." Danny opened the passenger door of the truck for Alisa. Dana and JC rode in the back with the others so she and Danny could be up front.

Catfish drove the truck up to Nana's front door. "Danny, you take care of your wife. We'll get that mess cleaned up down yonder."

"I want to see. I need to know what JC is making Gwen look at." Alisa said.

"You've been through enough for one day. Go on inside and get cha somethin' to eat." Catfish gave her a warm smile.

"Don't let anybody hurt Gwen, Catfish. She protected me, fed me, and did what she could. Promise me, Catfish." Alisa wouldn't get out of the truck until she got her answer.

Catfish nodded. "I'll look after her, I promise."

"I'll hold you to that." Alisa stepped out of the truck and looked at everyone in the back. "Thank you all for coming to get me. You're good friends. Be kind to Gwen. She's not like the rest of them."

JC smiled at Alisa. "We all love you. Everybody here would do anything in the world for you."

"Thanks." She put her hand on JC's arm. "Everybody."

"Dana, you can get out here. You did a good job. I'd be happy to have you on my team any day," JC said. "You, too, Danny. Good work."

"Thanks. And thank you for coordinating the rescue." Danny took Dana's hand to help her down from the back of the pickup.

Catfish drove off toward the barn while Danny, Alisa, and Dana went in the house.

Pauline was in the living room with the kids. "You're home! Praise Jesus!"

Melissa walked in with Annie in her arms and her pistol on her side. "Is everybody okay?"

"Everybody from our team. The other team wasn't quite as fortunate." Danny took his boots off before continuing into the house.

"No injuries?" Tracey Reese asked.

"Nope. Not a scratch. Where is Nana?" Danny asked.

"She's still in her room praying. She hasn't been out except to get a drink of water or use the restroom since you guys left," Pauline said.

"We were praying with her, too." Kalie Reese put her arm around her mother's leg.

Danny had been pushing his emotions back all day, and he'd reached his limit. He began to sob as he held his wife close. "Well, I guess God heard your prayers."

Nana came in the room, followed by Rusty wagging his tail.

"Oh, thank you, Jesus, thank you, Lord. Hallelujah!" She threw her hands in the air.

"I'm so glad to see you both." Nana put her arms around Danny and Alisa. "Let's get you cleaned up and fed."

Alisa sighed. "Thank you, Nana. It's good to be back.

CHAPTER 8

Cursed be he that doeth the work of the LORD deceitfully, and cursed be he that keepeth back his sword from blood.

Jeremiah 48:10

The next morning, there was a knock at the door. Danny got up from the breakfast table. "I'll get it."

He walked to the front door and opened it. "JC, come on in."

"How is Alisa holding up?" JC wiped his feet on the mat before entering.

"Okay. As good as can be expected, I guess." Danny lowered his voice. "Did you guys get the barn cleaned up?"

JC stepped inside. "Somewhat. That's what I wanted to talk to you about. Try to keep the girls inside this morning if you can. We pulled the bodies over behind the barn, but we didn't have enough light to do much else with them. We have to find a way to dispose of them today. They were a bunch of dirt bags, so I'm not breakin' my back to dig graves for all of them. Not that I have the spare time to do that anyway. So, unless you or somebody else wants to dig holes or you have a better idea, I say we build a bonfire and throw them on top. We can drag enough tree limbs and brush to get a good fire going in an hour or so. It would take days to dig graves. If you want to burn 'em, Jack and I will help. If you want to dig, you're on your own."

Danny nodded. "I think a bonfire will work just fine."

"We still have two prisoners. We have to figure out what to do with them."

Danny furrowed his brow. "What do you suggest?"

"We need to form a tribunal," JC said.

"How would that work?"

"I recommend we have a representative from each farm to hear their case. Capital punishment would require a unanimous vote, and all lesser sentences would require a simple majority."

Danny rubbed his head. "How would the representatives be chosen?"

"That would be up to the residents of each farm. As for my family, I'm it. I assume Rocky would probably be the representative for their place, Korey for his farm, and Catfish if he wants to have any say in the trial. You guys have to decide who would be your representative. If nobody likes that idea, we can do something different. It's just a suggestion. But whatever we do, we need to get it wrapped up today. This whole ordeal is eating into our farming time, which is what we should be focusing on right now."

"Let me talk it over with Nana. Would you like a cup of coffee?"

"Sure. I need to talk to Miss Jennie anyway." JC followed Danny back into the dining room.

"Have a seat. Let me scramble an egg for you. We've got plenty of biscuits left over." Nana pulled a chair out for JC.

"Just a cup of coffee, Miss Jennie. I really can't stay."

"At least have a biscuit. You have to make time to eat sooner or later. Might as well be now." Nana poured JC a cup of coffee.

"Okay, just one." JC relented. "Miss Jennie, I've got that travel trailer that I talked to you about a while back. Catfish said he would pull it over here today if you don't mind. If things get any worse, we might need to circle the wagons. The only way we can build an effective security force is if we pool our resources."

Nana brought JC a plate with two biscuits on it. "Whenever you're ready, it's fine with me. Are you going to start living in it now?"

JC shook his head as he finished chewing. "No. We'll stay at our place as long as we can, but I have a feeling that times are going to get rougher before they get better. I'd like to have a plan in place before we need it."

"You've still got all that food up in the hay loft.

I've always said you and your family are welcome here anytime."

"Thank you, Miss Jennie." JC ate the second biscuit and chugged his coffee. "I've got to run. Catfish is going to be at my house in about ten minutes. We'll be on over in an hour or so. Danny can fill you all in on what we need to get done today." JC waved as he headed out the door.

Alisa wrapped three biscuits up in a paper napkin. "I'll be right back."

"JC asked that I keep everybody inside until he gets back," Danny said. "Besides, you can't go to the barn without an escort. I'm not making that mistake again."

Alisa smiled. "Thanks, but I'll make sure I always have a gun. I can't take being treated like a china doll."

"It's not just you. I think we should implement a buddy system; nobody leaves the house alone. We should only go out in groups of two or more; everybody should be armed, and at least one of those people should have a long gun, a shotgun, or a rifle." Danny looked around the table at the others.

Steven sipped his coffee. "I agree. I don't think that's an overreaction considering everything we've been through since we left Savannah."

Dana nodded. "It makes sense."

Danny looked at Alisa. "What do you think?"

She shrugged. "I feel like this is all my fault. Everybody has to live on pins and needles now because I got kidnapped."

Nana gave her a hug. "Shug, this ain't your fault. Them ornery rascals that took you, they're the ones to blame. The whole world out there is a-fallin' apart, and ain't one bit of it your fault.

"Them heathens up in Washington, DC and out in Hollywood, they're the ones that led this country away from obeyin' the Word of the Lord. And everybody just a went right along with 'em. They had time for everything except seeking God and walkin' with Jesus. This country ain't wanted nothin' to do with God for decades. Well, he finally shook the dust off his feet and left us to our own devices. And that's why we have to live the way Danny is sayin'. But it sure ain't your fault."

"Thanks, Nana." Alisa hugged Miss Jennie tightly and looked over at her husband. "It's a good plan, Danny. So, can you walk down to the barn with me to give Gwen something to eat?"

Danny took a deep breath and thought for a second. "It's not a pretty scene down there. Why don't you let me and Steven take her breakfast to her?"

"I can handle it. I want to see her anyway."

Danny stuck his hands in his pockets and proceeded to tell everyone what JC had said about the tribunal.

Alisa put her hands on her hips. "Capital punishment? Who's going to be our representative? Whoever it is, you better not vote to execute Gwen!"

"I'm sure everyone will take into consideration that Gwen helped you." Danny put his arm on her shoulder. "In the Wild West, horse thieves were executed. Both because they didn't have the resources to house criminals for long periods of time and to send a message to let people know that type of behavior wouldn't be tolerated. With no legal infrastructure or law enforcement, we're in an even tighter position that the Wild West. Unfortunately, our two choices are execution or letting them go, virtually unpunished. We just don't have the means to provide for a lot of middle-ground punishments. Compared to horse thievery, kidnapping is a lot worse."

Dana asked, "What about, 'Do unto others as you'd have them do unto you'?"

Danny pursed his lips. "I guess we have to consider who the *others* are in that statement. If *others* represent society as a whole, I would have trouble justifying setting kidnappers free to strike again. I certainly wouldn't want anyone to do that to me, especially after what we've been through."

Dana nodded slowly. "I guess I didn't think about it from that perspective."

Danny looked at Steven. "Would you be interested in being our rep on the tribunal?"

He shook his head. "Not really, why don't you do it?"

Alisa crossed her arms. "I'll do it."

Danny was surprised. "You want to be the representative?"

"Yes. I was the one who was kidnapped. I should have some say in what happens to the perpetrators."

Danny looked at Nana. "What do you think?"

"She's right, Daniel. Ain't nobody else got no more say about it than her." Nana continued cleaning up the breakfast table.

Danny shrugged. "I'll talk to JC. If it's not a

conflict of interest for the victim to be on the tribunal board, I guess you're it. About taking food down to Gwen, can we wait until after JC and the others get here?"

Alisa took his hands. "No, Danny. Please, I understand that justice is important, but so is mercy. She's down there, tied up in the barn, hungry and afraid. I know what it feels like, and she was there for me."

"Okay, let me get ready." Up to this point, he thought that Alisa had developed some kind of Stockholm-syndrome connection with the girl. But now he realized that Gwen really had made a huge impact in making Alisa's ordeal more palatable.

Steven stood. "Do you want me to go, as back up?"

Danny paused in the doorway. "That's probably a good idea. Bring your shotgun."

"Dana, can you and Nana walk Rusty after the dishes are cleaned up? And take him toward the creek. I don't want him near the barn until we've dealt with the situation." Danny grabbed his AK.

"Sure thing! See you in a while." Dana stood to help Nana clear the table.

Alisa poured the rest of the leftover coffee into a mason jar, stuck the biscuits in the pocket of her hoodie, and led the way to the barn with Danny and Steven close behind.

Steven opened the barn door and Danny stood with his rifle at a low-ready position until he confirmed that the prisoners were still tied up, in the positions they were supposed to be. Once he saw the two of them, tied to two separate support beams in the barn, he lowered the rifle.

Alisa walked in first. "Gwen, hey. I brought you some breakfast."

Gwen's hand and feet were tied around the beam, so that she could neither stand, nor walk. "Hey, thanks, but I really just need to go to the bathroom."

Alisa looked at Danny. "Can we cut her loose?"

"Get her one of those old coffee cans over in the corner and she can use the utility room." Danny took out his knife and handed it to Alisa. "Gwen, we're going to cut you loose. If you try anything, we'll shoot you."

Bret called out. "I've got to go, too."

Danny looked at Bret. His pants were wet. "You'll have to wait till JC and the others get here. Besides, looks like you already went."

"Can I have something to eat?" he requested.

"Resources are tight. We don't have enough to allocate to feeding you." Danny kept his eyes on Alisa and Gwen.

"You brought food for her. You can't let me starve to death!"

Danny glanced over at Bret. "I doubt you'll be around long enough for that to happen."

"So you're going to let us go?" Bret asked.

Danny just shrugged.

Bret called out to Steven. "Are you going to let us go?"

He answered, "I don't have anything to do with it. Your fate is in the hands of the tribunal."

Gwen came out of the utility room, rubbing her wrists. "Thanks, Alisa. Everything hurts from being in the same position all night."

"Sure. Can you eat something now?" Alisa offered her the napkin with the biscuits wrapped up in it.

"Yeah, thank you." Gwen sat on one of the hay bales and ate the food.

Bret called out, "Why does she get food and I don't?"

"Because, I'm in charge of the food." Alisa set the jar of coffee next to Gwen, walked over to the tool bench, and picked up an old pry bar. "Remember me?"

"You know I was just kidding," Bret pleaded. "I wouldn't have really done anything to you."

"I guess I can't take a joke." Alisa smiled and swung the pry bar into his hands, crushing his fingers.

"Agghh!" Bret screamed in agony, then continued to cry out in pain.

Alisa walked back to the tool bench and grabbed the duct tape. "I can't listen to that all day." She wrapped the tape around Bret's mouth and head.

Bret's face turned red as he fought to get enough air through his nose to keep up with the demand of his convulsing lungs.

"Can you breathe okay?"

He shook his head.

"Good, your comfort is our utmost importance here at the Walker Bed and Breakfast. Be sure to leave us a good review." Alisa kicked him in the kidneys as she walked away.

Danny and Steven just watched as Alisa vented her frustration on Bret.

Once he saw that she'd calmed down a little, Danny handed the zip ties to Alisa. "We can come back and give Gwen another break later, but we have to keep her tied up for now."

Alisa took the ties and dropped her head. "Sorry, Gwen. I have to do this."

Gwen walked back to the beam and sat down to allow Alisa to secure her hands and feet once again.

Afterwards, they left the barn, closing the door behind them. When they arrived back at the house, Catfish, JC, and Jack were pulling up with the travel trailer.

Jack jumped out of the back of the truck. "Hey, Alisa. How are you?"

"I'm okay, thanks, in part, to you."

"Hey, are Korey and Rocky coming?" Danny opened the door for Catfish.

JC nodded. "They're coming to help us clean up, but neither wants to be involved in the trial. They said they'd be fine with whatever we decide. I can't really hold it against them. Both of them were here for us when we needed them to help go get Alisa. But, I do need one of you guys to be on the tribunal. Did you decide who it would be?"

Danny looked over at his wife. "Alisa wants to serve if it's not a conflict of interest."

JC knuckled his forehead. "Are you sure about that?"

"I'm sure." Her voice was steadfast.

"I ain't got no problem with it." JC started walking toward the barn. "Let's get it over with."

"Right now?" Alisa sounded surprised.

"Yeah." JC snorted. "We've got things to do.

I'm only building one bonfire, so everybody that's getting burned needs to go at one time."

JC's crass way of discussing the situation made Danny feel uneasy, but what could he say? JC was right. It was mid-March, and they needed to be focusing on planting. Even if they worked around the clock, there was no guarantee that they'd be able to produce everything they needed to survive. Each day that was lost to chasing hoodlums around reduced those odds dramatically.

"So how are we going to go about this? Is someone going to represent the defendants? Are we going to set up a table? Should there be witnesses?" Alisa followed close behind JC.

JC exhaled a deep breath. "We don't have time for all of that. We'll tell them what they are accused of, let them speak their mind for a minute, decide if they're guilty, and carry out the sentence."

"What? Like just stand there and say I pronounce you guilty and then hang them?"

JC kept up his brisk pace as he walked toward the barn. "Hanging is sort of a hassle. You have to get a rope, tie it, keep the prisoners secure while you relocate them. A bullet in the head is quick, efficient . . . and humane. It works out better for everybody."

Alisa stopped in front of the door, blocking the latch for everyone else. "We should have some idea of a consensus before we go in here, don't you think?"

JC grinned. "You mean, prejudge, before the trial? If you want it to be fair, you should keep an open mind until you've heard their testimony."

Alisa didn't move. "Whatever, but if you guys want me to go along with executing Bret, I have to know that you'll let Gwen live."

JC put his hands out. "We need a unanimous vote for capital punishment. You don't have to cut any deals with us."

"Okay, but I need to know you'll treat her fairly. She helped me a lot."

JC looked her in the eyes. "I'll keep that in mind."

Alisa turned around and opened the latch. "Okay, let's try her first then, so she doesn't have to sweat being executed."

Jack whispered to Danny, "Should we be in here during the trial?"

Danny thought about the question. "I suppose it's okay. We're like bailiffs or something."

JC walked over to Gwen. "You're accused of being criminally involved in the kidnapping of Alisa Walker and the subsequent attempt to extort goods from our group in exchange for her release. You're also accused of being criminally involved in continuing to hold her even after we agreed to the exchange. How do you plea?"

Gwen lowered her head. "I didn't think up the plan, and I didn't have any say in how they carried it out. I tried to get Joey and Travis to take her back when they went to get the food."

JC stood with his hands behind his back. "After they left, it was only you, Alisa, and the other girl left in the house. You were armed and therefore could have overpowered the other girl in an effort to set Alisa free. By not doing that, you were an active participant in her abduction."

"I was afraid. I was afraid that Travis would kill me."

JC looked at Catfish. "I say she's guilty."

Catfish looked at Gwen. "If you'd let her go, we would've protected ya. But ya didn't. You was a coward with no regard fer nobody but yourself. Guilty."

Alisa stood between Gwen and Catfish. "That's not true. She protected me from that piece of filth over there. She fed me, untied me so I could eat and go to the restroom. She stuck her neck out for me. I say, not guilty. I think we should set her free and let her stay here with us."

JC shook his head. "No way. That ain't happenin'. She helped you, but she also helped her crew. She's guilty, and she ain't living anywhere around here. For sentencing, I recommend that she piles up the wood for our little bonfire, then stacks the bodies of her accomplices on the pile. Afterward, she'll be banished from a one-hundred-mile radius of this farm. And if I ever see her again, she'll wish she died an easy death right here, today."

Alisa took both of Catfish's hands. "No! Catfish, that's just as bad as killing her. Where is she going to go and how is she going to get there? You know what it's like out there. If we kick her out, she's as good as dead."

Catfish looked tenderly into Alisa's eyes. "Sorry, sweet pea. JC is right. She ought to have got you out of that place. She had her chance and she didn't. She's got to go. You don't know that she won't make it. If she travels smart, finds a community, and gets around the right folks, she could make it. But I have to agree with JC's sentence." Catfish turned to Bret. "And it's a heap lot better deal than that one is a-fixin' to get."

Alisa looked at Gwen. "I'm sorry. I tried."

Tears were streaming down Gwen's face. "I know. And they're right. I should have shot Jena and got you out of there."

JC bent down, took out his knife, and cut the ties off of Bret's feet. "Stand up. You're on trial."

Bret worked his way up the beam into a standing position.

JC pointed the knife at him. "You are being accused of kidnapping and extortion. How do you plead?"

Bret made an incoherent noise through the duct tape wrapped tightly around his mouth.

JC ran the edge of the knife between Bret's cheek and the tape, cutting it free. "How do you plead?"

"Not guilty. Do I get a lawyer?"

"Guilty. I recommend death by gunshot." JC turned away. "Catfish, how do you rule?"

"Guilty." Catfish stuck his hands in his overall pockets. "I concur with the recommendation, death by gunshot."

"Alisa?" JC said.

"Is she on the tribunal? You can't have a victim being a judge!" Bret's voice was frantic.

Alisa walked up to him. "No telling how many other girls didn't have someone like Gwen to get in your way."

"I've never done anything like that. I promise." Bret shook his head from side to side as he begged.

"Either way, now that society has melted into oblivion, you'd be free to be the real pervert that you are, if we set you free." She stared at him with her hands on her hips.

"No. I'll be kind. I'll do the right thing. I would never do that." Bret continued to implore her.

Alisa looked at him. "I hope that's true, but I can't see inside your heart to know for sure. And I can't take a chance that you're bluffing. Then I'd be responsible if you ever did that to someone else. If it is true, take the next few minutes to ask Jesus to forgive you and ask him to let you in his kingdom, because you're going to be meeting him, real soon." Alisa turned back toward JC and Catfish. "Guilty. I agree, death by gunshot. I ask that the tribunal grant the convicted five minutes to consider his life and ask forgiveness of his maker."

JC looked at Catfish who nodded. JC looked at his watch. "Five minutes granted."

Bret began screaming hysterically. "I want to appeal. This isn't fair! I haven't killed anyone! You can't just kill me! Oh please, please, please!"

Alisa looked at him. "You're wasting time. You really need to be asking God to forgive you."

Bret just hung his head and continued to cry.

Steven handed his shotgun to Danny and walked over to the condemned man. "Would you like to ask God to forgive you? Do you want me to pray with you?"

Bret looked up. "I want you people to forgive me! I want you to let me go! Who are you anyway?

You can't judge me. None of you are any better than I am."

Steven lowered his head. "I'm not judging you. And I'm no better than you. I needed to be forgiven just like you do. Jesus came to earth to die for my sins and for yours. All you have to do is accept the free gift."

Bret spoke softly to Steven. "Bro, please, get me out of this. Talk to your boy. Tell him to let me go and he'll never see me again. I swear."

Steven sighed, walked back over to Danny, and retrieved his shotgun. "I'll be waiting for you guys outside."

JC looked at his watch. "Time's up. Alisa, you, Jack, and Danny wait for us outside."

"Can Gwen come outside with us?" Alisa stood by the girl.

"No. She needs to see this. She needs to remember this, every time she thinks about bringing somebody over here to get even or every time she thinks it might be okay to come back to town. Because if either of those things happen, I'll kill her. Remembering this might save her life."

Alisa turned away from JC and stormed out the door.

Danny and Jack followed. Seconds later, Danny heard the loud crack of JC's pistol. The sentence had been carried out.

Steven glanced over at Danny. "Swift justice, huh?"

Alisa was sullen. "Yeah. I don't know who the bigger monster is."

Jack didn't appreciate that comment. "Hey,

Alisa. I understand that you're upset, but my dad risked his life. Heck, he risked my life to come save you. He's doing what he believes is right, what he thinks has to be done to keep you and everyone else around here safe. This is a different world, and you should be grateful that there is somebody around who can make the tough calls. And remember, no one else had a clue how to effect your rescue. So they could have all had the best intentions about coming to get you, but chances are, you would have rotted away, tied up in that house if it wasn't for that monster in there."

Alisa started crying and walked back to the house.

Jack shook his head. "That came out a little harsher than I intended it to."

Danny nodded. "I think she knows you're probably right. And she appreciates what your dad did, and what you did." Danny patted him on the back. "And so do I."

Catfish walked out the barn door. "Who wants to volunteer to help gather firewood?"

Danny gave a somber nod. Knowing that the kindling would be used for the pyre gave him a different feeling than building a campfire. It caused him to examine the frailty of life and left him with a cloud of melancholy hanging over his head. "Ichabod," he whispered to himself. Yes, they had been successful in the ambush, survived the raid on the house, and brought Alisa home safely. Justice had been meted out, but he felt no glory in any of it.

Catfish looked at Steven and Jack. "Does that mean you two would rather drag the stinkin' corpses to the wood pile?"

Jack shook his head and quickly followed Danny. "No, I'll help Danny with the wood."

"Me, too." Steven did likewise.

"Hee-hee-ha." Catfish's giggle was slightly sadistic.

Danny, Jack, and Steven soon had a fair pile of wood stacked roughly three feet high at the center.

"That should do it. We'll let Gwen load the bodies and we'll get them lit up. The buzzards are getting antsy." JC pointed at the carrion birds circling overhead.

Gwen turned her head in disgust as she dragged one after another of her fallen acquaintances to the site of the pyre. "I can't get them on top of the wood."

Steven leaned his shotgun against the wall of the barn and walked over to help her.

Danny felt a pang of guilt, knowing he should help as well. He picked up Steven's shotgun and took it over to the tree where Catfish was standing. He leaned his rifle and the shotgun against the tree. "Can you watch these?"

Catfish gave him a nod, and he walked over to the wood pile to assist Gwen and Steven. Jack also helped out, and all the bodies were finally lying atop the pile of brush and timber.

JC walked over to the pile, took out a lighter, and started a small fire near the center. He stood and walked back over near the barn. "This isn't going to smell like apple pie, so you guys might want to head on back to the house. Catfish and I will watch the fire and make sure it doesn't go out or get out of control."

Gwen stood motionless near the growing flames.

JC pointed at her. "Hit the road. Make sure we never see you again. If we do, you'll wish you'd died here today."

"Can I at least go back to my house and get my things before I leave town?"

"I don't care what you do. Just make sure you are out of the county by sundown."

Gwen walked lifelessly toward the gravel path which led out to the main road.

Danny, Steven, and Jack walked back toward the house.

Alisa came running out of the house toward Gwen.

Danny sprinted to catch up with her. "Hey, wait up."

Alisa slowed her pace so Danny could reach her. "I put together a few things to help Gwen get to wherever she's going."

Danny looked at the small backpack that Alisa was carrying. "No guns, right?"

"No. Some food, our little camping stove, water purification tablets, and a canteen."

Steven and Jack soon reached their location.

Alisa looked at Jack. "Please don't tell your dad. I just want to give her a few things to help her survive, and I don't want to fight about it. But I'm going to do it either way because it's the right thing to do."

Steven stuck his free hand in his pocket. "I've got that one-person tent. We never even used it.

And we should give her a Bible. She's going to need someplace to go for hope."

Danny nodded, and Steven ran toward the house.

Jack smiled at Alisa. "I won't say anything."

Alisa patted Danny on the arm. "Tell Steven to meet us out by the road on the other side of the hedgerow. I'll have Gwen wait there until he comes."

Danny looked at Jack. "Can you relay that message? I don't want to leave Alisa alone."

"She's not going to hurt me, Danny."

He grinned. "I know, but we have to travel in twos. Buddy system, remember?

"Come on then." Alisa resumed her brisk pace.

They caught up with Gwen right before the end of the long gravel drive. Alisa presented her with the backpack. "Here's a few things to help you get by."

Gwen's eyes welled up with tears as she took the backpack. "Thank you."

Alisa hugged her. "You'll be okay."

Gwen nodded.

Danny looked back toward the house. "Steven has a couple more things to give you if you can hang out for a while."

Minutes later, Steven arrived, carrying the tent and a small New Testament Bible. He handed them to her while he caught his breath.

"Thank you."

"The tent is brand new." Steven breathed heavily between words. "The Bible is small, so it won't take up a lot of room or weigh you down, but if you read it, it will be worth more than gold."

She flipped through the pages. "No one ever gave me a Bible."

"It will change your life." Alisa smiled.

"I could use that." Gwen looked closer at the pages. "Maybe I will read it. I listened to what you were trying to tell Bret. You guys all think God will listen if I talk to him?"

"I know he will. He can't wait to hear from you," Steven said.

"I've got a lot of things to think about." Gwen stuck the small Bible in her back pocket. "And plenty of time for thinking."

"Take care," Alisa said.

"Thank you for everything, Alisa." Gwen began walking away.

"I wish I could have done more," Alisa said.

She turned around for one last look. Gwen's face was filled with regret. "I could have done more. I wish I had done everything I could have."

CHAPTER 9

But let all those that put their trust in thee rejoice: let them ever shout for joy, because thou defendest them: let them also that love thy name be joyful in thee. For thou, LORD, wilt bless the righteous; with favour wilt thou compass him as with a shield.

Psalm 5:11-12

Danny held Alisa's hand as they found a seat for church Sunday morning. Dana and Steven had done a remarkable job of cleaning the blood stains off of the dirt floor. Danny had spread some hay around on the floor for good measure, but the lingering memory of what they had done in the exact same location just two days earlier made it difficult for

Danny to maintain an attitude of worship inside the old barn. He looked over at the spot where JC had executed Bret. Then, his eyes moved toward the beam where Gwen had been held, awaiting her sentence. He wondered if she had survived the past two nights on her own.

He looked over at Alisa and ran his finger along the side of her beautiful brown hair. A feeling of gratitude swept in and washed away all of the dirtiness from the events of those days. "I'm so glad you're okay. I was going out of my mind when I didn't know where you were."

She clutched his arm with both hands and sighed. "It's good to be home."

As they sang the old hymns that Nana had selected for the morning, Danny focused on rejoicing with his wife and his friends rather than paying attention to Catfish's poor timing and out-of-tune notes on the harmonica.

Steven had prepared another great message, on hope and perseverance from II Corinthians 4. Danny listened and drew strength from the words of encouragement. Danny glanced over at Rusty who was sitting near the door, facing the opening.

The old farm dog had been ever vigilant since Alisa's abduction. Even though Danny had kept him from seeing the prisoners and dissuaded him from sniffing around the ashes where they'd disposed of the bodies, Rusty somehow knew something had happened that wasn't quite right. Rusty had taken to staying up all night, even though people from the group were keeping an around-the-clock watch for unwelcome guests.

Danny turned to look at Rusty again when he noticed him stand up suddenly.

Rusty made a low growling, "woof."

Danny patted Alisa on the leg. "I'll be right back."

JC had noticed the movement in Rusty as well and walked to the door to meet Danny, with his snub-nosed revolver drawn. "Draw your weapon and let's have a look around outside."

Danny pulled his Glock from his waist and followed JC's lead out the door. "Did you see anything?"

"Nope, but Rusty did. Could've been a rabbit, could have been something worse."

Rusty barked again, but louder as he looked toward the hedgerow that ran along the road.

JC opened the door and yelled inside, disrupting the service. "We've got company!"

Danny saw two people dressed in military clothing and carrying rifles come around the opening of the hedgerow. He thought quickly about how poorly suited he was to engage a hostile with a rifle at a distance.

"Don't shoot!" the bearded man from the road yelled. He held his rifle by the barrel and waved his hands.

Danny looked closer. "Nick? Cami?"

By now, everyone from inside the barn was standing around the barn door. Danny was elated to see his sister and ran toward her. Nana followed him, moving faster than he'd seen her move in years.

When he reached her, Danny hugged Cami as

hard as he could. "Long trip, huh?"

"Yeah, long trip." She laid her weary head on his shoulder.

Danny stepped back to look at her. She was very thin, but no visible injuries. "You're okay? Do you need medical attention?"

"No, just a hot bath, a big meal, and a soft bed." She smiled.

"In that order?" Danny winked.

She tousled his hair. "In that order."

Danny shook Nick's hand. "Good to have you back. It's been a little rough around here."

Nick let out a tired laugh. "Rough around here?" He looked at the house, the barn, and surveyed the fields and tree line. "You ain't seen rough yet."

Danny's joy was tempered by the foreshadowed grief that Nick implied. "I guess you guys saw some hard scenes out there, huh?"

Nick's face was extremely slender, weathered, dry, and seemed ten years older than it'd looked when Danny saw him less than three months earlier. His face was reminiscent of that first pitiful cow that Danny had seen in the graveyard, when all of this nightmarish reality was merely a bad dream. There was no going back to that time, so Danny knew better than to entertain such a thought. This was how life would be from this point forward — the new normal. Danny had to accept it for what it was.

Nick's distant eyes looked toward the road they had just come in on. "Unimaginable. People are starving, killing each other, fighting over scraps, and doing the unthinkable just to stay alive, just to continue their miserable existence for one more day."

Danny could tell that Nick didn't want to get into any more detail. "Well, you're home now. Come on in and let's get you something to eat."

Nick turned and looked Danny in the eye for a moment. It was as if he had something to tell him, something urgent, and something Danny needed to know right now. Danny waited for him to speak but heard nothing.

Danny was caught off guard by what he thought he saw on Nick's face. Was that fear? No, it couldn't be. Nick was a soldier; he had been through two tours of duty in the desert. Nothing scared him anymore.

Finally Nick broke his empty stare, put his hand on Danny's arm, and smiled. "That sounds like a plan. Let's go eat."

The church service was over. All the attendees gathered around to express how happy they were that Nick and Cami had made it home.

JC patted Danny on the back. "You were scheduled for night watch tonight. I'll cover your shift. Enjoy being with your sister tonight."

"You guys aren't going to hang around? Nana is going to cook up a storm." Danny could see JC's disappointment. Seeing Cami return was a painful reminder that his son Chris was still not home. And over a month after the event, the odds were getting slimmer and slimmer.

"No, I'm setting up some trip wire alarms around my place. I want to get that done before dark."

Danny shook his hand. "You'll have a reunion

soon, and if you're scheduled for night watch, I'll return the favor."

JC forced a smile. "I hope you're right."

Alisa walked up and took Danny's hand. She had evidently figured out why JC was feeling so low. "Bye, JC." It was the first time she had spoken to him since he'd banished Gwen.

He turned to wave then motioned for Jack, Melissa, and Annie to follow him home.

Danny took Nick's backpack and carried it the rest of the way to the house. Alisa did the same for Cami. Danny looked over at his sister. "I missed you. I prayed for you every day; we all did. I'm glad you're back."

When they reached the porch, Cami plopped down in the swing. "Me, too. And thanks for the prayers. We were in a couple of situations where I knew it was God who got us through them. Have you had any trouble around here?"

Danny set Nick's pack against the porch rail. "Yeah, Alisa was kidnapped."

Cami had begun unlacing her boots, but she stopped. "Oh no! Are you okay?"

Alisa leaned Cami's pack next to Nick's. "Yeah. My hero came to get me."

Danny blushed. "JC actually organized the rescue."

Nick sat next to Cami on the swing and removed his boots as well. "Were you able to neutralize the threat or are they still out there?"

Danny leaned against the rail and gave a brief synopsis of the ordeal.

Nick pointed to his pack. "In that top pouch, I've

got a pair of Crocs. Can you get those for me?"

"Sure. Cami, do you have Crocs in your pack?" Danny unzipped the pack and retrieved the rubber shoes.

Cami leaned back. "Yes, please!"

Alisa pulled Cami's Crocs from her pack and handed them to her. "We had to fight our way here, also. We lost the car in the first shootout, then almost lost Steven in the second."

Cami's eyes lit up as she put the rubber shoes on her bare feet. "Wow!"

Alisa gave them the condensed version of the trip from Savannah to Nana's.

"I'm sure you guys have your own stories to tell. It's been more than a month since the lights went out," Danny said.

Cami looked over at Nick and took his hand. "Yeah, but I think we need a good night's sleep before we'll be ready to relive it."

"You guys can have our bed, and we'll crash on the floor in our sleeping bags tonight." Alisa took Danny's hand.

Cami shook her head. "As long as the RV is still in one piece, we can sleep there."

Danny lowered his brow. "But the bedroom in the RV is full of supplies. You'd have to move all of that."

Cami waved her hand. "Nope. We can sleep on the pullout couch. We'll relocate the supplies tomorrow. It will be easier. All of our clean clothes, hygiene items, everything is there. Besides, it will give me a sense of normalcy to be around my own stuff." She looked at Nick. "We haven't had much normalcy lately."

Nana walked out on the porch with a plate of leftover biscuits from breakfast. "Y'all eat these to get something in your stomach. Lunch will be ready in about twenty minutes. I've got a pot of coffee going for you, too."

"Thanks, Nana." Cami took a biscuit and passed the plate to Nick.

The two of them quickly scarfed down the last crumbs from the plate.

Alisa took the empty plate. "I'll take that in for you. Do you want me to find you something else to eat right now?"

"I think that will tide us over till lunch. But if the coffee is ready, I'd love a cup." Nick smiled.

Alisa nodded and took the plate inside.

"How long has it been since you ate?" Danny asked.

"We ate this morning, but not much," Cami said. "When we left DC, we had two weeks of food. By scavenging for greens and cattails, we stretched it out to three weeks. This past week, we've been living on whatever we can kill and scavenge."

Nick ran his fingers through his beard. "The deer are already getting thin. In fact, all the wild game are becoming scarce. We saved one pouch of the dehydrated Mexican chicken with rice. The raccoons seemed to like it so we've been using it for bait."

Danny felt terrible, knowing that his sister had been living off of raccoon, but he figured it was much better than starving.

Alisa came outside with two piping hot cups of

coffee. "Here you go. Enjoy."

"Thanks." Cami took a long deep smell of the aroma. "We had two boxes of single-serve instant coffee in our bags. We shared a cup every day for the first two weeks, and I've been dreaming of this moment ever since."

Nana prepared a huge lunch which was enjoyed by all. Once the guests had left, everyone pitched in to help boil water so Nick and Cami could each take a long, hot bath. Afterwards, Danny, Alisa, and Rusty walked Cami and Nick down to the RV.

Danny carried Nick's backpack. "JC will be standing watch over the cattle tonight, so he'll be keeping an eye on your RV also."

Nick held Cami's hand as they walked. "That will be great. We haven't been able to both sleep at the same time since we left. One of us has had to stand guard while the other slept."

Cami looked over at her little brother. "And after pushing hard to cover twenty miles a day on foot, you need more than five hours of sleep before you get up and do it all over again. But, we're home now."

Nick unlocked the heavy-duty latch and opened the door to the RV.

Alisa followed Cami up the stairs and set her pack near the kitchen table. "Need anything else?"

Cami hugged her. "No. You guys have been great."

Nick immediately began pulling the cushions off the couch to pull out the bed. "Thanks for everything. Tell Nana we'll try to make breakfast, but if we don't. . ."

Danny put his hand in the air. "I know. We'll see you at breakfast, lunch, or whenever. Sweet dreams."

Cami blew Danny a kiss. "Good night."

Danny and Alisa called for Rusty to follow them back to the house, leaving the two road-weary travelers so they could get some much needed rest.

CHAPTER 10

Open rebuke is better than secret love.
Faithful are the wounds of a friend; but the
kisses of an enemy are deceitful.

Proverbs 27:5-6

Danny quickly put his hand back up on the table
and sat up straight in his chair when Nana walked in
the dining room at breakfast Monday morning.

"Daniel, you better not be feedin' that cat from
the table! I'll put both of you out in the barn." Nana
set a bowl of brown sugar oatmeal on the table and
walked back into the kitchen.

Danny grunted his disappointment at having
been caught and looked over at Alisa and Steven,
who were both snickering. Puddin' was not deterred
by the rebuke and continued to claw at the leg of his

pants for another morsel of the country ham fat he'd been feeding her.

Dana scowled at him. "What are you giving her, Danny?"

"Ham."

She tilted her head in disbelief. "Ham or fat?"

"Ham fat."

"Danny, she's getting obese. You can't feed her all the time."

"You said it was all fur."

Dana huffed. "I said it was all fur when we left Savannah. Thanks to you and Nana, now it's fur and fat."

"We don't have country ham very often. Nana only makes it on special occasions. Puddin' smells it cooking and feels left out if she doesn't get any. Besides, we only have five more hams. Once they're gone, you won't have to worry about me feeding it to her anymore."

Alisa butted in. "Isn't the special occasion supposed to be your sister coming home? It doesn't look like there's going to be any ham left."

"Nana has two slices hidden in the kitchen for Nick and Cami." Danny cut into another piece, separating the fat which he would wrap in a napkin to give to Puddin' at a more opportune time.

"And you've seen this supposed secret ham?" Alisa asked.

"Nope. Don't have to. She always does that if someone isn't at the table."

Dana peered at the last slice of ham on the plate in the middle of the table. "How does she keep the ham from going bad without a refrigerator?"

"Country ham dates back to before refrigeration. It's cured in a smokehouse with plenty of salt and a little bit of sugar. Once it's cured it just needs a cool, dry place. The store where she bought these just had them hanging on a wooden pole in the middle of the aisle. Gives the place a nice aroma."

Dana looked out the window toward the barn. "Can you cure beef like that?"

Danny looked over at Nana who had finally sat down to eat a few bites. "I'm not sure."

Nana split open a biscuit and put some jelly on it. "You can smoke cure anything in a smokehouse if you got salt. We used to make beef sausage and cure it in the smokehouse when I was young. Didn't nobody have no Frigidaires when we was a-growin' up. I've heard of people smokin' fish. I'd have to be mighty hungry to eat a smoked fish, but I reckon some folks like it."

There was a knock at the back door. Danny's heart jumped. He quickly remembered that Nick and Cami were probably stopping by, but after all he'd been through since the EMP, jumpiness was to be expected, and perhaps even healthy in small doses. Nevertheless, he pulled his shirt up over the handle of the Glock in his waist as he stood up. "I'll see who it is."

Danny walked out the door to the back porch and then unlocked the exterior door of the enclosed porch area. "JC, hey, come on in."

JC wiped his feet. "Nick and Cami are on their way. I don't mean to butt in on breakfast, but Nick said he was going to fill everyone in on what they saw on the way here and thought I should probably hear it also."

Danny patted him on the back. "You're always welcome. Come on in."

"Get in here and get ya somethin' to eat," Nana said.

"A cup of coffee would be fine, Miss Jennie." JC took a seat at the large dining room table.

"You have to eat. You ain't sick, are ya?" Nana brought a plate with a slice of ham on it and set it in front of JC.

JC took a biscuit and cut the ham to make a sandwich out of it. He looked over at Danny. "Did they tell you anything yesterday?"

Danny shook his head. "Nick said it was a rough trip but was too tired to get into any specifics."

JC nodded as he finished chewing, then said, "It will be good to get some intel on what's happening in the rest of the world. We'll be able to plan better what we need to do around here."

"Did you get your place wired up with booby traps?" Danny asked.

"Just some simple trip alarms. Nothing dangerous. The last thing I need is for Rusty to come over there and start sniffing around and get himself blown up. Or worse, have Annie trip one and get hurt. I'd never forgive myself." JC looked under the table. "The cat is pawing my leg."

Dana's voice dripped with sarcasm. "Danny taught her to beg. Isn't that a cool trick?"

"She just wants the fat from your ham," Danny explained.

JC looked at the piece of fat on the edge of his plate as he took another bite of his biscuit, as if to tell Danny he was welcome to it but not to expect him to participate in the delinquency of the overfed pet.

Nana reached across the table and took the fat. "Better save that for Rusty. He'll be mad as the devil if he smells ham meat and don't get a taste of it."

Nick and Cami walked in the back.

"Hey!" Cami said to everyone as she walked in.

"How did you sleep?" Alisa asked.

"Oh my goodness! I could have slept all day, but our tummies were growling." Cami went to the kitchen and poured coffee for her and Nick.

"There's plenty to eat. I've got ham for both of you in the kitchen, and I'll make y'all some eggs." Nana left her unfinished plate to go prepare plates for the newcomers.

Cami set the coffee cups on the table and took a seat. "Nana, thank you for this beautiful breakfast."

"Ain't no trouble. I got all these other ones in here to feed." Nana's voice came from the kitchen. "Y'all go on and eat your oatmeal 'fore it gets cold."

Nick spooned some onto his plate. "I take it you guys already said grace?"

"Yeah, we did," Steven said.

Nick took a bite then looked over at JC. "Danny said you coordinated the rescue mission. I guess you have some training."

"NYPD, retired. Plus a few years in the military."

"That was a heavy operation for a beat cop."

JC was the type who held his cards close to his

chest. "Yeah, well, I just did what needed to be done."

Danny tried to read between the lines. He could tell there was more to JC than he was letting on, but he was obviously done talking about himself.

"Whatever your training is, it's going to come in handy. It's a real mess out there." Nick didn't seem convinced that he knew all there was to know about JC's experience either.

Alisa blurted out, "Danny had another dream."

Nick and Cami both stopped chewing and looked around the table at the others as if they hoped someone would tell them it was only a joke. No one spoke.

Cami placed her biscuit back on her plate. "What about?"

Danny explained the details of the vision, trying to rush through his dissertation while Nick and Cami ate. He did not relish the memories. Each time he had to repeat it his pulse quickened, and he felt unsettled.

Once he'd been through the particulars of the dream, he said, "Alisa and Steven both think it's about a war. Do you think we'll be attacked by whoever did this to us?"

Nick sipped his coffee. "Your dream could very well be about war, but I don't think we'll have to worry about Russia or China."

Dana asked, "Is that who you think did it?"

Nick shook his head. "No, we think it was North Korea, although they could have been working in concert with one of the others. At any rate, Cami and I stuck around long enough to find out what was going on. That's part of what took us so long to get here. Two days after the attack, the entire Ohio-class submarine fleet launched a coordinated attack against the rest of the world to level the playing field."

Steven listened attentively. "Nuclear?"

"EMP. High altitude detonation of Trident II missiles from every sub in the fleet. We turned off everybody's lights. The joint chiefs deliberated, and some wanted to respond by nuking all of our enemies, but in the end, they decided a like-kind response was the best course of action."

Alisa leaned in as she listened. "We wiped out the entire world's power grid? How many missiles did that take?"

"We have fourteen Ohio-class subs, each with twenty-four Trident II missiles, but considering each missile has up to eight 475-kiloton warheads, we certainly didn't have to launch them all. Thirty or forty would probably generate an EMP that would cover every major land mass on earth with massive overlap sectors. I suspect we lit off double that for good measure." Nick continued eating his oatmeal.

Steven asked, "How will we ever get the power back if we shut down every country that produces transformers and electronic components?"

Nick tried not to laugh as he sipped his coffee. "Good question. But, considering that China and Germany are the primary producers of those goods, the president and the joint chiefs both estimated that an invasion from those countries was a larger concern than not having them around to build transformers."

Dana wrinkled her nose. "Germany? They're a staunch ally of America."

"Sure they are, as long as you're well-armed and alert to your surroundings. History hasn't been kind to anyone that's been overly trusting of the Germans." Nick sopped his plate with a biscuit.

JC asked, "If you don't think the dream is about an invasion, what do you think it pertains to?"

"Resource wars. People are killing each other over a can of soup in the cities. Soon, there won't be any cans of soup left in the cities, and they'll figure out where the food is. Large bands are already forming to go on raiding missions in the populated areas. They're hitting warehouses, scavenging grocery and restaurant supply trucks that are stranded on the highways, and doing whatever they can to survive. By the time all of those resources are used up, you'll have very well-organized groups of marauders. And, in this type of environment, the worst of the worst will be the ones that survive. The next logical step in the equation will be for the bands to begin looting farms.

"Of course, many of them will try to institute various forms of neo-feudal systems. The raiders will act as the lords, killing off anyone they see as a threat and forcing the rest to live as serfs, in slave-like conditions. The serfs will do all the work and produce all of the goods, while the lords take what they want and leave just enough for them to survive.

"Anyone who wants to move up in the organization so they can eat better will have to be a warrior and prove their loyalty to the lords.

Eventually, the lords will get greedy and begin to fight over other territories."

Dana tilted her head to one side. "How do you know it will turn out like that? Most people are nice and would rather help their fellow human beings."

Nick shrugged. "It's already happening. We ran across five families that were fleeing Greenville two days ago. They were all from an upscale neighborhood. There were only two men in the group when we saw them. Before they fled, they had set up a block watch and were attempting to maintain civility when a raiding party from the next subdivision over killed all the people on block watch one night and began going house to house, taking goods, killing anyone that resisted and taking captives."

"You mean like sex slaves?" Steven winced in horror.

"No, like slaves for labor. Pre-teen girls and boys." Nick lowered his head. "Sex slaves would be a waste of resources in the present economy. Women are prostituting themselves for a single meal. You'd have to feed a slave three times a day just to keep them alive. And when I say girls are prostituting themselves, I'm not talking about loose women and junkies who were like that anyway; we're talking young professional women and young mothers who are trying to feed their children."

Danny looked down at the floor. He felt sick at his stomach. Even with the dreams, he'd never imagined such unfathomable suffering could be happening right here in America. "The group you ran into, where were they going?"

"The survivors from those five families were headed to Nantahala National Forest to try to get by, living off the land." Nick took a deep breath. He was visually shaken up by the anguish of the refugees he'd encountered. "None of them looked like they were trained nor equipped for what they were trying to do. The chance of any of them making it for more than three months in the woods is next to zero."

Danny turned toward his sister. "How long did you guys hang around after the EMP?"

Cami replied, "Three days. Looking back, we should have left right away, but like Nick said, we wanted to know what the military response would be so we'd have a better idea what we are all in for, long-term.

"We had bought dirt bikes, and rigged up jerry cans so we'd have enough gas to get home after the EMP. We even bought the bikes on Craigslist with cash so there would be no paper trail. But, as it turned out, the Pentagon took it upon themselves to search our house and take the bikes for 'safekeeping.'

"Friday morning after the lights went out, the Pentagon sent a Humvee to pick us up."

Dana asked, "They still have cars that work?"

Cami nodded. "Oh yeah. Most all military equipment is hardened against EMP.

"Anyway, back to my story. They told us to pack a bag, we'd be staying in government housing inside the wire. Government housing turned out to be barrack-style tents which they set up all around DC. By noon Friday, the military had an area cordoned off, extending from the Pentagon, across the river, around Capitol Hill and the White House, all the way back to the State Department. That whole area essentially became an extension of the Washington Naval Yard. Anyone without a government ID was evicted from the area. Anyone with a government ID wasn't allowed to leave."

"How did you get out?" Danny asked.

Cami sipped her coffee. "We got clearance to go back to our house to get some more personal items. Once there, we bribed our armed escort."

"With what?" Alisa quizzed.

"Our rainy day fund." Cami lifted her eyebrows. "We kept ten thousand in cash, inside the wall. It wasn't going to be worth a dime once there was nothing to buy, so it seemed like a good deal. Our escort was probably thinking of deserting anyway. Nearly half of all the military and government workers had figured out that it was only going to get worse and decided to go AWOL by the third day. All the bigwigs, the president, senators, and upper-level staffers were all ferreted off to COG bunkers Thursday night. Everyone still in DC by the third day was expendable, and we all knew it."

"What's a COG bunker?" Dana asked.

"Continuity of government. The military has remote underground locations spread all over the country, with EMP-hardened communications equipment, food, water, power, and security."

"Sounds like they were prepared for this event. Why didn't they tell the rest of us to get ready?" Steven crossed his arms.

Cami held her palms up. "Like I told Danny

before all of this happened, the Congressional EMP Commission, EMP Task Force, some media personalities, and a few politicians have been harping about this for years. No one paid attention."

"I never heard nobody say they was a-gonna turn the lights off till Danny had his vision," Nana protested.

Cami smiled. "Well, (Mike Huckabee, Ted Koppel, former CIA director James Woolsey, they've all been sounding the alarm for years, but it didn't get good television ratings, so the networks quit providing them a platform.")

Steven smirked, "Ironically, the networks sealed their own fate."

"Along with the fate of the nation," Alisa added.

"And the world," Dana commented also.

"No point in dwelling on the past. We need to focus on how to prepare for when Genghis Khan decides to extend the mongrel empire into Miss Jennie's farm." JC sounded serious.

Steven stuck a finger in the air. "I think you meant Mongol. A mongrel is like a mixed breed dog, like a mutt."

JC didn't crack a smile. "I meant what I said."

Danny pursed his lips. It was a fairly accurate analogy for Bret, Travis, and the lot who had abducted Alisa. He figured their type would be the ones who'd excel in the present environment. "A mongrel empire, indeed," he muttered to himself.

Nick wiped his face with his napkin and set it in his plate. "We'll have to pick a spot to defend. Speaking of Mongols, mongrels, and empires, one of Rome's mistakes was trying to hold too much territory with too little resources. If we spread out too thin, we'll end up losing everything. And by everything, I mean everything. We'll lose every inch of property, and those of us who don't die will wish we had. I recommend we scavenge everything we can to build as much housing as possible." Nick picked up the salt shaker, pepper shaker, and several toothpicks from the holder. "This is Nana's house." He set the salt down. "Here is the barn." He placed the pepper several inches away from the salt. Then, he began forming a box between the salt and pepper with the toothpicks. "We should form two rows of housing between the barn and the house. That will leave a common area in between for cooking, eating, and meeting together, like a fort. We'll put our RV along this line, closest to the road. JC, you should move your travel trailer on the same line."

JC nodded and picked up the toothpick representing his travel trailer and moved it to the second row. "Good plan, but I've got a wife and a baby. I want my trailer on the back line, furthest from the road."

Nick picked up the toothpick and toyed with it in his hand. "I understand, but the housing we'll be able to build will be little more than ramshackle shacks. You'll be better protected in that trailer than most anyone else."

JC pulled the toothpick out from between Nick's fingers. "With all due respect, I'm walking away from my farm and a very well-constructed house to go along with your plan. I figured we might have to circle the wagons when I heard about Danny's dream, so I'm okay with abandoning my property.

But, if you want me to go along with your plan, my trailer stays here." He put the toothpick back in the second row. "Otherwise, I'll take my chances at my house."

Nick said nothing, but put both hands in the air as a symbol of his acquiescence.

Danny tried not to let it be too obvious, but he let out a gentle sigh of relief. Nick and JC were the two men in the group who might be able to put a plan together that could keep everyone alive. Given the circumstances, their combined skill sets were crucial elements to the viability of the entire community. Danny looked over at JC. "Do you think the Reeses will go along with the plan?"

JC leaned back in his chair. "They have to. This is going to be an all-in or all-out kind of thing. Anybody who wants to tough out the zombie apocalypse on their own is welcome to do so. We'll be their friend; we'll trade with them, whatever, but they have to know we can't offer them any support or charity once they walk away."

Nick crossed his arms and nodded. "I agree with JC."

Steven looked at Nana. "Do you think Catfish will move to the farm?"

"Faster than a chicken on a Junebug. I'd sooner sleep under a tree than set foot in that man's house. It looks like a bunch a hogs've been livin' in there." Nana stood to begin clearing the table. "You could put him in the hay loft and it'd be a step up from where he is now."

Nick handed his plate to Nana. "Would you be open to having more people sleep in the house? We could probably move the stuff from the back porch out to the barn. And maybe have some other people bunk up together."

Danny caught Steven and Dana looking at each other out of the corner of his eye. When he looked to confirm what he was sure he'd just seen, they had both looked away.

"I reckon," Nana said. "As long as that filthy heathen Catfish don't think he's sleepin' in this house."

Alisa raised her hand. "It would be tough to fit another bed in our room, but we could stack storage items up against the wall to make more room in the rest of the house."

Nick shook his head. "Good idea."

Danny immediately saw the play she'd just made to ensure their privacy. He gave her a wink and a smile to show his appreciation. Tight quarters were fine, as long as they had a place to get away from it all and be alone.

Cami held Nick's hand. "In fact, Alisa, maybe we'll bring some of our stuff out of the RV and stack it against that wall in your room later today. Once we get moved into the RV bedroom, the couch will be available for others, maybe the Reeses."

"We'll help you," Danny said. "How will you move the RV?"

Nick shook his head. "I'm not sure. I was hoping that Rocky's tractor still worked. Otherwise, we'll have to hope Catfish's truck can push it."

"I'm going home to get a couple hours of sleep. I'm beat after my night watch shift." JC stood up and pushed his chair under the table. "I'll go get Catfish in the morning and have him come over to move my trailer. Afterwards, I'll have him drive me out to the Reeses'. I'll try to convince Korey to bring his family over here. It would help if I could give them an idea of where they're going to be sleeping. It's hard enough to uproot a family, but if they feel like they're going to be an inconvenience or there's no room for them, we might not be able to get them out here. We need every trigger finger we can get if we want to survive. You guys keep that in mind when you figure out where they're going to sleep."

Danny got up and walked JC to the door. "Thanks again for taking my shift last night."

"No problem at all. Talk to you later." JC closed the door behind him.

After helping Nana get the kitchen cleaned up, Danny and the others began helping Cami and Nick clear the supplies out of the RV.

Nick instructed them where to take each box and bin. Some items were brought back to the house to be stored upstairs in Danny and Alisa's room, but much of it was taken to the hay loft.

As Danny hoisted the last bin up the ladder and into the loft, he said to Nick, "We have all of our supplies stashed along the wall in Dana's room, so we've still got plenty of space in our room if you want to clear out some more bins from the RV."

Nick smiled. "Thanks, we'll manage with what's left in the RV. We just needed to get the boxes cleared off the bed. But I'll take you up on letting us use the space. I've got some critical items in that metal shed that I'd like to keep in the house."

"Oh, like what?" Danny began climbing back down the ladder.

"A bunch of stuff. We'll start pulling it out tomorrow. I think Cami and I still need to rest up for the remainder of the day."

"Yeah, you probably need a week of R&R after your trip. I know how tired we were after just a few days."

It had taken less than an hour to clear out all the boxes with everyone's help. Cami and Nick went back in the RV for a nap while Danny and the others finished the daily chores.

Steven grabbed an ax from the tool area of the barn before they left. "I guess Danny and I will go collect firewood if you girls want to take care of the chickens and the rabbits."

"Sure," Dana said.

Danny kissed Alisa on the forehead. "Stay close to the house. And make sure one of you has a shotgun, even around the house."

"I've got the revolver." Alisa pulled her jacket up to reveal the handle.

"Good, but you should always have a long gun nearby as well. Steven will have his shotgun, and I'll have the Glock. If we see any small game, we might take a shot with the shotgun, so don't be alarmed. If we have trouble, I'll take two quick shots with the Glock. If you hear that, get Nick and come find us."

Alisa nodded and stole another kiss. "Okay, be safe."

Danny grabbed the saw and retrieved Steven's

shotgun from the corner of the barn. "Let's go get some wood."

Steven walked beside Danny toward the forest. "Nick and JC seemed like they were in a bit of an alpha-male competition back there."

Danny handed the shotgun over to his friend as they walked. "I think they're just trying to find their respective places in all of this. They're both leaders, and they seem to respect each other, but I suppose it'll be a process to figure out how different leadership roles are going to be delegated going forward."

Steven nodded. "And I totally understand JC's point, not wanting to put his family on the front line. I suppose I'd get an alpha syndrome if I were in his shoes."

Danny chuckled. "We're blessed to have them both. We wouldn't stand a chance without them."

"Have you given any thought as to where we should put the wood?"

"I was thinking of ricking it up alongside of the propane tank. It would provide some protection against an attack. I'd hate to see that thing blow up because it caught a bullet."

Steven glanced over. "Good idea. We could use firewood to form defensive firing positions all around the camp. It has to be stacked somewhere, might as well make use of it while it's in storage."

"Good plan. I like it," Danny said. "I thought I saw you and Dana look at each other when Nick was talking about bunking up."

"I don't know what you're talking about." Steven tested a small, barren tree to see if it would bend or break.

Danny grabbed a twig from the tree and folded it in his hand. It snapped. "Looks pretty dry."

Steven swung the ax at the base of the tree a few times. "If I notch this out, I think we'll be able to push it over."

Danny watched as Steven chopped. "You still sound pretty certain that there's nothing between the two of you. I thought the only problem before was that she wasn't a believer. Now that she's accepted Jesus, what's the deal?"

Steven paused and pushed on the tree. It still needed a few more good chops. "There's a lot going on right now. We've got to build a fort, raise our own food, provide our own security, learn to get along with everybody; besides all of that, I'm responsible for coming up with a message for church every week." Steven resumed chopping.

Danny waited for Steven to pause again, then gave the tree a good push. It began to creak over. It wasn't big enough to come crashing down, but it eventually fell. "But, we have a lot of down time, also. Once the sun sets, we can't get much accomplished. Any night you're not working security, you've got time . . . for friends . . . or whatever. Dana doesn't strike me as the needy type."

Steven took a couple more whacks to break the tree free at the base. "She must; you put a lot of effort into getting her hitched."

Danny pulled the tree to confirm it was completely severed from the stump. "I'm not worried about her. She's got options."

"Like who? Catfish?" Steven's voice suddenly got defensive.

"Like Jack. That kid looks like an Abercrombie model."

"He's seventeen!"

Danny looked at the tree. "We don't have any way to haul the wood back. I say we drag the whole tree to the house and cut it up there."

"That's fine. Why did you bring up Jack? Did she say something about him?"

Danny grabbed a limb and started pulling. "It's just the way of nature. He'll be eighteen soon, then there will only be four years between them. He's mature for his age, and smart. If I saw the two of them out together at the movies, I wouldn't think anything of it. He could pass for twenty."

Steven huffed as he struggled to hold the ax and the shotgun in the same hand so he could pull a limb from the tree. "Who's to say he'd have any interest in a cougar five years older than him?"

Danny fought back a grin. Steven was confirming what he already knew. "Four, but then there's the brother. He's about my age. He'll probably be back soon."

Steven's voice became more irritated. "You don't know that."

"Bro, relax! I'm just saying." Danny had to really work at not laughing out loud. Even so, he wasn't finished goading his friend. "And suppose he shows up wounded."

"What's that supposed to mean?"

"Dana has a natural instinct for being a nurse. She took very good care of your leg when you were injured. If Chris comes home and needs a little medical attention, the Florence Nightingale Effect might take over."

Steven dropped his end of the tree. "Are you just making this garbage up to manipulate me into dating Dana?"

Danny could see that Steven was becoming seriously upset. He released his end of the tree as well and paused. "Steven, I care about you. I know that you and Dana had a connection before. I'm simply trying to point out that she's a very pretty girl amongst a possibly growing number of eligible bachelors. If you don't feel that way for her anymore, that's fine, but get it figured out now. I don't want to see you wallowing in regret once that ship has sailed."

Steven took a deep breath and looked across the field toward the house where the girls were tending the rabbit hutches. "I do like her, Danny."

"Then what's the hold-up?"

Steven bit his lip as he stared at Dana in the distance. "Savannah."

"I don't get it. Did you guys do something I don't know about? We all make mistakes. You ask God for forgiveness and move on."

"No. It's not that."

"What then?"

Steven shook his head and looked down toward the ground. "I was going to leave her when the EMP went off. I insisted that we walk away and leave her to die. What would have happened to her if I'd done that?"

"That didn't happen." Danny put his hand on

Steven's shoulder.

"Thank God. Thanks to Alisa insisting that we bring her."

"Okay, but now she's here, and you're here. She likes you, Steven. She doesn't blame you."

Steven began to cry. "But how could I have abandoned her? The girl I love. I don't deserve her, Danny. She'd be better off with Jack or Chris. I just want her to be happy and safe."

Danny hugged his friend. "Bro, you need to think about what you are doing right now. You're blaming yourself, punishing yourself by not letting Dana know how you feel. In the process, you're punishing her too. The person you're trying to shield from the evil monster you think lives inside you; she's getting hurt by your imposed protection."

Steven snorted. "Kind of ironic, huh?"

"Kind of proud." Danny looked him in the eye.

Steven knuckled his forehead. "Proud?"

"Yeah, you're too proud to forgive yourself. You asked her to forgive you at your first church message in the barn, in front of the entire group. I saw her. She was bawling. She completely forgave you.

"I guarantee you that Dana never gives a second thought to being told she couldn't come along. She remembers that you relented and finally said it was okay for her to come with us. She's grateful. You, on the other hand, won't forgive yourself. Despite the fact that Jesus, the King of the universe, has forgiven you, you won't. It sounds like pride to me; like you have higher standards than God. You think that you're more righteous than Christ, and that he was wrong for forgiving you. Or worse, you think the blood of Christ isn't good enough to cover your sin of abandoning Dana, which you never did. Either way, I'd say you have some soul searching, especially if you intend on being the spiritual leader around here."

"Wow!" Steven's face had a look of shock.

"I'm not trying to beat you up. You were doing a pretty good job of that yourself. I just want you to look objectively at what you're thinking, what you're doing, and how it's affecting the people around you, especially Dana."

Steven sighed. "Well, that was pretty offensive, but I needed to hear it. You're right. I've got some soul searching to do."

The two of them dragged the tree to the side of the house and proceeded to chop and saw it into firewood. Next, they cut and processed two more small trees. Neither one said much.

CHAPTER 11

> They which builded on the wall, and they that bare burdens, with those that laded, (every one with one of his hands wrought in the work,) and with the other hand held a weapon.
>
> Nehemiah 4:17

Danny stumbled out of bed and put his jeans on. He was still not accustomed to the early mornings and tough manual labor. He nudged Alisa. "Time to wake up."

She covered her head with the pillow, and her muffled voice responded, "No! We were hauling boxes, feeding animals, and working in the garden all day yesterday. I'm beat. Can't I sleep through breakfast?"

Nana yelled from the bottom of the stairs. "Y'all come on. The biscuits is gettin' cold."

"If you're brave enough, sure, go ahead." Danny looked his shirt over to consider if he could wear it one more day. It was dusty from hauling wood but not sweaty. He gave it a quick sniff test and put it on. Since there were no washing machines and the only detergent was what they'd stockpiled, the standard for *dirty clothes* had been lowered by several rungs. Socks and underwear were put on fresh every day, but shirts were expected to be worn two days, if possible. The goal for jeans and pants was to wear them until they were visually soiled. With the amount of farm work the group had been doing, that was typically three days or less.

"Let's do it all over again." Alisa threw the covers off and put on the same pair of cargo pants she'd worn the day before but went straight to a clean tee-shirt.

Danny winked at her. "You're chicken to sleep through breakfast."

"Has anyone ever done it?"

"Cami tried it once, when we were kids. Once."

"What happened?"

"Crawl back in the bed and find out for yourself."

Alisa flung one of the pillows at him. "Quit messin' with me, Danny Walker! It's too early and I'm in no mood."

Danny winked, gave a mischievous grin, and blew her a kiss as he headed to the breakfast table. Danny took two steps at a time to get downstairs faster. Dana, Steven, Cami and Nick were already at the table.

"Where's Lisa?" Nana asked.

Danny bit his tongue slightly to keep from laughing. "She said she's going to sleep through breakfast and that we could eat without her."

Nana walked over to the foot of the stairs. "Now listen here, young lady, you best get down here at this table 'fore I have to come up there and drag you down by the hair of your head! The sun has been up for an hour and . . ."

Alisa came bounding down the stairs, "Coming, Nana!"

Danny fought to contain his amusement as he looked to see the reaction of the others at the table. Steven, of course, was snickering. Dana looked like she was trying to figure out what was going on. Cami appeared to be having flashbacks, and Nick was grinning from ear to ear.

"Oh." Nana looked surprised to see Alisa so quickly. "Steven, you say grace."

Danny regained his composure as Steven asked the blessing over the food.

Alisa reached under the table and pinched the side of Danny's leg as hard as she could. She whispered, "You better hope that I don't find out that you had something to do with that little scene."

Danny winced in pain as he pried her fingers from his thigh. "Ouch! You've already tried, convicted, and punished me."

She winked as she passed the plate of pancakes. "It's the apocalypse. Justice moves swiftly."

After breakfast, Danny poured another cup of

coffee, went out front to sit under the tree to be alone, and read a few chapters from his Bible before the day was completely devoured by chores. A soft, cool breeze rustled through the tree limbs, which were slowly turning green with new leaves. Down by the creek was a long, meandering patch of wild daffodils, mixed in vibrant yellows and pure whites, with bright green stems. "Tomorrow is the first day of spring." Danny wanted to keep track of seasons and holidays to maintain a sense of normalcy in an otherwise chaotic world. He took a deep breath. "It even smells like a fresh start." Danny thought about the dystopian landscape they'd had to travel through to get to Nana's and how dreary it had looked when they arrived. But now, the flowers, the new growth on the trees; maybe the worst was behind them and this was a new beginning. Danny smiled, looking up at the wonders of creation around him as he read through the Book of Psalms.

Suddenly, all of his thoughts of a fresh start were shattered as Catfish drove down the gravel path pulling a trailer full of pigs. The hogs were held on the flatbed trailer by a makeshift cage constructed of wood pallets that had been coupled together using bailing wire. The image was a jolting reminder that everyone was moving to Nana's farm for mutual defense. The daffodils were in bloom, but America was heading into the darkest of winters concerning God's judgment for forsaking His Word and His ways.

"Ichabod," Danny whispered to himself. The glory of God still appeared through the renewal of creation, but it had most certainly departed this cursed nation.

Catfish leaned out the window of his truck. "Where does Miss Jennie expect me to keep my hogs?"

Danny got up and walked toward the vehicle. He waved his hand to disperse the smell coming from the creatures. "Downwind."

Catfish chuckled, letting a dribble of tobacco juice drip from his lower lip. "You'll get used to it."

Danny looked over at JC, who was getting out of the passenger's side. "Maybe so, but I still think we should build them a pen on the back side of the barnyard."

"All right. I'm gonna let 'em waller about with the cows till we get 'em somewheres else to go," Catfish said.

Danny noticed the bullet hole in Catfish's windshield. He walked closer to the truck. He turned to JC. "Did Catfish make you mad on the way over?"

JC snickered. "No."

Catfish waved his hand. "Just a little misunderstandin'."

"I'll say." Danny crossed his arms as he waited for an explanation.

Catfish put the vehicle in park and cut the engine. "When the lights got turned out, there was free gas all over the creation. Every car on the road had several gallons just a-sittin' there, like a peach waitin' to be plucked. All these heathens 'round here done sucked up all the gas from the cars on the road, so I've had to hunt a mite harder to keep my truck runnin'. I went to get a little fuel from a car in some feller's driveway. He didn't take too kindly to it at all."

"Catfish! You've been stealing gas?" Danny let his mouth hang open.

"Well, folks got different ways of sayin' what stealin' is and what it ain't, times bein' what they are." Catfish shrugged innocently.

Danny crossed his arms. "I guess the guy who shot your windshield has a pretty clear definition of stealing and a pretty good idea about how he handles thieves, times being what they are."

"Hmm," Catfish snorted as he examined the bullet hole. "I reckon he does." He started the engine. "Anyhow, I'll have to be a mite more stingy about galivantin' around town."

"How much fuel do you have left?" Danny asked.

"Oh, less than fifty gallons." Catfish slowly pulled away and drove his pigs over toward the barn.

JC shook his head. "He's got gas stashed in coffee cans, plastic buckets, and milk jugs. I don't necessarily approve of the way he acquired it, but it will come in handy."

Danny watched as Catfish drove off. "Is he going to drive you over to the Reeses' place?"

"Yep. Did anyone talk to Rocky about moving over here?"

Danny nodded. "Nick went over there yesterday evening. He explained the concept, but Rocky thinks because he can see Nana's house from his porch, that's close enough."

JC slowly shook his head. "With just the two of

them in that house, he wouldn't stand a chance. I understand, he doesn't want to walk away from his home. I feel the same way, but we've all got to do whatever it takes to survive. If you don't mind, why don't you help Catfish with moving my trailer? I'll go talk to Rocky, see if I can persuade him."

"No problem." Danny patted JC on the back as he walked toward the creek.

Danny picked up his Bible, which was next to the tree, and brought it back in the house. Next he called Steven to help out moving the trailer.

Steven carried his shotgun as they walked toward the trailer. "I thought a lot about what you said yesterday. But I'm not sure she still likes me."

"I am," Danny said, matter-of-factly.

"How?" Steven looked at him curiously.

"She said she loves you."

"I never heard that."

"It was after you were shot, you were lying over in the grass, not in great shape. She prayed and asked God for a miracle, to get you back to Nana's safely. When she was praying, she told God she loved you."

"I didn't know all of that."

"You do now."

"And that's when Catfish showed up with the truck? Right after she prayed for a miracle?"

"Yeah."

"Hmm." Steven was quiet for a while. "I remember her giving me water and feeding me. She's a really great girl."

Danny nodded. "She is."

"But what am I going to do? I can't ask her to go

to the movies."

Danny shook his head at Steven's thick-headedness. "All you have to do is quit pushing her away. Just be nice. Of course, if you want to move things along, you could ask her to go for a walk."

Steven smiled. "I guess I could do that."

They reached the trailer and helped Catfish get it hitched up. It was soon in position, just where JC had requested it be parked. Shortly thereafter, Danny heard the sound of Rocky's tractor coming down the hill toward the gravel drive. "I guess we should go tell Nick and Cami that it's time to move the RV."

Catfish moved his truck out of the way, while Steven and Danny walked to the RV.

Danny knocked on the door of the RV. "Hey, guys, Rocky is coming with the tractor."

Cami's voice came from inside. "Thanks, we'll be right out."

JC was standing on the back of the tractor as Rocky drove around the back of the barn.

Steven looked the tractor over. "At least tractors don't have computers. Hopefully most farmers will be able to keep things going until they run out of gas."

Rocky let out a sarcastic laugh. "Ha! Now that's a good one, tractors don't have computers. John Deere has been putting proprietary computers in their tractors for years. They come with a lifetime licensing agreement for the software that run the computers, so farmers technically never own the tractor. What's worse, they can be prosecuted under copyright law for attempting to make alterations to their own tractor. You can't even work on it without a licensed diagnostic computer to tell you what's wrong."

Steven looked surprised. "Wow. Well, I guess they can't be prosecuted anymore."

Rocky smirked. "Yeah, guess not. Anyway, I got sick of being cornered by Deere and the other corporate giants, and rebuilt this old 1975 International Harvester Farmall. Did most of it myself."

"It's a nice-looking classic tractor. And it runs great." JC jumped off the back and inspected it from the front and side.

Rocky smiled. "At least we'll have a tractor until we run out of gas."

Steven asked, "Think we could use it tomorrow to get the front field broken up? Nana wants us to fill that entire field with corn. It would be a heck of a job if we had to do it all by hand."

"Sure. I'll go ahead and get it plowed after we finish moving the RV. But won't a field of corn right by the road paint a giant target on the farm?" Rocky cut the engine.

Danny said, "It will, but we're putting melons, beans, tomatoes, potatoes, and strawberries on the back side of the farm. Corn is the most high-profile, but it's also the easiest thing to grow en masse. We'd be able to produce way more than we can eat, so if we have beggars coming around, we can put them to work harvesting, then pay them in corn for their work."

Rocky adjusted his red, International Harvester cap. "If looters don't have it cleaned out by the time it's ready to harvest."

Nick crossed his arms. "We could put an observation post up in the hedgerow along the road."

JC looked toward the hedgerow. "Won't do us much good without comms. We can't afford to allocate more than two people for security on that corner. With all the other tasks, even two would be spreading us thin. Suppose four or five guys come through and decide they want to pick corn. Two people can't engage five looters with no way to call for backup."

Nick winked and pulled his keys from his pocket. "We put a few goodies away in the metal shed next to the RV. I did the best I knew how to protect them from an EMP. Why don't we go see if they still work?"

Danny had been itching to know what was in that shed. "All right!"

"You got comms in there?" JC's voice was optimistically curious.

Nick removed the lock and opened the shed. "We'll know in a minute." He took out two .50 caliber ammo cans and removed a strip of foil insulation tape that covered the seam where the lid met the base of the first can. He pulled the latch and opened the lid. He removed a piece of cardboard lying on top of the contents, which acted as an insulator between the can and whatever was inside. Nick pulled out a Mylar bag and handed it to Danny. "Will you do the honors?"

"Sure." Danny took out his pocket knife and cut the Mylar open. Inside were two boxes, each individually wrapped in heavy-duty aluminum foil.

Nick opened the other can, removed a second Mylar bag, and retrieved two more boxes, giving one to JC and the other to Cami. He took one of the boxes from Danny and began to open it.

Danny followed his lead as did JC and Cami. Danny pulled the foil back to reveal a cardboard box. "Baofeng. Professional FM transceiver."

JC had his unit unboxed and quickly attached the antenna. He gave Nick one of his rare smiles. "Good call."

Nick keyed his mic. "This is November Foxtrot calling Juliet Charlie. Do you read me?"

JC keyed his mic. "Loud and clear, November Foxtrot."

Steven quizzed JC. "How did you know who he was talking about?"

"Juliet Charlie, that's my initials, JC."

"Got it." Steven nodded.

"Them is some fine doohickeys till the batteries play out." Catfish admired one of the units.

Nick nodded. "If everything in the shed survived the EMP, I've got that covered. Danny, give me a hand with that large box."

Danny carefully helped Nick remove a large box covered in aluminum foil and foil insulation tape, which was roughly half the size of a door. "Solar panels?"

Nick nodded. "Yep, 100 watts. I have four of them."

"Don't you go to shreddin' that tin foil. We can save it. Might need it for somethin'. Miss Jennie'll tan your hides if she finds out you're a-bein' wasteful." Catfish helped Danny and Nick remove the aluminum foil without tearing it up.

Rocky helped Steven pull the second panel out of the shed. "You must have spent a fortune on all of this."

Nick shook his head as he pulled the panel from the cardboard box. "100 dollars on the charge controller, little more than that on the inverter, 550 for all four panels. I might have another 100 in cables and connectors." Nick pointed to the two large 370 amp hour batteries. "Those bad boys set me back about 400 bucks each. Still, the whole system, even with the protective material I had on, it cost less than two grand. Considering we knew this was coming, it seemed like a worthwhile investment."

JC nodded. "All of this is a game changer. What did you pay for the radios?"

"Like twenty-five dollars each." Nick pointed to some other ammo cans in the back. "I've got a few rechargeable batteries, a shortwave radio, and a couple other things back there.

"After we decided to splurge on getting the RV, everything else was sort of small potatoes. Then, Danny had his first dream, which came true. After that second dream, we made getting ready for this our top priority." Nick pulled the charge controller out of one of the ammo boxes and began connecting the wires.

"Smart move," JC said. "Between these radios and a few trip-wire alarms like I've got set up over at my place, I think we can lock this place down pretty good."

Alisa and Dana came walking up. Dana was carrying a bucket and Alisa had the AK-47, in keeping with the standard security protocol.

Alisa surveyed all of the electronic components for the solar charging station. "What's all of this?"

Danny gave her and Dana a quick rundown of what Nick was doing.

"So, we have a radio that works?" Dana asked.

"Yeah, but no radio stations. The US military made sure they turned off the lights for everybody," Steven answered.

Nick paused what he was doing. "Cami, bring me that ammo can on the bottom of the stack."

Cami brought that can over to Nick. He opened it and took out a small AM/FM/shortwave receiver and handed it to Dana. "One of those cans against the wall has some batteries. If someone wants to fish those out, we'll get this thing working. Who knows? Perhaps we will find a ham operator who had the forethought to put away a radio and a way to power it."

Dana examined the radio. "This will pick up a ham radio?"

"Yeah, if you click the single-side band button, the one that says SSB, it will. Once you get the batteries in it, just keep scrolling through and looking. There's also a long cable antenna in the box. The higher you can get that hung, the better your odds of catching a signal." Nick continued connecting the solar components.

"What's in the bucket?" Danny asked.

Alisa rolled her eyes. "Don't ask!"

"Chicken poop and rabbit poop. Want to look?"

Dana offered the bucket to Danny.

He put both hands in the air. "I trust you."

"Nana says we have to build a compost bin to mix the poop with leaves, paper, and forest debris so it can break down to be used as fertilizer. She said it might kill the vegetables if we put it directly on the plants." Dana swung the bucket back and forth.

Catfish shook his head. "You can put rabbit poop straight on the garden. It won't hurt nothin'. But she's right about the chicken droppin's. They'll burn your garden up if you don't let 'em break down first."

"Good to know. Do you want to tell her she's wrong about the rabbit poop?" Dana smiled at Catfish.

"Best you go on and put 'em all in the compost. Might help everything else break down faster anyhow." Catfish pointed to the trailer with which he'd brought his pigs. "I got some wood pallets over yonder that you can use for your compost bin. Just string four of 'em together with the bailin' wire. Don't need no top."

"Thanks." Dana looked around. "Any volunteers to help me build the poop box?"

Steven raised his hand quickly. "I'll give you a hand."

Alisa looked puzzled and began to raise her hand as well. Danny grabbed it before she could and lightly shook his head.

"Great. Let's go build a poop bin." Dana carried the bucket toward the pallets, and Steven walked beside her, carrying his shotgun.

Alisa stuck her tongue in her jaw. "What just happened?"

Danny shrugged. "Just let nature take its course."

Alisa frowned as she watched them walk away. "Nature is fine, but he needs to stop leading her on if he's not interested. After his public apology in the barn, she was expecting a little more interest than what she got."

"We talked for a little while yesterday. I think he saw the light," Danny said.

Alisa crossed her arms. "I hope so. If he hurts her feelings again, he'll see lights all right."

Once the solar generator was set up, Nick hit the power button on the inverter. "We've got juice!"

Everyone clapped and whistled.

JC asked Nick, "How hard is that to relocate?"

"Not hard at all. Why?"

"If it's easy for us to move, it'd be easy for someone else to haul away. We might want it closer to the house."

"Good call." Nick looked around. "This isn't the best exposure for the panels anyway. We could move the entire shed to the courtyard. Then, I could hang the inverter and charge controller right over top the batteries. I've got enough cable that we can reposition the panels every morning to an eastern exposure and each afternoon for a western exposure. That would maximize our solar collection time."

"And, it would be secure." JC looked the system over.

Rocky interrupted, "If you don't mind, I'd like to go ahead and get your RV moved. I need to get started on the field right away if I'm going to get it plowed today."

"Of course." Nick tossed the RV keys to Cami. "Cami will turn the steering wheel and guide it into position."

Rocky started the engine of the tractor. "Okay, I'll get the tow chain hooked up. I'll try not to tear anything up."

"The EMP took care of that. Not much left to tear up, mechanically speaking," Nick said.

Rocky had the chain hooked up within minutes. He pulled the RV to the position between the barn and the house as Nick directed.

"Looks good." Nick gave Rocky a thumbs-up.

Catfish unhooked the tow chain and handed it to Rocky, who drove off to get his plow.

Nick began unhooking the system so it could be relocated. "Catfish, can you pull your truck around so we can set this all up in what will be the courtyard?"

"Yep. I'll be around directly with the vehicle." Catfish adjusted his overalls and went to get his truck.

Everyone worked together to roll the metal shed over on its side so Catfish could pull it to the yard with a makeshift harness of rope and two ratcheting tie-down straps. Next, everyone pitched in to help Nick affix the charge controller and inverter to the inside of the shed wall. The two large six-volt batteries were connected in series to create a twelve-volt cell, which was compatible with the rest of the system.

Nick plugged in the chargers for the radios.

"Once the batteries and radios are fully charged, we can decide what other applications will have priority. It looks like a big system, but it's actually fairly limited in what we can actually run with it."

"On the bright side, most of our electronics are fried, so we won't need much." Alisa stuck her hands in her pockets.

Nick chuckled. "Yeah. We can run a couple of lamps, a hot plate, fans, maybe even a refrigerator as long as it doesn't have a circuit board. If Nana's fridge sucks too much electricity, we can power the little one in the RV. It's small, but could make a big difference for preserving leftovers and such."

Danny glanced over at JC. "Did you get anywhere with Rocky?"

JC sighed. "He agreed to position some of his preps in the barn, but he doesn't want to leave his house to move into a shack 300 yards over. I see his point, and I hope we don't get taken by surprise, but, our security force won't be able to have a guard up on the hill to watch his house around the clock."

Catfish yelled out his window. "JC, we best get a move on if we're gonna go over by the Reeses' place. I still got to get my gasoline supply to bring over here. And my toothbrush."

"You ain't fooling nobody. You don't use a toothbrush." JC waved to the others as he got in the truck.

Alisa held Danny's hand as Catfish and JC drove away. "What if we built a really cute place for Rocky and Pauline? Maybe they would move then."

Cami smiled. "If you guys can build something with a little space and a good roof, I'll help Alisa decorate. I'm sure that would go a long way with convincing them to come."

Nick smiled and put his arm around Cami. "We can give it a shot. If we build it and they don't move, it will be available for anyone else who wants to come."

Nana yelled out the back door. "When y'all get done fixin' your spaceship, come on to the table. Lunch will be ready."

"Thanks, Nana," Cami yelled back. "She's determined to make sure none of us starve."

"Should I run and get Steven and Dana?" Alisa asked.

Danny winked. "I'll make sure Nana saves something for them to eat. Why don't we let them take their time with the compost bin?"

"Okay." Alisa carried the AK in one hand and held Danny's hand with the other as they walked back to the house.

CHAPTER 12

If the ax is dull, And one does not sharpen the edge, Then he must use more strength; But wisdom brings success.

Ecclesiastes 10:10 NKJV

Danny lay on his bed, scrolling past the static on the shortwave radio.

Alisa walked in and continued towel drying her hair. "Finding anything?"

"Nothing." He glanced up. "How was your bath?"

"Cold. It takes way too long to boil water for a hot bath. First you have to pump the water, then you have to get the fire going and position the grate so the pots don't tip over. And all the pots that fit on the grate will only fill the tub halfway. By the time you've gone through the entire process again to fill the tub all the way, the water from the first round is already cold. It's just not worth it. So, I fill the tub with one round of hot water, then just put enough cold water to make it like a foot deep and make it work. It's such a hassle."

Danny continued pressing the button to scan the frequencies. "A lot of folks are dying because they don't even have water to drink. It could be worse."

She bit her lip and looked at the bed where Danny lay. "I know. I don't mean to complain, but I'm exhausted from planting corn all day by hand."

He looked up at her. "I understand. I wasn't trying to make you feel bad; I just wanted you to be grateful for what we have. And I totally know what you mean. It would have been nice to come in from the field, take a nice hot shower, and relax. Farming is hard work, especially the way we have to do it. But once again, it could be worse. At least Rocky plowed the field with his tractor."

Alisa twirled her wet towel up and snapped it right by Danny's feet. POP!

"Hey!" He jumped up from the bed. "What was that all about?"

"You just gave me a great idea!" She slung the towel over her shoulder like a weapon.

"And that's the thanks I get? Being beat with a wet towel?" Danny scowled.

"If I had wanted to hit you with it, you'd have a red mark on your foot the size of a tomato. I just wanted to wake you up so you'd be as excited as I am."

Danny set the radio on top of a plastic bin full of

supplies which he was using as a nightstand. "Okay, let's hear your idea."

"Have you ever seen a camping shower?"

"Probably not. Why?"

"Well, I was thinking we could make something like that. Basically, it's a black water bladder with a hose that's like a foot and a half long. The hose has a little nozzle that you squeeze when you want the water to spray out. You fill it with water, let it hang in the sun all day to get hot, then you have a nice warm shower waiting for you at the end of the day."

Danny shook his head. "Too bad you didn't think of buying one of those when we still had stores, online shopping, and free shipping on orders over thirty-five dollars."

Alisa began twirling the towel again. "Is that a criticism?"

Danny shielded himself from the fury of the towel. "I meant to say, too bad I didn't think of buying one when they were available."

"That sounds better." She slung the coiled towel back over her shoulder. "Anyway, it's a simple design. We would just need to put a hook in the ceiling over the bathtub. Then we could hang a five-gallon bucket from the hook with a small length of garden hose coming out the side, near the bottom. The hose could even have the sprayer on it. We just need to figure out how to get the hose to stay in the bucket and not leak around the opening. Even if it leaked a little bit, that would be fine since it would be hanging over the tub anyway, and it only has to hold the water for a few minutes. Especially since showers use less water than a bath, we would conserve so much time pumping and boiling water. And less water boiled means less firewood that has to be collected to boil it. Heck, we could heat enough water on the grate at one time for three or four people to get a shower. Seems like something where we could all put our minds together and come up with a solution."

"Rocky rebuilt his tractor. I'm sure he can figure out how to make a piece of hose stick in a bucket without falling out." Danny tried to envision Alisa's suggestion. "I think I'm following you for the basic principle, but you lost me on heating the water. I thought you said the camping shower was heated by solar."

"It is, but I'm just trying to figure out the mechanics of using the gravity-fed water delivery system for now. Heating the water is the smaller issue."

Since he was responsible for collecting firewood, Danny was stuck on heating the water with the sun. "But, the camping showers, they heat up in the sun because they're black. So all we have to do is pump the water for the showers in the morning and let it sit in a black container all day. We could even set it up on the roof so it never gets hit by the shade. We could use buckets, milk jugs, whatever, as long as we can paint them black."

"Yeah, that should work."

Danny continued pondering possible solutions. "So I'm trying to envision the camping shower. Does it look like the water bladders that Nick and Cami have for their backpacks?"

Alisa looked confused. "What water bladders?"

"I guess they're what the military uses instead of canteens. It's like a heavy-duty plastic bag with a drinking tube so the soldiers can just bite down on the end and suck whenever they want a drink."

She ripped the towel off her shoulder and popped it again, this time barely grazing his leg. "That's exactly what I'm talking about!"

"Give me that!" Danny grabbed the towel and took it out of her hands. "Enough with the towel popping!"

"You're no fun. I'm going to go ask Cami if I can use one of her water thingies to make a shower."

Danny twirled the towel into a tight coil and popped the back of Alisa's leg as she was heading for the door.

"Ouch! Danny! I didn't pop you that hard!"

"Don't dish it out if you can't take it." He grinned mischievously.

Suddenly, the radio came to life. "This is your eight o'clock nightly update from Pickens Radio. I'm Ranger Dave."

Danny dropped the towel and turned to walk slowly toward the radio. Alisa froze, motionless in her tracks.

The report continued. "We don't have a lot of new reports for this evening. I did finally hear from another ham operator who has a system that survived the blast, so at least I know I'm not just talking to myself, so a big shout-out to K4CDM if you're listening. K4CDM is dealing with the same things the rest of us have to face. No stores, no emergency services, and very little information.

"Our community here, just outside of Pickens, South Carolina, is coming together well to provide for security, which is becoming an increasing problem. As resources in nearby Greenville are drying up, desperate people who have managed to stay alive this long are pouring into the countryside in search of supplies. Most folks around here are not in much of a position to help more than perhaps a meal or two, and many of the desperate refugees are turning aggressive. Many others were already in the aggressive stage when they left the city. Unfortunately, they make up a large portion of the survivors.

"It's been exactly five weeks today since the EMP. If you're still alive at this point, you fall into one of three categories. Either you were prepared for such an event, you weren't prepared but knew someone who was prepared enough to be able to share, or you weren't prepared but you've taken what you needed by force. Everybody else is either dead or will be soon.

"If you fall into the first two categories, be aware, the last category thrives in this environment, so you need to get organized and do whatever is necessary to protect your family. And make your mind up now. Hesitation might cost you your life.

"On to the next topic. I have not been able to pick any civilian radio signals from anywhere around the world. That fact convinces me that this was a worldwide event, most likely military in nature. The few military signals that I have intercepted have all used heavy encryption, which tells me very little other than the fact that they are active.

"Once again, if anyone is out there who has the ability to transmit, please call in on this frequency and let me know that you are out there. Every little piece of information will help us put together a better picture of what is going on around the country and around the world.

"Those of you who are able to listen but not transmit, God bless, stay safe, and take care of each other. Until tomorrow, this is Ranger Dave with Pickens Radio signing off."

Danny picked the radio up and looked at it as if it might spring back to life as it just had. He turned to look at Alisa, who stood motionless in their bedroom doorway.

She put her hand over her mouth. "We're not alone. I can't believe how good it feels just to hear someone else's voice coming over a radio."

Danny put his shoes on. "I'm going with you."

"Where?"

"To the RV. Aren't you going to ask Cami for the water bladder from her backpack, for your shower invention?"

"I completely forgot. I was so wrapped up in the news broadcast." Alisa picked the towel up off the floor and hung it on the door knob.

Danny pushed in the telescoping antenna of the shortwave radio and carried it with him as he led the way downstairs and to the RV. Alisa followed close behind.

When they arrived at the RV, Danny knocked on the door.

Cami answered the door in her sweat suit. "Hey,

come in. I thought you guys would be asleep by now after planting corn all day."

"Did we wake you?" Danny walked up the stairs into the RV.

"No. Nick just got in from getting his bath. It's such a long process, and only one person at a time can get their bath. Whoever ends up last in line could be waiting for hours."

Alisa smiled. "I might have a solution for that, but Danny has something important to tell you first."

"What? Tell me." Cami took a seat on the couch.

"We picked up a radio transmission. Some guy, he's making his own news show. Not that he had much news to share." Danny sat next to Cami.

Cami called toward the bedroom. "Nick, you're gonna want to hear this."

Nick came into the living room. "Hey, guys, what's up?"

"They heard a transmission on the shortwave," Cami said.

Danny told Nick everything they'd heard.

"That's a start. Did you write down the frequency?" Nick leaned against the door frame.

"No, but I haven't changed it." Danny handed the radio to Nick.

Nick set the radio down on the counter and scratched around to find a notepad and a pen. "We need to keep a log. We should write down what we heard, when we heard it, and the frequency." He scribbled down the pertinent information.

Alisa added, "He said he'll be back on tomorrow evening at the same time."

"Good." Nick kept writing. "You said eight o'clock, right?"

"Yeah, eight." Danny said.

Cami looked at Alisa. "You said you had something to tell us?"

Alisa explained her ideas.

Nick put his palm on his forehead. "I can't believe I didn't think of that. We would be able to use the shower right here in the RV. We've got extra water bladders, so we can make two of the camping showers. In fact, I've got some black duct tape so we can heat them in the sun, at least for the first shower they're used for every day. I like the bucket idea also. The bladders will eventually wear out, and the bucket shower will be more resilient."

Cami went in the bedroom and made some noise as she tried to locate the spare water bladders. She returned and handed one to Alisa. "Why don't you try rigging this one up, and we'll see what we come up with for the other. We'll use which ever design works better for all subsequent models."

"Awesome. Thanks! This is really going to help things be a little more normal." Alisa grinned as she looked over the plastic pouch and tube.

"What a fantastic idea. Hopefully we'll be able to come up with some more inventions like that. The problem is, everyone is so tired from trying to keep up, there's not a lot of time left over for creative thinking." Nick walked Danny and Alisa to the door.

Alisa waved as she walked down the stairs. "I hate doing things the hard way, so I'll keep thinking. Good night."

"Sleep tight, guys. Danny, take the radio with you, in case you feel like scanning some more." Cami handed him the shortwave.

"And the radio log." Nick handed him the notebook also.

Danny kissed his sister on the cheek before he left. "Good night."

The next morning after breakfast, Danny asked Alisa, "Have you seen Steven? I need him to help me with the last two rows of corn."

"He's helping Dana feed the animals."

"I thought you usually did that with her."

Alisa shrugged. "Guess I've been outsourced."

"Unemployed, huh? Can I interest you in a career in agriculture?"

"What kind of retirement plan does it have?"

"The same as all agrarian careers, a six-foot hole in exchange for a lifetime of service."

"Sounds too good to be true. It must be a competitive job market. Are there any positions available?"

"As a matter of fact, one just opened up. And despite the less-than-optimum retirement package, it does offer a fantastic work environment and an opportunity to work with one of the best trainers in the industry."

"Now, you're overselling. Let me get my boots."

Danny winked. "I'll fill a couple jugs with water and meet you on the back porch. Don't forget your rifle."

"Sounds hostile. What happened to the fantastic work environment?"

"It's just a formality, you know, insurance requirement."

Danny grabbed the water, a bag of seed corn, and made sure his pistol was secure in the holster that JC had given him. It was a cheap canvas holster that kept the gun secure via a strap which snapped shut. While it wasn't the best, it beat the heck out of his old method of carrying his pistol in his waistband, which JC called Mexican carry.

Alisa soon appeared with the AK slung over her shoulder. "I hope I'm getting paid for training."

Danny led the way toward the barn to get a hoe and a shovel. "Think of it as an internship. The life lessons and the experience should be considered adequate compensation."

"In other words, I'm not getting paid."

"You're really catching on to the corporate culture. I think you'll do well."

When they reached the barn, Danny opened the door and walked in.

Steven's voice called out. "Hey, I'm in the loft. Don't get spooked and shoot me."

"You're fine." Danny pursed his lips and looked at Alisa. He picked through the tools, selecting an old hoe and a spade shovel which he handed to Alisa. "This will be good for busting up any large chunks of soil. Rocky only ran the disc plow over the field once because we're trying to conserve fuel."

Steven came climbing down the ladder. "All the animals are fed. We can help with the corn if you need us to."

Danny picked several pieces of hay out of

Steven's hair. "Must have been a rough day for feeding cattle."

Steven glanced over at Dana who had just climbed down the ladder and was beginning to blush. "Uh, yeah. That loft is kind of dangerous. You have to watch your step."

"Yeah, tell me about it." Danny nodded. "Catfish will be moving in up there today or tomorrow. That should put a damper on the ambiance. We only have the two rows left in the cornfield. You guys can go look for firewood if you want."

Alisa brushed some hay off the back of Dana's shirt. "Unless you guys need a chaperone."

Steven grabbed an ax and a saw from the tool bench. "I think we can manage."

Dana led the way out the barn door without saying a word. Steven followed her with only a quick wave to Danny and Alisa.

Alisa crossed her arms and watched them walk out of the barn. "Looks like nature is taking its course."

Danny took the tools from Alisa and leaned them against the support beam. He held her hand and spun the ring on her finger around and around. "You know, there's nothing stopping us from rolling in the hay." He leaned in and kissed her.

She kissed him then pulled away. "Except those two rows of corn that need planting."

"I forgot to mention, this is union work; we get paid by the hour, not the job." He leaned in for another kiss. "And Catfish is moving in up there. This might be your last chance to live out that country music video in the hay loft."

She giggled, bit her lower lip, and began climbing the ladder to the loft.

Later that afternoon, Steven and Dana showed up at the back of the cornfield. Steven surveyed the row Danny and Alisa were working on. "You guys still not done yet? Nana said lunch will be ready in fifteen minutes."

Alisa was following Danny and covering each seed with the hoe as he planted them. "Management and labor had to iron out a few things to get through contract negotiations."

Dana furrowed her brow. "What are you talking about?"

Danny fought back a laugh. "Just tell Nana we will be finished in a little while. Don't wait for us; go ahead and eat. We'll eat when we get back."

Steven looked at Danny curiously. "Whatever. See you in a while."

Danny and Alisa continued working diligently together to finish planting the corn. He glanced behind him to give her a smile from time to time. He'd been worried that rushing to get married along with the strain of surviving the unprecedented challenges of life after an EMP would strain their relationship. But for now, it was only pressing them closer together.

At every moment, he was in a state of heightened awareness, being conscious of every movement, every sound, and every potential threat. It kept him from ever being completely relaxed, but with each passing day, he was acclimating to the new reality and making a conscious effort to not let it affect the way he treated Alisa.

Danny remembered the playful days back in the restaurant when he, Alisa, Steven, Dana, and the rest of the crew would laugh and joke with barely a care in the world. Those days were gone, but they were learning to laugh and play again in spite of the difficulties. Danny was learning to live life on life's terms.

JC's family moved into their trailer on Nana's farm late Wednesday afternoon. Catfish moved into the hay loft early that evening. The members of the Reese family were still sorting through their belongings and trying to decide what to bring and what they had to leave behind. It was no easy decision, but Korey had said that he knew the move had to be made sooner or later. It was agreed that Catfish would ferry a load of their belongings over to Nana's for church on Sunday, then help the Reese family relocate the remainder of the items they'd be bringing, after lunch. Rocky and Pauline were still sitting tight in their home across the creek and had no immediate plans to move to what was now being referred to as Fort Jennie, a term coined by none other than the eccentric Catfish.

Wednesday evening, everyone presently abiding at Fort Jennie gathered around the radio in Nana's living room to listen to the eight o'clock broadcast from Pickens Radio. Ranger Dave had no new information but did announce that Sunday evening, a group from his community would be playing some bluegrass music directly following the eight o'clock update.

"Wow, bluegrass, that will be cool." JC was seldom moved to such excitement.

"What does anybody from New York City know about bluegrass?" Nana scowled.

"I listened to country when I was in the military. I guess you could say it was a gateway drug to the harder stuff."

Steven lowered his eyebrows. "We're still talking about bluegrass music, right?"

JC snorted. "Yeah."

Nick smiled. "It will be nice to have some form of entertainment. I think we could all use the distraction. An idea that Melissa brought up to me earlier today was the need for a larger communal cooking and dining area. For now, the best solution seems to be eating in shifts. I think we can put together some rough picnic tables in the courtyard to eat at when the weather is nice. JC has volunteered the wood from his cattle barn for the tables. Hopefully we can have those together by Sunday so we can all eat lunch together, then have a place to listen to the radio as well.

"It would be a very big project and consume limited resources to build a permanent shelter for the picnic tables, so I think the best solution for inclement weather would be to revert back to eating in shifts at the dining room table. I'm opened to hearing what everyone else thinks."

Danny nodded. "I agree with your plan. It makes sense."

Nana said, "I can't fix enough food for all these people in that little kitchen every day. I'm gonna need a place to cook outside. Besides, we have to cook with wood whenever we can so I can save the gas for bad weather. It's gonna have to have a roof on it. Don't expect me to be out there cookin' in the middle of the summer with no roof over my head."

Jack looked at JC. "Dad, since we're tearing up the barn anyway, can we use a section of the metal roof to make a shelter for Miss Jennie's outdoor kitchen?"

JC nodded. "We can do that."

Nana hugged Jack and kissed his cheek. "God bless you, child."

JC stuck his hand in the air and made a circular motion. Next, he moved his hand back and forth. His family, even little two-year-old Annie, understood the military signals, rallied around him, and began moving out. The Castell family bade everyone good night as they retired to their travel trailer.

Dana yawned. "I'm turning in for tonight." In a very conspicuously inconspicuous manner, she glanced at Steven, said, "Good night," and turned to go upstairs.

Likewise, Steven made eye contact with her, said, "Good night," and quickly looked away.

Danny chuckled and looked at Alisa, who had also witnessed the poor acting meant to throw Nana and the others off the scent of what was going on between the two of them.

Nick and Cami were next to leave. "We'll see you guys in the morning," Cami said. "And your shower bag worked great, Alisa. Good job with that."

Once all the good nights were said, Danny and Alisa headed up to their room. It had been another long day, and they would sleep well.

CHAPTER 13

But if any provide not for his own, and specially for those of his own house, he hath denied the faith, and is worse than an infidel.

1 Timothy 5:8

POW! Danny jumped out of bed and grabbed the AK from the corner of the room.

Alisa sat up in the bed. "What was that?"

"Gunshots! Here! Take the Glock and lie in the floor. Hide under the covers until I get back. Just leave a space big enough to see if anyone is coming in here. If you see someone, shoot them!" Danny threw on his jeans and stuck an extra magazine in his back pocket.

"No, Danny. I'm coming with you!"

"No, you're not. Do what I said! I'll be back."

Danny softly closed the door behind him and gently walked down the stairs.

Steven was up and had his shotgun. "Where did it come from?"

"Sounded like the back. Put your boots on. If you step on something sharp, you'll be down before the shooting starts." Danny looked out the front window.

Steven quickly stepped into his boots but didn't bother lacing them. "Ready."

Danny turned the knob of the front door carefully. "We'll go out the front and try to flank them."

Steven followed him out the door and around the side of the house. Danny walked low, next to the structure, and peeked around the corner, near the chicken coop. Just then, he saw a bright light shining near the trailer and heard JC's voice scream, "Freeze!"

He saw a dark figure silhouetted against the tactical lights from JC and Nick's rifles. The figure dropped a dead animal and a shotgun.

"Don't shoot. It's just me," Catfish's voice called out.

Danny shook his head. "It's Catfish."

He and Steven walked around the back to see what all of the commotion had been about. Nick and JC approached from the other side, lowering their rifles.

"What happened?" Danny asked.

"Seen a coon headin' for the rabbit hutch. Once they figure out where to get free vittles, they'll be back every night. Coon is good eatin', too." Catfish bent down to retrieve his shotgun and his kill.

"It better be. It just cost the whole compound a good night's sleep." JC did not sound happy about being woken up over a raccoon trying to get in the rabbit hutch.

"What 'cha want me to do, JC? Let him clean out the rabbits and the chickens so you can get your beauty sleep? Trust me, you could sleep till the resurrection and it wouldn't make you no purdier." Catfish seemed hurt by the lack of appreciation for standing guard.

Nick rubbed his weary eyes. "We need to protect the animals, but we also need to sleep past . . ." he paused to look at his watch. He sighed. "Past 4:30."

Danny looked at JC. "What about Jack's air rifle? Maybe it could be a permanent part of the night watch arsenal. Whoever has night watch can still eliminate threats to the smaller livestock, and everybody else can sleep right through it."

Steven yawned. "If we hear a gunshot, then we'll know it's a real threat, and we can come running."

JC nodded. "Good idea. Think we can wait till tomorrow to dig it out?"

Catfish held the dead raccoon up. "Don't bother me none. I'll be gettin' this one skinned out. If there's a chicken or rabbit missin' come mornin', don't blame it on me."

Nick waved as he returned to the RV. "But that was a good drill. Everybody did a good job handling the threat."

"Thanks." Danny turned to go back inside.

"Think you'll be able to go back to sleep?" Steven asked.

"Not a chance. Nana is probably already up, which means everybody might as well get up."

Steven set his shotgun in the corner when they came in the door. "I want to check on Dana, make sure she's alright."

"She's probably huddled up with Alisa. Come on up," Danny said.

Nana was waiting inside with her housecoat and shotgun. "Did ya get 'em?"

"Just a raccoon trying to get at the rabbits. Catfish killed it," Danny said.

"He eats those nasty vermin. He best not think he's cooking that filthy coon in my kitchen." Nana went back into her room and closed the door.

When Danny and Steven got upstairs, both of the girls were hiding under the blanket, on the floor behind the bed, just as Danny had instructed Alisa.

"All clear?" Alisa stuck her head out.

"All clear," Danny said.

"Hey," Dana said as she crawled out from behind the bed.

Steven smiled at her. "I wanted to make sure you were okay."

"I'm fine. Thanks for checking." She smiled back.

"Okay, then. See you at breakfast."

"See you there." She waved as he walked out the door and down the stairs.

"I'm going to try to go back to sleep." Dana carried the old revolver which she kept by her bed.

"Good luck. Nana's already awake." Danny grinned.

Dana gave a disappointed sigh and closed the

door behind her as she left.

"I guess we can lie back down until Nana starts banging pots and pans." Danny laid the AK on top of a stack of buckets containing the long-term storage food they'd brought from Savannah, prior to the EMP.

Alisa lay down and covered her head with the comforter. "It's worth a shot."

Danny curled up beside her and closed his eyes.

It seemed like only seconds later when he heard Nana call up the stairs.

"Get on down here. Breakfast'll be ready in a minute," she said.

Danny looked around. The glimmer of daybreak was illuminating the room. "The sun is coming up. We must have been asleep for at least two hours."

"I needed it." Alisa rolled out of bed and got dressed.

After breakfast Danny, Alisa, Steven, and Dana set off to the backfield to plant sweet potatoes. Nana had sprouted several of the potatoes in a small garden bed near the house. She had then taken cuttings from those and planted them in a hodge-podge selection of containers. Danny carried fifteen of the cuttings in various plastic containers: peanut butter jars, cottage cheese containers, and yogurt cups in a wheelbarrow. Alisa packed an old milk crate holding twelve empty soda cans which had the tops cut off and drainage holes poked in the bottom to accommodate one sweet potato cutting each. The cuttings would take root in a couple of weeks, as long as the soil in the containers was kept moist.

Dana hand-carried another four containers, and Steven carried the hoes and shovels to work the ground.

Danny stopped at the edge of the woods. "Let's put a couple plants right here. They'll blend in with the undergrowth and, unless someone knows they're here, most people will walk right by them."

Dana stood, holding two plastic containers in each hand. "Aren't we going to plant rows of sweet potatoes in the garden? If you put a bunch of them here, we won't have enough for rows."

Danny took a shovel from Steven and began to dig. "Sweet potatoes are very prolific. If we put two plants here, they'll take over this entire area, as long as something doesn't eat them before they have a chance to start growing."

"Like what?" Steven asked.

Danny removed one of the cuttings from a container and planted it in the hole. "Rabbits, mainly. They love the sweet potato greens."

Alisa helped him pat the dirt around the freshly planted cutting. "I love the greens also. I couldn't believe Nana had never heard of eating them."

Danny gave her a quick kiss before brushing the dirt off his hands. "Eating sweet potato greens is kind of a new thing. We were blessed to work in a restaurant that served them, but it wasn't a popular dish in the South, like turnip greens or mustard greens."

Dana followed as Danny led the way to the next location with the wheelbarrow. "Sounds like the perfect survival food. You get the vitamins and carbs from the potato, a green vegetable from the top, and the whole thing just looks like some random vine if you plant it near the edge of the forest. So even if we have looters, they'll probably never find all of our sweet potatoes."

"As long as they're not rabbits," Alisa chuckled.

The group found several other inconspicuous locations to plant some of the cuttings. The rest were put in the freshly plowed rows in the backfield. Once they finished with the sweet potatoes, they planted several rows of squash, melons, turnips, and a few more rows of green beans, then headed back to the house for lunch.

Steven brushed the dirt from his knees with his free hand as he walked. "I think these pants qualify as dirty now."

"Those pants qualified as dirty two days ago." Danny pushed the wheelbarrow full of the empty containers which would all be used again to start the next round of crops for a later harvest.

When they arrived back at the house, JC's family was unloading some of their personal effects from the back of Catfish's truck and bringing them into the trailer.

"Need a hand?" Danny offered.

JC looked the group over. "I appreciate the offer, but I think we can handle it."

"It's no bother at all." Steven reiterated the offer.

"Look, uh, no offense, but you guys are pretty dirty. I know it's just a trailer, but I'd like to keep it clean as much as possible. We might be here for a while."

Danny looked at his shirt and pants, which were heavily coated in dirt from the garden. "Oh, yeah.

We'll get cleaned up, and if you need any help after lunch, I'll give you a hand."

"We should be done by then, but I might need you for something else." JC adjusted his ball cap.

"Sure, what's up?" Danny asked.

"I want to set some trip alarms along the back property line. I'm less worried about the hedgerow that runs along the road and the creek, but the fence that runs along the back pasture and the woods running behind the house, I'd like to know if someone is coming through back there."

"What do you have in mind?"

"I made some trip-wire alarms out of mouse traps and fishing line. When sprung, they'll set off an emptied-out shotgun round that has the powder, but no shot in it. If someone trips the line, it will scare the heck out of them and let us know they're on the property."

"Sounds clever. Why wouldn't you use live rounds? Maybe that would kill them and we wouldn't have to worry about them coming back."

Rusty was standing next to JC, wagging his tail. JC bent over to pet him on the back. "Like I was telling you about the alarms I set up over on my place, you wouldn't want the dog to set one of those off by accident. Or worse, one of us. Still, since you and Steven are typically the guys gathering firewood, it would be good for you two to know where the trip lines are located. Even if it's not dangerous, we don't want to set them off by accident if we can help it. If anyone else goes to the back property line for wood or any other reason, they'll always have one of us three to point out where the lines are."

"That sounds like a good plan." Danny nodded.

"What about a map?" Alisa asked. "Could you make a diagram of where each one of the trip wire is? If they're set up for a long period of time, even you guys might forget exactly where you put them."

"That's a good idea," JC said. "You draw pretty good. Why don't you come with us and make a map?"

"I paint," she replied. "That's a little different than mapmaking."

"Close enough. At least people will know it's a tree if you draw it."

Steven ran his hand through his hair. "Could we blaze the trees that have a wire attached to them? If we blazed the side facing the house, anyone approaching from the back wouldn't see the blaze anyway."

"What's a blaze?" Alisa asked.

"Like on a trail. It's a small patch of paint to let you know you're on the trail," Steven explained.

"Fantastic idea." JC smiled.

Dana added, "Since we're most likely to get hit at night, we could paint the blaze with a dark color. It would be easy to identify in the daylight, but nobody would see it at night. We wouldn't be back there collecting wood or hunting at night anyway, right?"

"Right." JC snapped his fingers. "Another good idea. Since the blazes will be painted with a dark color, nighttime trespassers won't see them if they use the back woods as an avenue of retreat.

"So, all of you meet by my trailer after lunch.

Jack, Danny, and I will set the alarms. Dana and Steven can paint blazes, and Alisa can draw a diagram."

"See you in a bit." Danny waved.

"Hang back, I've got something else to discuss with you." JC gave Danny's arm a light tug.

"Sure." Danny waved Alisa and the others on. "I'll catch up, guys."

"Don't be late getting to the table." Alisa winked and blew him a kiss as she walked off.

"What's up?" Danny asked.

JC looked around. "Catfish wants to go on an expedition tomorrow."

Danny shook his head. "I don't like any of the words in that sentence -- Catfish, go, expedition, tomorrow. When you string them all together, I like them even less."

JC snorted. "I get that. I felt the same way when he approached me about it. But hear me out. There's a lot of supplies out there on the road, and if we're going to make this place into a fort, we're going to need it."

"You're talking about stealing! We need the protection of God more than anything we're going to find out there on the road. And if we start stealing, I think we lose that protection. Look at Catfish. His window got shot out trying to boost gasoline from someone. I think that was his warning from God, and it might be his last." Danny's voice became a bit louder and higher pitched as he protested.

JC put a hand in the air. "Settle down. No one said anything about stealing. Let me finish."

Danny crossed his arms and listened reluctantly. "Go ahead."

JC looked toward the road. "There is a place out on US 29 that sells utility sheds. Some of them are really nice. They look like little cabins, metal roofs, windows, top-notch."

"How is taking one not stealing, and besides, how in the world would you ever move them?"

"I've got the cash in the house to buy a couple, provided we can locate the owner. About moving them, that isn't such a big deal. Have you ever seen one of those being delivered?"

"No."

JC continued explaining. "They usually come in on a flatbed truck with a tilt-up bed that has a winch to pull the shed up on the bed."

"Which we don't have." Danny really wanted no part of this conversation.

JC kept talking. "Once the shed is delivered, it can be repositioned using what's called a mule. Basically, it's a really small forklift that lifts one side of the shed. The back side of the shed is put on a small set of wheels."

"We don't have those things either."

JC nodded. "I know. Just listen. The place that sells the sheds probably has a mule. We would only need two pairs of the wheels, then we could pull it with the truck back to the farm."

"How would you get the shed up to put the wheels under it?"

"Two truck jacks. We jack up one side, slide the wheels under, put tire chocks down, and then do the other side."

Danny crossed his arms tighter as he shook his head. "Seems like we could just build sheds out of the wood from your barn. It wouldn't be much harder than all of this."

"Trust me, it would be a lot harder, especially with no power tools."

"Can't you charge power tools with the solar generator?"

"You've never built anything with battery-operated power tools, have you? Those batteries from Home Depot are garbage. They last about fifteen minutes, and that's if you happen to get a good one that still takes a charge after six months."

"Why are you telling just me about the mission? This is everyone's decision. Heck, Nick is the one you'll have to convince."

JC put his hand on Danny's shoulder. "If you're in, it will be a lot easier to convince everyone else to go along with the plan."

"Why me? I just live here. You and Nick are the security and administration for the whole group. Steven is the spiritual leader, or at least he's trying to be."

JC shook his head. "Don't sell yourself short. People listen to you, maybe more than you know. You're the guy who has the dreams. We're pretty much all here and have some basic level of preparedness for this situation because of your dreams."

"Great. So if Catfish's expedition goes south and someone gets hurt, it's my fault."

"Don't think of it like that."

"Then how should I think of it?"

JC looked around the property. "Think of it like, if we get hit hard by a big gang of ruthless criminals, scumbags like Nick said to expect, will you know that you did everything you could to protect the people you love? At least that's the way I'm thinking of it."

Danny did not want to think of it like that. But JC was right. He had to do everything he could to keep Alisa, Nana, Cami, and everyone else as safe as possible. "And then, that's it? We're just getting a couple of sheds?"

JC looked back toward the road. "We're going to need fencing."

Danny exhaled. "Fencing? Where will we get that?"

"There's an old Owens Corning plant on 81. We can scavenge some of their fencing. It's not like they have anything left to protect with a fence. Anything of use or value has already been looted."

"And that's it? Sheds and fence?"

"And gas."

Danny threw his hands in the air as he repeated what JC had just said. "And gas. JC, this is stealing."

JC lowered his head, then looked back up to stare directly into Danny's eyes. "Danny, it's been five weeks since the EMP. Any unclaimed, unprotected resources still out there now are going to get taken by someone. The question is, will they be used for good, to defend the people you love, or will they be used by the bad guys, to fortify positions that they can use as a base to come pillage your unprotected property? I think you're having a little trouble envisioning the America of tomorrow, so let me paint you a little picture."

JC sarcastically swiped his hand across the sky. "Come with me to the magical land of tomorrow, a land where Mad Max would soil himself from fear at the thought of venturing out from behind a heavily armed, gated wall, a mystical place where Rambo and Clint Eastwood shiver in panic and anxiety. Why? Because the animals running the show in the world of tomorrow are the worst of the worst, sociopaths that take what they want and kill everyone who gets in the way. And let me remind you, your pretty young wife has already been through enough for one apocalypse. If I were you, I'd beg, borrow, or steal to make sure nothing like that ever happened to her again."

Anger flashed through Danny's mind at the thought of Alisa being hurt or abducted again. JC had pushed the right button. "Okay, whatever it takes . . . within reasonable, moral boundaries."

JC patted him on the back. "We're not taking anything by force. If anyone lays claim to any resources while we're taking them, we'll walk away, as long as they don't engage us."

Danny grimaced. This was not what he wanted to be thinking about. Times were hard enough; he hadn't expected them to get harder. But it seemed as though they might, and he, most assuredly, wanted to keep Alisa as safe as possible. "What do we do next?"

"We need to get Nick on board. I'd rather have you with me than Catfish when I go talk to him."

"He's probably in the trailer with Cami, getting

cleaned up for lunch. Want to talk to him now?"

JC shook his head. "Definitely not before lunch, and I'd rather catch him when it can be just the three of us. Cami is great, but she's another person that would need convincing if she's involved in the conversation."

"Hmm." Danny thought about when they could get Nick alone. "We could ask him to double check the trip wires after we're done setting them up."

"Good idea. He'll be tired, so he won't have much fight left in him to argue. You better go get cleaned up and get to the table before Miss Jennie starts yelling."

"Okay, see you after lunch." Danny grinned as he walked away.

Danny washed his face and hands in the plastic wash basin on the back porch. He changed his clothes and headed to the table for lunch.

Shortly after lunch, the four friends worked with JC and Jack to get the trip wires set along the perimeters of the property. They finished around 5:00, so Danny and JC would have just enough light to use an inspection of the trip lines as a ruse to get Nick off to where they could speak in private. Danny found him and Cami by the solar shed, moving the panels in order to squeeze the last bit of energy from the remaining sunlight.

"How's it going?" Danny asked.

"Not bad," Nick replied. "We're producing plenty of juice to keep the batteries charged for radios, flashlights, the small fridge, and JC's night vision scopes."

"That's fantastic! It seems like such a small thing, but a handful of batteries is completely changing our life."

"Especially when it comes to security, the flashlights, radios, and night vision may end up saving our lives." Nick finished setting the last panel at the best angle to get the most sun.

"We set up some trip wires along the back property line in the woods and a few more where the cornfield meets the pasture. JC wanted you to look it over and let us know if you think we missed anything."

Nick dusted his hands off. "Sure. Cami, do you want to walk with us?"

"I think he had some other security matters he wanted to discuss with you as well." Danny wanted to infuse just the right amount of drudgery to make it sound like more of a task than a relaxing walk in the woods.

Cami looked over her shoulder toward the house. "Nana probably needs some help with dinner. Besides, I need to get cleaned up and we only have one bathroom. If you think you'll be okay without me, I'll have a nice pot of hot water waiting for you to take a shower when you get back."

Nick gave her a quick kiss on the lips. "Sounds good. See you in a bit."

Danny led the way to JC's trailer. "Here is a copy of the map that Alisa made. It helps us to remember where all of the booby traps are located. None of them are dangerous, so we wouldn't get more than a bad scare if we accidently tripped one anyway, but the map is a nice thing to have."

Nick smiled as he looked over the map that Danny handed him. "She did a good job on this. We can incorporate this information into a larger map when we split the property up into zones. If we're ever attacked, it will be easier to say *zone one* or *zone two*, rather than *over by the creek* or *behind the barn*, especially if one of the alarms is tripped. Someone could say, *a wire was tripped in zone four*, and everyone would know exactly where the threat was coming from."

JC was waiting when they arrived at the trailer. "Let's go check 'em out."

As they walked back toward the woods, JC looked over at Nick. "I was talking with Danny, and we were thinking that if things get as rough as you say, we're going to need to fortify this place a little more heavily."

Nick shrugged as he walked. "We're doing everything we can."

"Maybe," JC said, "and maybe not. Catfish seems to think there's a lot of resources out there that no one has claimed yet."

"Catfish's idea of claiming resources is what civilized folk call looting."

"I know," JC chuckled, but it didn't sound like a sincere laugh. "But, I don't want to be too quick to dismiss him. He's been out there on the road more than any of the rest of us, except you and Cami, of course. So, the rest of us have to rely on you, Catfish, and a five-minute radio show that says the same thing every night, to figure out what it really looks like out there. Going on what you told us, it sounds like things could get a lot worse."

"It's going to get worse."

JC looked over at Nick. "Then, if there are unclaimed resources out there, they'll probably be used against us. Is that a fair analysis?"

Nick sighed. "Riding around with Catfish stealing gas is a good way to catch a bullet. Do that a few times and you won't be around long enough to find out."

"I'm not really talking about gas. At least, not just gas." JC continued to lay out a cohesive plan for salvaging fence, fuel, and the sheds.

Nick shook his head and looked at Danny. "What do you think about all of this?"

"I think we have to do what we can to keep the farm secured. Alisa has already been kidnapped. I know we're taking more precautions now, but how prepared are we to hold off the zombie hordes you told us about? I don't want to go through that again."

"And if you get killed trying to scavenge fence or steal gas, that's not going to help Alisa." Nick stopped walking and let his rifle hang from the single-point sling.

Danny looked down for a moment as he thought about the predicament. He looked back up at Nick. "Do you have a better idea?"

Nick exhaled a long, deep breath. "No. I guess I don't."

"That means you're on board then?" JC asked.

Nick continued walking toward the forest. "It means I don't have a better idea." After a few more steps, he said, "I'll work with you guys. If we can come up with a plan that minimizes the risk, we'll execute it, but I don't want to be responsible for leading anyone into a death trap. And right now, with the level of training this group has, we're doing good to keep this place safe, much less thinking about going outside the wire for a raiding mission."

JC nodded. "I agree 100 percent. We need training. I've been pushing for that since before you got here. I get a lot of flak because there are so many other chores to do. People have to figure out what they are not going to do in order to provide time for training."

Danny walked close behind JC and Nick. "The gardens are in, for the most part. We'd be able to dedicate more time to training."

Nick paused again. "I guess I don't understand why we're scavenging the sheds rather than travel trailers. I mean, they'd already be on wheels. We would be exposed to an attack for a lot less time hooking up a trailer hitch than trying to load a shed on these wheels that may or may not be at the location."

JC answered, "I've got the cash to pay for some sheds. They're a couple thousand bucks. A travel trailer is big money."

Nick snickered. "Who are you going to pay? Are you going to stick the money in the top drawer of the office? Some goon will just break in and steal it five minutes after we're gone."

"I'm just trying to do the right thing here, trying to be ethical." JC replied.

Nick nodded. "I understand. But you have a good point about the resources we don't take, being used against us. I don't know. I should probably sleep on it; it's been a long day. And don't say anything to anyone else until the three of us are in agreement about how we should proceed."

Danny added, "Until the four of us have agreed, don't forget about Catfish."

Nick pursed his lips. "Three of us. Catfish's risk analysis skills leave something to be desired, as evidenced by the shiny new bullet hole in his windshield."

JC laughed. "Yeah. Sounds like a plan."

The three men gave a cursory inspection of the trip wires, then headed back to what was being called the compound.

"I'll see you guys later." JC waved as he headed toward his own trailer.

"You guys aren't eating with us?" Danny asked.

JC shook his head. "First night in the trailer. We want to eat together as a family tonight. Don't worry, we'll be seeing plenty of each other."

Nick waved. "Cami and I have night watch tonight. Did you get your night vision scope set up on the air rifle for raccoons?"

JC stopped and adjusted his ball cap. "Oh yeah. I almost forgot. I'll bring it by after dinner. I've got that second Starlight scope also. I could set it up on my rifle I guess. I don't mind having the Benjamin as a community weapon, but that rifle is my baby."

"I've got a spare AR or two in the trailer. We can use one of those for the community night vision rifle if you don't mind giving up the scope."

"Sounds like a plan." JC stepped into his trailer and gave another wave as he closed the door.

Danny cocked his head to one side. "A spare AR or two?"

"We knew hard times were coming. Come on, let's go eat." Nick put his hand on Danny's shoulder as they walked back to the house.

CHAPTER 14

He teacheth my hands to war, so that a bow of steel is broken by mine arms. Thou hast also given me the shield of thy salvation: and thy right hand hath holden me up, and thy gentleness hath made me great. Thou hast enlarged my steps under me, that my feet did not slip. I have pursued mine enemies, and overtaken them: neither did I turn again till they were consumed. I have wounded them that they were not able to rise: they are fallen under my feet. For thou hast girded me with strength unto the battle: thou hast subdued under me those that rose up against me.

Psalm 18:34-39

Danny Walker had created a monster. Trying not to get caught by Nana or Dana, he hurriedly dropped another piece of egg to the floor as Puddin' had progressed to biting his pant leg if her belly wasn't filled from the breakfast table.

Alisa saw what was going on. She pursed her lips and rolled her eyes at him.

He shrugged as he looked at her, hoping for a look of sympathy. He received no gestures of compassion.

Nana walked into the dining room and set a plate of biscuits on the table. "Daniel, you take these on over to JC's trailer. I thought Cami and Nick would be eatin' with us, so I made too many."

"Nick said not to expect them when they have night watch. I think they eat while they are on lookout, so when their shift is over, they just want to go to bed," Danny replied.

Nana set a jar of homemade blackberry jelly next to the biscuits. "All the same, I like to have extra, in case they're hungry. You get on over there. And take this jelly with you."

"Yes, ma'am." Danny stood, picked up the plate and the jar, and headed for the door.

Rusty greeted him as he walked outside.

"Hey, boy." Danny paused, set the jelly jar on the outside window seal of the porch, and gave Rusty a pat. He took one of the biscuits from the plate and fed it to Rusty. "I'm sure JC won't miss one biscuit."

Danny picked up the jelly and proceeded toward

the trailer, with Rusty trailing close behind. He knocked on the door.

Catfish answered the door. "Miss Jennie's biscuits! I declare. That's a fine thing to have waitin' fer ya of a mornin'. Get on in here."

Danny handed the plate to Catfish, who took a biscuit then passed the plate around to JC and his family. "Nana sent over some blackberry jelly also."

Catfish didn't finish chewing his biscuit, nor did he cover his mouth when he asked Danny, "What do you think Nick'll say about us runnin' into town for a few things."

It had been specifically discussed that the conversation would stay close-knit for the time being. Danny glanced at Jack and Melissa, who were giving each other curious looks.

JC grabbed a biscuit and opened the door. "Come on. Let's go outside."

Danny walked out, followed closely by Catfish.

"Be right back," JC said to Jack, Melissa, and Annie as he closed the door of the trailer behind him.

JC looked at Catfish. "We're trying to stay low-key with all of this. We need to get a consensus before we can go around announcing what we have in mind. Politics."

"Never was one much for politickin'." Catfish took a second biscuit out of the pocket of his filthy overalls.

A shiver went up Danny's spine as he considered eating anything that had been in Catfish's pocket. "I think he'll come around to the idea. Just out of curiosity, do you know of any places nearby that sell travel trailers?"

Catfish motioned toward the road. Bits of biscuit fell out of his mouth and got caught in his beard as he spoke. "Right before you get to town on 24. Lakeview RV. They've got some purdy trailers. Wouldn't mind havin' one of them myself."

JC scowled at Danny. He'd obviously misspoke by mentioning trailers to Catfish. "I know the place. It's about five miles from here. A lot of fifth wheels. We don't have the setup to move those."

Catfish chuckled. "If they sell fifth wheels, you know they'll have the hitches for 'em. Besides that, they have plenty smaller trailers. But puttin' a fifth-wheel hitch on my truck would be a mite easier n' tryin' to get a shed up on wheels."

"The thing is, I've got the money to pay for sheds," JC protested.

"If there's anybody around to pay. I reckon if anybody is around at the RV lot, they'd be willing to make you a deal, seein' how business is so poorly these days. Might be that they'd be willing to trade a RV for one of them tubs of canned goods you got up in the hay loft. Hungry folk can't eat no trailer."

JC grunted as a sign of his frustration with the situation. "At any rate, we're going to have to start training, whether we go on a scavenging mission or not. Danny, why don't you go get Steven, Alisa, and Dana. Tell them to hurry up with their chores and meet up at the back of the barn. I'll get Jack and Melissa. Catfish, you go get Rocky and ask Pauline if she can watch Annie while we drill."

"Are you planning to take the girls on the

scavenging mission?" Danny asked.

"No, but if all the men go, they'll be here alone. They need to be able to operate as a cohesive unit to defend the farm. And if we ever get attacked here, we'll need every person in the compound to know how to fight, cover their lanes, and take directions in battle. Knowing what to do and how to do it will make everybody feel better also. Think about taking a test; you're much less nervous if you studied up and know the material. And there's a pretty good chance that we'll get a pop quiz before all of this is said and done."

Danny nodded. "That makes sense. Should I wake Nick and Cami?"

"They need their sleep. Nick already knows this stuff, and Cami is probably further along than most." JC turned his attention to Catfish. "I know fuel is getting tight, but you should run over to the Reeses' place and see if Korey can come train with us. Bring the kid too. He's old enough to shoot; he's old enough to train. You won't be able to bring all of their things on Sunday in one load anyway. Go ahead and make a run with whatever they have packed up."

"I'll do it." Catfish headed off to get Rocky before driving out to the Reeses' farm.

Danny patted his leg for Rusty to follow him back to the house. "We'll get the chores knocked out and meet you at the barn in an hour."

JC walked back up the stairs to return to his trailer. "Sounds good. Make sure everyone brings their weapons and any gear they may have."

"Sure thing." Danny waved.

He was back at the house in minutes. He walked upstairs to his room where Alisa was putting on her hiking shoes. "JC wants us to do some security training today after the chores are done."

"Okay. Any reason for the rush?"

"No, not really." Danny retrieved the tactical vest from the closet that JC had given him.

"No, or not really? That's two answers to one question."

"No."

"Hmm. You're not telling me something."

Danny avoided the questioning and placed magazines for the AK-47 in the pocket on the vest. "I don't know what you're talking about, but make sure you wear a belt so you can put the pistol holster on it."

"Don't lie to me, Danny. Tell me it's a secret. Tell me you don't want to talk about it, or don't say anything at all, but don't lie. I don't want us to do that."

Danny felt a pang of guilt in his stomach. He sighed. "I'm sorry, I won't do it again. You're right, there's something, but I'm not at liberty to discuss it."

"Are we getting attacked?" Alisa's voice was frantic.

"No, no, nothing like that."

"Then what? I won't say anything."

Danny huffed. "You just made me admit I wasn't being honest, and you said it was okay to tell you I can't talk about it. But when I tell you that, you give me the third degree. That's not fair."

"Danny! You said there's something. Now my

imagination is making up all kinds of horrible things. I didn't say scare me to death. Don't you trust me not to say anything?"

Danny was backed in a corner. He sat down on the bed next to her. "Nothing is definite. We're just thinking of going out to look for some resources."

"What kind of resources?"

"Like I said, nothing is definite. We may decide not to even go."

"But if you do, what will you be looking for?"

"Fence, gas, stuff to make the compound more secure in the event of an attack."

Alisa strung her belt through the hoops of the pistol holster. "If you go, I want to go also."

"Out of the question."

"Why?"

"Because, it just is." Danny led the way to the door.

She grabbed his arm and turned him around. "Danny, I need to do something like that. Since I was kidnapped, I feel like a victim. I need to be involved in something that makes me feel like I can take care of myself. You have to understand how I feel."

Danny shook his head. "It doesn't matter what I say anyway. JC would never allow it."

"You already asked JC?"

"No."

"Then how do you know what he'll say?"

"Alisa, you can't go. If all the men leave, you'll have to stay here to be part of the security team. It's not like you'd be doing nothing. Someone has to stand guard over the compound."

"Cami, Dana, and Melissa can stand guard. They all know how to shoot. Well, Dana is getting better anyways. She can hit a milk jug with a shotgun. That's good enough to watch over the farm while we're gone."

"I think you're not getting it. You just can't go."

Alisa crossed her arms and sat back down on the bed. "Because you say so. It has nothing to do with JC. Don't blame it on him. Why don't you want me to go, Danny?"

"I'd be worried about you."

"I'm no china doll. I can take care of myself. Plus, I'd be worried about you if you go, and I'd have to sit and wait to see if you ever come back or not. You can't do that to me, Danny."

Danny took a deep breath. "If you're there and we get in trouble, I'll be focused on taking care of you and I won't do what I have to do for the good of the team. And you don't have to worry about me not coming back. If any situation looks the least bit sketchy, we'll roll out. No fighting, no discussion; we'll leave right away. JC and Nick both know what they're doing. They'll keep us safe."

Alisa stood up and stuck the Glock in the holster. "Then why can't I go?"

Danny sighed. "We're arguing about something that may never happen. Let's get the chores knocked out so we're not late. If there is even going to be a scavenging mission, we'll fight about it when we know for sure. Agreed?"

Alisa followed Danny down the stairs. "It's a discussion, not a fight. I'm not arguing, I'm just speaking my mind. I'm allowed to have an opinion, right?"

Danny's patience was wearing thin. "If you and Dana want to take care of the chickens and rabbits, Steven and I will check on the cattle and water the seedlings."

"Fine!"

Danny found Steven. "Hey man, want to help me check the cows and water the containers?"

"I was going to help Dana."

"Yeah, well, you don't want to be too available. Chicks don't like that. Makes you look clingy."

Steven peered into Danny's eyes. "Is this the same person who was telling me to make my move earlier this week? Now I'm being clingy?"

Danny avoided eye contact. "I'm just saying, don't overdo it."

"Trouble in paradise?" Steven asked.

"Bro, we haven't hung out in a while. Can't I hang out with my best friend? And, we have security training after the animals are taken care of. I don't want you guys to get lost in each other's eyes and lose track of time."

Dana walked in the room. "Hey, cutie, Alisa wants me to feed chickens with her. Girl time, you know. I'll see you in a bit."

Steven gave her a kiss. "Have fun." He turned to Danny. "Looks like I'm all yours."

"Great. Bring your shotgun ammo sling that you made. You'll get a chance to try it out during training."

"So you guys are obviously having a spat. Do you want to talk about it?"

Danny shook his head. "No. It's just close

quarters. We need a few minutes apart. We eat together, sleep together, work together; we're around each other twenty-four hours a day. Everyone needs a little fresh air once in a while. And when you don't get it, little things bug you. You'll understand in a few weeks."

"I don't know. I'm still making up for lost time." Steven picked up one of the starter containers as they walked on to the back porch. "Let's get these seeds watered."

"Yeah. Let's get it done." Danny grabbed a bucket as he led the way toward the hand pump.

Once the chores were completed, Danny and Steven grabbed their weapons and their gear and headed toward the barn. The girls joined them shortly thereafter.

JC, Melissa, and Jack arrived next, all wearing full tactical gear.

JC looked at Dana and Alisa. "Where are your weapons?"

"Right here." Alisa patted the Glock on her side.

"Here's mine." Dana put her hand on the handle of the revolver in her pocket.

JC shook his head. "You don't even have a holster?"

"No." Dana didn't seem to think it was a problem.

"I'll find something for you. But you girls need long guns. A pistol is effective at close range, if you're trained." JC sighed, "We don't even have enough ammo to train you to a level of proficiency where those would ever be more than a last-resort gun. Steven, if I give you my deer rifle to use, can you give Dana your shotgun?"

"Sure."

"And Alisa, why don't you take Dana's revolver and give it back to Miss Jennie. See if she'll let you use her shotgun."

"Right now?" Alisa asked.

JC nodded. "Yeah, we're waiting on Catfish, Korey, and Rocky anyway."

Alisa took the revolver and walked briskly toward the house.

JC motioned to Jack. "Go get the .308 for Steven."

"Be right back." Jack hurried off toward the trailer.

JC drilled Dana on the basic functions of the shotgun. "Let's see you unload and reload."

She fumbled to find the pump release, but eventually depressed the small lever and pumped out the shells until it was empty.

"Could have been faster, but okay. Let's see you reload." JC stood with his arms crossed.

She picked up the shells from the ground.

"Make sure there's no grass or dirt on any of those before you put them back in the shotgun."

Dana carefully wiped each shell with her t-shirt before reloading it.

JC watched. "Tonight, (practice unloading and reloading over your bed. Then you won't have to worry about wiping the shells off every time. You need to do it until you can load shells without looking at what you're doing. In a firefight, you have to be looking at who is coming at you, not your weapon.) And this is different than when you trained to go get Alisa. That was close range. A shotgun is a good weapon at close range, but it's not very effective over fifty yards. If you're responsible for covering a particular area and someone is coming toward you, you'll have to wait for them to be within range. It's hard, but you have to do it. Peppering them at a distance might cause them to have to take cover, but it wastes ammo unless you know someone else with a rifle can get a kill shot from the maneuver."

Dana looked like she was trying to take it all in, but it didn't seem to be making sense to her.

JC patted her on the shoulder. "Don't worry, it seems overwhelming now, but we'll go over and over all of this until everyone knows it inside and out."

"Thanks." She smiled.

Catfish pulled up next to the barn with Korey and Jason Reese in the truck.

"Hey, guys." JC waved and walked toward the truck. "We'll train first and help yous get the truck unloaded next."

Catfish laughed.

"What's funny?" JC asked.

"Yous. I ain't never heard such Yankee talk. I reckon yous is Yankee fer y'all."

"Are you kiddin' me? Catfish! People in the South don't even understand you. It's like you're just making up words as you go."

Catfish spit with the accuracy of a sniper, sending tobacco juice flying three feet and landing precisely six inches from JC's shoe. "Least my made-up words ain't Yankee talk."

"Whatever." The look on JC's face was somewhere between angry and amused.

Jack and Alisa returned with their respective weapons, and finally, Rocky came walking up from the direction of his house.

JC began talking. "The first thing we are going to do is range cards. We'll have a card for each defensive position in the compound.

JC held up a clipboard with concentric half-circles at the top and several lines for writing at the bottom. "The first card will be for the barn loft lookout position. I think Catfish has labeled it the crow's nest. It has a pretty good view over the cornfield, the back pasture, all the way to the woods. Each of these concentric half-circle lines represents a given distance. So let's say they are fifty yards each. Most anything you can see from any position in the compound is going to fit on the card, if we say each ring is fifty yards." JC paused to make a quick sketch. He held the card up. "So I've made a rough drawing of the cornfield, starting here at the 200-yard mark, and this is the tree line at about 100 yards back here. We'll put in the fence, the hedgerow by the road, and then we'll know how far away any approaching hostiles are. Why is that important?"

Jack answered quickly. "So we can adjust the elevation of our weapon to compensate for the drop of the bullet."

JC nodded. "That's right. Depending on the weight of your bullet, barrel length, and other factors, your bullet is going to lose altitude in its trajectory. As we all train with our individual weapons at different distances, you'll learn how much you have to adjust for fifty yards, 100 yards, or 200 yards to still make the shot. Then, you can look at the range card for every defensive position in the compound and know how far away your target is. A 5.56 round won't drop as fast as a 7.62x.39 round, and Steven's .308 will be different than Catfish's 30-30. We'll learn all of that on the range after Nick wakes up. We'll go over troop movement until then so Nick and Cami can get another hour or two of sleep. I'm sure when any of you have night watch, you'll appreciate the same consideration."

"Everyone who was on the raid to bring Alisa home will remember some of this, but bear with us for the sake of those who weren't at that quick training. Other portions of the training will be new for most all of you, except Jack and Melissa. They know this stuff inside and out, so if you have questions, feel free to ask them."

JC spent the next two hours going over hand signals then drilling to see how much the group was remembering. Next he explained formations. He split the group up into fire teams and drilled them on formations and maneuvers.

Danny noticed that his fire team, called Alpha team, consisted of Catfish, Steven, Jack, Korey, and Rocky, the likely members of the scavenging run. JC put himself as the team leader of the other fire team, which conspicuously consisted of Melissa, Dana, Alisa, and ten-year-old Jason. No one on that team was likely to be slated for the mission. JC regularly abandoned his fire team during the training to observe Danny's team focusing on how they worked together as a team. Danny caught Alisa's scowl and knew she'd figured out why such attention was being given to the Alpha team.

Two hours later, Nick walked up. "You guys started without me?"

JC quipped, "We were waiting for you to show us the important stuff, like shooting."

Cami was close behind Nick. "Well, we do appreciate you holding off on that."

JC put his hand in the air and addressed the group. "Everybody, take fifteen minutes, go get a drink of water, or whatever you need to do, and we'll set up some targets when you get back."

"I need to get our rifles. Danny, you and JC walk back with me to the trailer." Nick led the way.

"Did you get a chance to think it over?" Danny asked.

Nick obviously knew what he was talking about. "I did."

"Catfish knows where there are some travel trailers. It would be quicker than trying to load and haul storage sheds," Danny said.

"Trailers would be more practical. What do you think?" Nick looked at JC.

"I hate it. But then again, I hate this whole mess. And I have that little girl to think about. I've got my wife to protect, a son to look out for, hopefully another one that will need a safe place when he finally gets home. The more I wonder about Chris, the more I want to do to make sure I don't have to worry about the rest of my family. I have to take all of that into consideration when I'm trying to figure out where the moral high ground is."

"You said you have some money." Danny walked close behind JC and Nick. "What if you took it, and maybe some provisions? We might be able to locate the owner and work out a deal for some trailers."

"Or we could get there and find a band of marauders already using the location as a forward operating base to go on raids," Nick said. "A place like that is a perfect base camp for a looting expedition."

JC exhaled deeply. "If it's not already inhabited, that makes the case for taking the trailers that much stronger."

Nick opened the door for Danny and JC to go in the trailer. "I say we go for it. If no one is laying claim to them, we'll be fortifying our own compound and reducing the resources of a potential problem location."

"Yeah, I agree." JC walked up the stairs and into the trailer.

Danny followed. "I'm in. If we can find the owner, we'll offer to trade. If he's not there I guess we just have to take them. It's not like we could leave a note. Anyone could find that note and come looking for us. That's just asking for trouble."

"You got that right." Nick closed the door behind them. "Due to the sensitivity of the subject, I think we should try to tell people one at a time. I'd rather not have to deal with an outraged group if we're going to have a lot of opposition. Talking to everyone separately will allow us to address their individual concerns. A group uprising tends to give people who previously had no issues with the mission a reason to object."

"I'll break it to Steven and the girls." Danny nodded.

JC stuck his thumbs in the top of his tactical vest. "I'll talk to Rocky, and my family, of course."

"Who should talk to Korey?" Nick asked.

JC shook his head. "Definitely not Catfish. Even if it weren't morally questionable, he'd make it sound like it was. I guess I can talk to Korey. You guys ready to go shoot?"

Nick picked up his and Cami's rifles. "Ready. Danny, will you grab that ammo can?"

Danny picked up the green, metal box. "Sure."

Once back at the barn, JC set up targets at twenty-five, fifty, seventy-five, and 100 yards. He set up two firing lines and assigned Nick to work one of the lines and Jack to work the other, coaching each shooter as their turn came up. Danny went first, and Nick worked with him as his coach.

Nick took Danny's AK-47. "Your rear sight is adjustable. We'll set it on the number one which represents 100 meters. JC is training everyone with yards, so that's roughly 110 yards. If your rifle is shooting straight, you should be coming in just a hair lower than where you are aiming. So, for the seventy-five yard target, you'll be shooting below the bullseye, and even lower for the fifty. Does that make sense?"

Danny took the rifle back and looked at the rear sight. "The number two is for 200 meters and the three is for 300? Should I change it if I have to shoot further?"

Nick scratched his head. "That's the purpose of this range, so you can get used to your weapon and be able to calculate where you need to aim at different distances without making any adjustments to your sights. You've been in a firefight or two. Imagine having to make adjustments to your sights while you're being shot at."

Danny furrowed his brow. "Yeah, I see what you're saying. That wouldn't be good."

"Okay, whenever you're ready, start with the fifty-yard target." Nick stepped behind Danny.

Danny took aim and fired.

"Dead center, good shot, but you're a little high. You'll have to aim a little bit lower, beneath your bullseye."

Danny took another shot and hit very near the bullseye.

"Great," Nick said. "Try for twenty-five yards."

Danny continued to shoot at the varying distances, getting a feel for where the round was going and how much higher or lower he had to shoot. Two magazines later, he was able to toggle back and forth between the targets with a moderate degree of accuracy.

Steven was next. It took a while longer for him to shoot as he had to work the bolt action on JC's .308 each time he fired, and reload the magazine after every four rounds. With a little help from Nick, Steven was soon shooting fairly close to the bullseye as well.

Steven stepped back so Nick could work with Catfish and his lever-action 30-30 for a while.

Danny patted Steven on the shoulder. "That was some fine shooting. We've got a little time; want to grab a seat under the tree?"

"Yeah. Sounds good. Training was kind of fun, but it takes a lot out of you." Steven walked beside Danny toward the old oak around by the front of the barn. "You and Alisa seem to have made up."

Danny nodded. "She doesn't like me to be overly protective of her."

"After what happened to her, it's understandable."

"I tried to explain that." Danny reached the tree, leaned his rifle against the trunk, and took a seat.

Steven did the same. "Deep down, I'm sure she appreciates it."

Danny looked over at Steven. "So, I think we can get some trailers, then the compound would be able to accommodate everyone."

"Really? Where in the heck are you going to find trailers in the middle of the apocalypse?"

Danny proceeded to lay out the basic strategy of the plan as well as the reasoning behind the mission.

As he listened, Steven began shaking his head, slowly at first, then gradually more quickly. "No. No. No. That's stealing, and it's wrong, and I want no part of it."

"But Steven, if we don't take them, they'll be used as a fortification for raiding parties."

Steven looked stunned. "Danny, are you listening to yourself? You are the raiding party. The second you set out to take something that isn't yours, you become the very thing you're trying to defend against. Are you missing the irony here?"

Danny continued to explain the rationale to Steven but to no avail.

Steven sat with his arms crossed. "It sounds like you guys have already legitimized this mission in your own minds, so I can't stop you, but don't expect me to come along. And, I'll highly recommend to Dana that she have no part in it."

"Well, we can agree on that, anyway. If Dana went, which I doubt JC would allow anyway, then Alisa would want to go, which I definitely don't want."

"I sure hope none of you gets shot. That would jeopardize the entire group." Steven stood up, grabbed his rifle, and walked away.

Danny could feel the coldness in Steven's withdrawal. He felt bad that this was going to be an issue between them, but his mind was made up, and he'd already committed to Nick and JC.

Danny made his way back over to the group. Alisa had just finished shooting. "How did you do?"

"It's a shotgun. You don't have to be a sharp shooter to hit anything with this. I wish we had bought another rifle." She looked at the AK hanging from Danny's shoulder.

"I guess there will always be things we wished we'd have done differently, but in the end, we're a lot better off than most people. I talked to Nick and JC. It looks like there's definitely going to be a scavenging mission."

"Have fun." Alisa's response was sullen.

"Not today." Danny put his hands on her shoulders. "Steven is not at all on board with the mission. He really doesn't understand the need. In fact, he's mad that we're doing it. I doubt he's talking to me right now. I can't stand to have him and you both giving me the cold shoulder. Who am I supposed to hang out with? Catfish?"

Alisa looked away to try and conceal her smile, but Danny saw it.

He ran his fingers through her hair. "So what do you say? Can we be friends?"

She took his hand with hers. "Just don't treat me like a baby, Danny. I can take care of myself."

He gave her a quick kiss on the lips. "Okay, but try to understand that God gave you to me, and I feel a certain responsibility for keeping you safe, especially after what happened to you."

JC walked up to Danny. "Did you talk to your people?"

Danny nodded and glanced at Alisa. "She knows; she understands why we have to do it. Steven, not so much. He's completely against it. Did you talk to Rocky?"

"Yeah, he hates it, but he's coming. Do you think Steven will come around?"

"No, I don't. He's pretty ticked off that we're doing it, but I don't think he'll try to get in the way of us going."

"As long as Korey comes on board, we should still be okay. I'd like to have at least a four-man security team, Catfish at the wheel and two people to cut the locks and get us hitched up."

"How do you feel the training went today?" Danny asked.

"It went good. Everyone did their best. Some people still need some work." JC grinned. "Let me correct that statement; most people still need a lot of work, but we'll do the best we can with what we have to work with. I wanted to develop a minimum level of proficiency amongst those who would be guarding the compound. We'll spend all day tomorrow drilling for the mission. Then, we'll rest up on Sunday and hit the trailer sales lot at first light on Monday.

"Later next week, we'll do another firing range, stretching the targets out a little further, 50, 150, 200, and maybe 250 yards. Then we'll see how well those skills translate over for the group. We'll set up targets at random spots out in the field, and people will have to use their range cards to figure out how far away the target is. I also want to build a small fortification around Miss Jennie's front porch and make a range card for that position. It has a good view of the drive which is a very likely avenue of approach, due to the natural boundaries of the hedgerow along the road and the creek running up the side of the property.

"Our biggest concern with training is ammo. Nick is going to have Cami make an inventory sheet on Monday. She'll spend the whole day going around to everyone and finding out exactly how much ammo we have so we can budget how much can be spent on training. We have to plan on never being able to resupply our ammo. I've got a ton of 5.56, so does Nick. I've also got a nice stash of .308 and shotgun ammo. You're the only one in the group with an AK, so as nice of a gun as it is, you're limited to how good you'll ever get with it because of the ammo situation."

Danny adjusted the sling of his rifle. "So make every shot count, even in training, right?"

"Even in training." JC nodded. "How much ammo do you have?"

Danny peered up toward the edge of the barn roof as he ran the calculation. "I started with 400 rounds, shot some training, blew through a few mags in firefights; probably about 275 rounds left."

"That's not much. And when it's gone, it's gone. I know you feel comfortable with that AK, but you should talk to Nick about letting you get his extra AR. I've got thousands of rounds of 5.56. So does Nick, and all of us are already trained, so we only need to shoot a minimal amount to stay sharp, make sure our weapons are zeroed in, plus whatever we need for hunting and defense."

Danny gritted his teeth and looked at Alisa. "We should have bought a lot more ammo."

"No sense kicking yourself. You did good. You prepared as best as you knew how, and everyone in your group got here safely. It could have been a lot worse." JC gave Danny's shoulder a squeeze.

Danny gave a light smile. "Yeah, thanks."

JC waved as he walked away. "I'm going to go have a chat with Korey. I'll see you guys later."

"Bye," Alisa said.

"You're welcome to eat dinner with us. Nana always makes plenty," Danny said.

JC turned to answer but kept walking. "Thanks, but we'll probably eat in the trailer tonight. It's our family time."

"Okay, see ya later." Danny waved.

CHAPTER 15

But thou, O LORD, art a shield for me; my glory, and the lifter up of mine head.

Psalm 3:3

As was becoming the norm, Danny awoke Saturday morning still exhausted from the day before. He turned over to look at Alisa, who also looked tired. "I'm crawling back in the bed after church tomorrow."

She put her finger on his nose and smiled. "Good luck. The Reeses are moving to the compound after church."

"Why did you have to remind me?" He rolled back over and covered his head.

Nana's voice rang out from the foot of the stairs. "Y'all get on down here. It's time to eat."

Alisa got up and jerked the covers off of Danny. "Rise and shine, country boy."

He made a vain attempt to cling to the covers, a symbol of the extra sleep he so desperately desired. "Okay."

The two of them quickly got dressed and made their way to the breakfast table. Grits and eggs were both readily available, so they were the two staples for the morning meal. The coffee was becoming gradually weaker as Nana rationed and rebrewed the grounds to make them last longer.

Danny hurried to get his chores done so he could meet the scavenging team behind the barn. Alisa helped him since Steven was still not speaking to Danny, other than forced courtesies and saying what had to be said for the morning's division of labor.

They arrived at the back of the barn where Nick and Cami were already waiting.

Nick handed an all-black AR-15 to Danny. "I spoke with JC last night. We decided the two of you should get trained up with this rifle. It's just like the one that's being used for night watch, except for the night vision scope."

Danny passed the rifle to Alisa to look over. "Thanks, that's great. Is it just like yours and Cami's?"

"Similar. Ours are Rock River Arms, slightly more high-end. This one and the night watch rifle are DPMS. They sold for less than $600 each before the EMP, but still very good guns. We figured they'd be our backup guns if anything happened and we lost our rifles on the way home. Or as it has turned out, we figured they'd be more useful than the $1200."

"Fantastic, thanks so much," Alisa said.

Nick handed a couple full magazines to Alisa. "You, Cami, and Melissa will be the primary defense for the compound while we're out on Monday, so you need to get up to speed on this weapon today. Danny, I assume you'll want to have your AK on Monday, right?"

"Yeah, I do."

"Okay then, let's do some shooting."

Alisa asked, "Should we be shooting so early in the morning?"

"Rocky had night watch last night. If he's sleeping with earplugs, the shots shouldn't bother him all the way over on the other side of the creek."

"I assume his watch went okay last night? No major events?" Danny asked.

Nick snorted. "Yes and no. No major events with animals or invaders obviously, but Pauline came running down here in the middle of the night. It scared him half to death, thinking something had happened to her."

"Is she okay? What happened?" Alisa looked concerned.

"No big deal," Nick said. "She had a bad dream, dreamed that Rocky was shot on the scavenging mission."

Danny didn't like the sound of that. "In my world, bad dreams are a very big deal. Are you sure you should be so quick to write it off?"

JC and Jack walked up as they were speaking.

"Did you tell them about Mrs. Cook's nightmare?" Jack inquired.

Nick nodded. "We were just talking about it."

Danny turned toward JC. "Do you think there could be anything to it?"

"Not really. She's never had a dream come true before."

Danny looked at the ground in front of him. "Neither had I, until three months ago. There's a first time for everything."

Nick rubbed his chin. "I don't think we can scrap such an important mission over what is probably just a case of Pauline being worried about her husband. That's a pretty normal dream for anyone who has a loved one going into a potentially dangerous situation."

"I agree." JC nodded. "Danny, if it were you having the dream, that would be a different story. I'd walk away from the mission in a heartbeat."

"Yeah, well, we still have to get through the next two nights." Danny knuckled his brow.

"Who's going to fill in for Rocky? At training I mean. Since he had night watch, you'll be missing your fourth lookout," Alisa said.

Danny knew exactly where this was going. "It's just training. We don't have to have a person in that position. We can just pretend Rocky is standing there."

"Wow." Alisa held the AR with one hand and put her other hand on her hip. "Did you get promoted to tactical coordinator? I didn't know. Congratulations. I'll see if I can get Nana to bake a cake to celebrate."

"I'm your husband. I don't have to be tactical coordinator. It's just training, Alisa. Don't get so bent out of shape."

"If it's just training, what would be the harm in me standing in for Rocky?"

"It's just not necessary."

JC pursed his lips. "I hate to get in the middle of this, but it would help to have another body standing in for Rocky, but not if it's going to cause friction. Danny, you can say no if you want. And Alisa, it's only if you promise not to rub it in his face. No I-told-you-so."

"Pinky swear!" Alisa's face lit up. "Danny, I'm sorry. Like you said, it's just training. After all, the better trained I am, the more I'll be able to protect myself while you're away. Can I? Please?"

Nick, Jack, and JC were all looking at him, and he knew they thought that Alisa should fill in. He did not, but he'd promised that he wouldn't be overprotective of her and that he'd let her live her life. And there was no way to argue that more training wouldn't make her safer. "This, in no way, implies that you'll be going on this or any other mission." Danny stuck his index finger in the air to emphasize his point.

Alisa bit her lip. "Thank you, Danny. And of course, I know that; you don't have anything to worry about."

"Hmm." He pursed his lips. He had plenty to worry about.

Nick spent the next several minutes going over the function of the AR-15 with Danny and Alisa. Then, they took turns firing the weapons at the various targets left out from training the day before.

Catfish soon arrived with Korey.

Danny shook Korey's hand. "So you got sucked into this, too."

"Yeah," Korey laughed. "I guess we'll be living in one of those trailers, so I figured I better go along and earn my keep."

"Where's the little guy?" Danny asked.

"I don't want him or the girls worrying about me while we're out on Monday, so I didn't want him to know what we're doing today. I practically had to hogtie him to keep him from coming today."

"You'll all be out here tomorrow, living life in the compound."

"Yep. It's tough on Tracey, and the girls. They'll miss their house, but it's a different world, and we have to do what we have to do."

The team practiced getting in and out of the truck for twenty minutes, with JC timing them and pushing them to move faster and faster.

It seemed like such a monotonous task to Danny, but he trusted Nick and JC, who assured the group over and over that the precious seconds lost, getting in or out of the truck, could cost a life.

Next, they practiced backing the truck up to Catfish's old flatbed trailer, which stood in for the travel trailers. Assorted types of locks were placed on the coupler to mimic the various hitch locks that would likely need to be cut off. Danny and Korey were responsible for cutting the locks and getting the trailer hooked up while Catfish backed up the truck and the others stood guard.

"Everybody is doing great. Let's put another lock on the coupler and run the whole operation from the top." Nick pointed to Alisa. "Switch with

Korey. I want to make sure he's trained to handle a security position in case we need him there."

"Okay." Alisa got in the bed of the truck, between Danny and Nick, where Korey had been sitting in the previous drills.

Everyone returned to the truck once more and Catfish drove around the barn, as if they were just pulling up to the trailer lot. The team bailed out of the truck in a precise order, depending on their positions. Danny waited for the rear security team, Nick and Korey, to sweep their area and yell, "All clear." Danny and Alisa dropped the tailgate, set their weapons on it, and retrieved the cutting tools from Danny's backpack. She handed him the hacksaw and held the bolt cutters in case he needed them.

Danny had sawn through a piece of rebar, drilled out the keyhole of an old lock, and cut another lock with the bolt cutters in the past three rounds of training. His arms were getting tired.

"Want some help?"

Danny stood back. "Go ahead."

Alisa positioned the bolt cutters on the old lock and began to squeeze. She put all of her strength into the task. Finally, the blades of the cutters bit together with a snap and the old lock dropped to the ground. "Voila!"

"Good job." He couldn't deny that she was a real trooper and put her heart into everything she did.

Nick began clapping. "You all did a bang-up job. Give yourselves a hand."

They all clapped.

JC addressed the group before dismissing them.

"This mission is a little bit of a touchy subject for some of the other folks living in the compound. The less we talk about it, the less of an issue it will be. Everybody, go home, get some rest. And be ready to roll out at five o'clock Monday morning."

Alisa reminded him, "We're moving the Reese family tomorrow, right?"

JC turned to Korey. "Since we're probably going to have a new trailer for you Monday, would you rather push your move back till Tuesday?"

Korey nodded. "Yep. Otherwise, it'll be like moving twice. The girls will be happy to have two more days in their home. And maybe Tracey won't be so anxious while we're out on the mission."

"Okay, then. See you all at church tomorrow." Nick waved and headed back to his trailer.

Danny smiled. He was happy for Korey's family to have another day in their home, but he was also happy to have a true day of rest. It was a much-needed break, especially with the mission on Monday.

Sunday morning, Danny and Alisa went to the barn early to straighten up before church. There was no way of making the venue look like anything other than a barn, but they could, at least, put the tools back in their proper place and arrange the hay bales in a manner that felt more inviting.

Everyone else living in the compound began arriving soon after. Catfish arrived with the Reese family just before Nana began singing from her handwritten song sheet. Even though they had postponed their official move date until Tuesday, the Reeses did not want to waste a trip and had loaded some of their belongings into Catfish's truck to bring over.

After four songs, Steven stepped to the front with his Bible, a notebook, and a sullen face. He opened the service with prayer, then flipped through the pages of his Bible. "I'm really torn on what to talk about this morning. I don't think I'm telling anyone something they don't know by saying we have a major split in opinion about tomorrow's mission. I know how I feel, but I also know how Danny and the men leading the team feel. I was tempted to use the pulpit as a vehicle to promote my agenda this morning. I'm not going to do that. I am going to talk about why I think it's the wrong thing to do, but I know that Danny, JC, and Nick are good people and what they are doing is being done out of love, so I'm going to talk about that. At the end of the day, we're all family now. We all depend on one another, and that means we're going to see things differently from time to time. We're going to have to look past our disagreements and focus on loving each other, like a family.

"I'm going to first start with a verse that I believe reflects the heart of Danny and the others. Turn with me to I Timothy 5:8, 'But if any provide not for his own, and specially for those of his own house, he hath denied the faith, and is worse than an infidel.' I think this verse represents the motivation of the team that is going out tomorrow." Steven continued to speak about the love, devotion, and self-sacrifice of the men who would be going out the following morning.

Steven flipped through the pages again. "Now, if you'll turn with me to Exodus 20:15. 'Thou shall not steal.' It's a very simple verse, with no need for an elaborate explanation. It doesn't have any criteria that need to be met before its application, nor does it provide for any exceptions. It's a hard and fast rule, and God saw fit to list it in his personal top-ten list of things he commanded us to do. It's my honest opinion that we find ourselves in our present predicament because of moral compromise. Our country and our culture found excuse after excuse to do away with moral absolutes, panning through grey areas until we found ourselves in such a condition that God Almighty had to turn his back on us, remove his hand of protection, and allow our ultimate destruction.

"Aside from all of that, I see tomorrow's mission as trusting in the flesh. I believe wholeheartedly that if we trust in God and honor his commandments that his providence will be our shelter and our refuge."

Nana shouted out, "Hallelujah!"

Her impromptu praise was loud enough and disruptive enough to break the seriousness and bring a grin or giggle to everyone in the barn, Steven included.

Steven smiled, then took a deep breath. "With all of that said, I would still like to go around the room and have each one of us pray for their safety tomorrow. We all know what a dangerous world it is beyond the hedgerow that separates Miss Jennie's farm from the rest of this broken world. I'll start, and then we'll go around the room until everyone has had a chance to pray. It doesn't have to be long, but this team does need God's protection."

Steven bowed his head and led in prayer. For the next half an hour, the rest of the attendees went around the barn, praying in turn.

Sunday dinner followed the service. As usual, Nana and Pauline Cook oversaw the food preparation efforts. Cami and Tracey Reese assisted with the meal, while Danny, Alisa, Steven, and Dana took care of setting up the outside eating area. Several wood boards pulled from the side of JC's barn sat atop a row of old metal barrels to make a serving table as well as a series of dining tables. For benches, more boards from the weathered barn were placed upon five-gallon buckets. Each eight-foot-long bench consisted of a bucket at both ends and one in the middle for support.

Since tomorrow's mission was such a subject of contention, the topic was avoided except for the low whispers amongst those known to be in agreement with each other on the matter.

JC accompanied Danny as he walked around to the hand pump in order to draw water for teaming off the iced tea. "Need some help?"

Danny handed him one of the buckets. "Sure. Nana brews the tea very strong, so we can mix it with cold water from the well. It's not exactly iced tea, but as long as we mix it right before we serve it, it's still relatively cold tea."

"Good enough for me." JC stood next to the pump as Danny began lifting and pushing the handle. "Listen, I've got some bad news."

"What happened?" Danny stopped pumping for a moment.

"Nothing terrible. It's Rocky. Pauline is hung up on that dream. She's convinced him not to go on the run tomorrow."

Danny resumed working the pump. "Oh. So, we'll be a man short. The security team is just precautionary, right? Can't we work with what we have?"

JC took the filled bucket and handed Danny the empty one. "We're totally exposed in an operation like that. I don't feel comfortable having any less than four people on security, to cover all four corners of the op. Splitting the security team into three zones leaves way too much room for someone to slip up on us."

"So, what are you recommending? We stay home?"

JC pursed his lips. "I hate to ask this of you."

Danny started shaking his head. He didn't need to hear the question. He knew exactly what JC was going to say. "You know, JC, this is exactly why I didn't want her to train. I knew something like this was going to come up."

"Danny, look. I understand exactly how you feel."

"You don't know how I feel!" Danny snapped back as he slung the bucket and started walking toward the dining area.

"Whoa, big guy. Settle down." JC didn't seem to take offense at Danny's attitude, but neither did he seem prepared to drop the subject. "Think about what you just said. I've got one kid out there, God knows where. I pray every night that he's alive and that God will bring him back, but the reality is, I have no way of knowing. My other son, I'm putting him in harm's way for the second time tomorrow. I understand that a wife is different, but don't think I don't love those two boys as much as you love your wife.

"Alisa is fast, smart, aware of her surroundings, and a natural when it comes to shooting. I'm not asking you to make any sacrifice that I'm not already making. And I wouldn't even consider putting her in if I didn't think she could handle it. Over the years, I've come to be a pretty good judge of who can take the heat and who's going to choke on game day."

"I thought you were just a beat cop. What do you know about how people will react in a shootout?"

"I worked as a beat cop. I never said that's what I was doing when I retired."

"I appreciate what you're saying, but it's not the same. Melissa is much better trained than Alisa. Why don't you put her in?"

"Danny, I'm going in. I'm putting my kid in. Melissa ain't going in. Somebody has to stick around for Annie. I can't leave my little girl in this world with neither one of her brothers, no mom, and no dad. That's too much to ask of her."

Danny felt a pang of guilt shoot through his gut. "Yeah, I'm sorry. I shouldn't have said that."

The two men made it back to the beverage area where Danny began mixing the strongly brewed tea with the cold water. JC set the bucket next to Danny's feet, patted him on the back, and said,

"Think it over. We'll talk later tonight."

Danny said nothing. He didn't want to think it over. He wanted to be back in Savannah, back at school, walking through Forsyth Park, holding Alisa's hand, and going to Leopold's for an ice cream. But none of that was ever going to happen again, so there was no use wishing for it.

After lunch, Danny helped Alisa, Dana, and Steven clean up. Then, Danny and Alisa went upstairs to take the nap he'd been waiting for all week.

Alisa closed the door, sat on one of the food storage buckets that was serving as a chair, and took her shoes off. "Dana overheard Pauline talking to Nana. Rocky isn't going out with you guys tomorrow."

Danny sighed as he kicked off his shoes and sat on the bed. "I heard."

"So, Nick and JC both know? Who's going to take his place?"

"Not you, if that's what you're hinting at." Danny lay his head on the pillow.

Disappointment was again scrolled across Alisa's face. "Danny, I don't think you understand what happened to me mentally when I was abducted. I've tried to tell you, but either you're not listening, you don't have the ability to empathize with my emotions, or you're too caught up in your own head to care. The powerlessness I felt, it's still with me. I still feel like a victim. I'm not going to get mad anymore, I'm not going to throw a fit, and if you say no, I'll be a submissive wife and do what you say. But, if you say no, I want you to understand what you are doing to me. You are imprisoning me in the past, in a perpetual state of being a victim. What happened to me is not your fault. I'd never blame that on you, but now I have a chance to prove that I can take care of myself, to break out of this prison of fear that's inside me, to face my monsters. If you take that away from me, you are what is standing in the way of my healing."

Danny listened as her voice cracked. He didn't have to look at her to know she was crying. So was he. Danny did understand how she felt, but she didn't understand his fear. He just didn't know if he was ready to face his monsters, ready to deal with the fear of losing her. He remained silent, but the tears continued to quietly roll down his face and onto the pillow as he drifted off to sleep.

Danny jumped up from the bed, stumbled to the corner of the room, and grabbed the AK-47. Half asleep, he tried to focus as he raised the rifle to a low-ready position. "They're coming, they're coming!" he yelled.

Alisa cried out from the other side of the bed, "Danny! What's happening? Who's coming?"

Confused, Danny surveyed the room as reality replaced the blurry vision he'd just seen. He lowered the rifle as he looked at Alisa, sitting on the bed with one hand covering her heart. In a low, mumbling voice, he repeated her question. "Who's coming?"

"Danny, put the gun down. I think you just had a bad dream. You scared me half to death. Sit down.

Do you want some water?"

Danny placed the rifle back in the corner where it had been. He took a deep breath and caught a bead of sweat with his tongue. "Yes, please." The familiar dry mouth following one of his nightmares needed more water than the few drops of salty perspiration sitting above his lip.

Alisa slowly stood up and made her way to the door. She put her hands on Danny's face and looked into his eyes compassionately. "I'll be right back with some water. And change your shirt; you're soaking wet."

"Thanks." Danny followed her instructions. The clean, dry shirt was becoming a sort of ritual, the last phase of his journey, back to reality from a distant land plagued by horror and fright. Danny sat back down on the bed and remained motionless while he waited for Alisa to return.

She returned quickly with a glass of water. "What happened? Another cow?"

Danny took a sip of water and set the glass on top of the bucket by the bed. "I don't know. I don't remember a cow. The only thing I remember was being out on a barren plain. It wasn't a desert exactly, but close. There was like some scrub brush growing and a few weeds here and there. Off in the distance, I saw a dust cloud. It was red. I remember thinking it was a dust storm, but as it got closer, I could hear the thunder of hooves charging in my direction."

Alisa handed him the glass of water. "Like horse hooves, or like cattle hooves?"

Danny took another sip and set the glass back

down. "I don't know. The only thing I could see was the dust cloud. But somehow, I knew that the source of the hooves and the billowing dust cloud was coming for me."

Alisa's face went white. "It's an attack. We're going to be attacked. We have to go tell JC and Nick, right now."

Danny nodded. "Okay, let me get my boots on."

Once they had their shoes on, Danny grabbed the AK and made his way down the stairs. Alisa followed close behind, buckling her pistol belt as she cleared the last stair. They passed Steven and Dana, holding hands and sitting in the swing on the front porch.

"Where are you guys running off to?" Steven asked.

"Danny had another dream. We have to talk to JC," Alisa said quickly in passing.

Steven trailed close behind with Dana following him as Danny and Alisa refused to stop on their way to JC's trailer. Danny knocked on the door.

JC came out and looked at the rifle in Danny's hand. "Is this an emergency?"

"I don't know," Danny answered.

"Do I need my gun?" JC rephrased his question.

Danny shrugged. "I had another dream. I don't know."

"Hold on one second." JC dipped back in the trailer. "Jack, we got an Ernie. Look alive." JC soon returned with his tactical vest and his rifle.

"What's an Ernie?" Alisa asked.

"We use Sesame Street characters for alert levels. It's less scary for Annie. But never mind that. What was your dream about?"

Danny was still processing the alert levels. "Ernie is which one? The orange one?"

"Yeah, Bert is yellow, Ernie is orange; Elmo is what you don't want to hear." JC motioned for Danny to get on with the explanation. "The dream, what was the dream."

Danny explained what he'd seen.

JC looked to Alisa. "Do you know what it means?"

"The dust was red. I think it's like a cloud of war. I think it means we're going to get attacked. The way the dust cloud was growing larger and the hooves getting louder, I think it's getting closer."

"I kind of gathered all of that, but how imminent do you think it is? Could this be happening within the hour, later tonight, tomorrow?" JC quizzed.

She shook her head. "I don't know. I guess since the cloud was a ways off, we probably have a little time, but not much. If I had to make an estimation, I'd say days. Definitely not months, and probably not weeks."

"So less than a week?" JC listened closely to everything she said.

"It's just a guess. I don't know."

JC patted her on the shoulder. "Don't underestimate yourself. I don't think God is going to bother giving Danny a dream unless it can be boiled down to actionable intelligence. You're his interpreter. If you say days, not weeks, it's probably days, not weeks."

"I never said I was his interpreter." Alisa stuck her hands in her pockets.

"Well, I have to go on something, and I'm going on that. Let's go tell Nick." JC motioned for them to follow him.

Jack was geared up and at the rear of the group by the time they arrived at Nick and Cami's trailer across the yard.

JC knocked.

"Be right out," Nick said.

"No hurry," JC said.

Nick and Cami soon came to the door. "Come on in," Cami said as she held the door open for Danny and his growing entourage.

JC gave Nick and Cami a quick synopsis of everything.

Alisa added, "Don't forget about the landscape, the scrub brush and the weeds."

Steven looked curious. "Do you think that's significant? The weeds?"

"It could be symbolic of the sparse resources. I'm not sure." Alisa shrugged.

Dana nodded. "That makes sense."

"The bottom line is, we're going to get hit soon, and we need to get ready." JC turned to Danny. "I need you to think about tomorrow. The whole operation hinges on your decision. I'm not going to run that op short-handed and put everybody at risk. And if we don't get the needed provisions to secure this place, we may all be dead this time next week."

Alisa took his hand. "Danny, what is he talking about?"

Danny grimaced and turned toward JC. "Go ahead, tell her."

"You sure about that?" JC quizzed.

Danny gave a reluctant nod.

"Alisa, would you be willing to fill in tomorrow? You'd be Danny's assistant on cutting locks and connecting hitches. That would allow me to put Korey into the vacant fourth security slot."

Alisa's eyes lit up, "Yes! Of course."

"Good, you know the drill. It will be just like training." JC looked as though he was surprised by her excitement.

Alisa hugged Danny and kissed him on his neck. She whispered in his ear, "Thank you!"

Danny was less ecstatic about the situation but forced a smile.

JC pointed at Steven. "It should be you going tomorrow. I appreciate your position on stealing, and that was a great little sermon you gave this morning; I just hope your conviction is still as strong when you're gurgling your last breath in a pool of your own blood, while you watch some sicko dragging your little girlfriend off on a dog leash to do who knows what to her."

Steven didn't respond to the comment but quietly stood up and left the RV. Dana looked like she had something to say, but kept her mouth shut as she slowly followed Steven out the door.

In fact, no one said anything. While Danny would have found a more discreet way to say it, he felt roughly the same way about the matter as JC did.

After a long moment of awkward silence, Danny said, "We should let Nick and Cami have their privacy back. Come on, everybody, let's go."

Cami held the door as they left the RV and

reminded everyone, "Don't forget about the news broadcast tonight. And we're supposed to have the bluegrass music right afterwards. We'll see you all by the picnic tables."

JC waved as he walked down the stairs. "Thanks, but I'm going to skip the entertainment tonight. I want to get as much rest as possible for tomorrow. Danny, I'm sure you'll let me know if the newscast has any pertinent information."

"Absolutely. It's usually the same old stuff, but if it's anything new, I'll relay the message to you. See you in the morning." Danny smiled as he waved to JC and Jack.

Alisa's voice was still full of excitement. "I'll see you tomorrow, JC!" Her salutation also seemed to serve as an assurance that she would, indeed, be included in the mission.

The turnout for what had been the highly anticipated Pickens Radio broadcast was light. JC and Jack didn't come, supposedly because they wanted to rest up, but Danny suspected it had to do with JC being irritated at the members of the group who weren't supportive of the salvaging mission.

Steven and Dana didn't come, after the harsh words from JC. Of course, they didn't know he wouldn't be there.

Nana, Catfish, Rocky, Pauline, Cami, Nick, Alisa, and Danny were all gathered around the radio before eight o'clock. The disagreement about the mission hung over the group, but everyone avoided the subject and tried to act cordial so they could enjoy the music when it began.

At eight o'clock on the dot, the radio sprang to life once again.

"Hey folks, I'm Ranger Dave. Thanks for listening to this special edition of Pickens Radio. First the news, then we have a special musical treat for anyone listening. A member of our community heard from a friend, who heard from a cousin, who heard from someone he ran into at a pop-up trading post, that a band of semi-well-organized ruffians were making their way around the area and extorting food and supplies in exchange for protection. The impression I got was that they're putting themselves out to be a self-proclaimed legitimate government who wants to institute order. In reality, they're probably little more than a local mafia.

"Now that I hear myself say it, sounds pretty much like the politicians we had before the EMP. But all jokes aside, just because someone comes around calling themselves governor this or mayor that, doesn't mean anything. So don't fall for it. Get organized and stand up for yourselves. If you let them push you around once, it will be harder and harder to resist.

"But like I said, this little news tidbit is coming down a long chain of the grapevine, so I can't confirm it as anything more than rumor."

Danny looked at Nick. "I don't guess that's anything worth disturbing JC over. Do you think?"

Nick shook his head. "Not really what we're looking for to be considered actionable intel.

There's no real who, what, where, or how many."

Ranger Dave continued the broadcast, going over the basics for new listeners. Afterwards, he introduced the musicians from his community, and they began to play. The bluegrass music was lively and fun, and everyone listening was soon clapping their hands or dancing around. Miss Jennie even knew the words to one of the songs and sang along.

The sound quality was pitiful compared to the standards before the EMP, but it had been more than five weeks since anyone had heard music over an electronic device, so no one complained. The band played for nearly an hour and the music did much to lift the spirits of the members in Danny's group who listened.

Afterwards, it was time for bed. Danny was still tired. The vision of the red dust cloud racing toward them from the horizon had robbed him of his chance to take a restful nap. He hoped there would be no more dreams. Danny desperately needed a good night's sleep before the mission.

Monday morning came early. Danny and Alisa were up well before daylight, even before Nana, so they could eat a good breakfast and gear up for the scavenging run.

A light tap at the back door preceded JC's entry. He was carrying a green tactical vest, similar to the one he'd given Danny. "Melissa is lending you her vest for today. You are both about the same size so the straps and buckles should be adjusted to fit you fairly well."

Alisa took the vest. "Thanks."

"Any new info from the radio last night?"

"Yes and no." Danny filled JC in on the hearsay that Ranger Dave had relayed the night before.

"There's probably some truth to it. It's a shame he didn't get more specific news." JC unclipped his holster holding a semi-automatic pistol and took two magazines out of his pocket, laying them all on the counter. "And here's my Glock. Alisa, you can wear it in the holster on the front of the vest. It's the same model as Danny's so you know what to do with it."

Alisa finished zipping up the vest. "I can't take your pistol. What will you use?"

"I've got my .38, as a backup. But I'll never be separated from my battle rifle. You and Danny will be cutting locks and hitching up the trailers, so it's imperative that you have a good sidearm in case we get hit and you can't get to your rifles right away."

Alisa stuck the Glock in the holster on the front of the vest. "Thanks again."

"No, thank you. You're a brave girl. I'm proud of you. And you, too, Danny. I know it takes a lot to put someone you love in harm's way."

Danny gave a slight nod and glanced over at his wife. "Thanks. I probably wouldn't even have her if you and Jack hadn't helped me bring her home."

"We all do what we gotta do." JC smirked. "Most of us, anyways. See you guys at the barn. We roll out in twenty minutes."

"We'll be there." Alisa walked JC to the door so it wouldn't slam shut and wake Nana.

Danny put a bowl containing the remainder of his oatmeal on the floor for Puddin', who quickly turned her nose up at the inadequate offering.

"Ungrateful cat." Danny shook his head. "These are hard times. We all have to make some adjustments." Danny found the leftover fried rabbit from Sunday dinner and tore off a few morsels to mix into the oatmeal. By shredding the meat very thinly, the picky feline would be forced to ingest some of the oatmeal. Oatmeal was heavily stocked in the compound, but rabbit was a treat they ate twice a week at most. Next, Danny picked out some gristle and bone to mix into another portion of oatmeal for Rusty. The reliable old farm dog would have eaten the oatmeal alone, without complaint, but it just didn't seem fair to not give him a taste of rabbit also.

After feeding the dog, Danny and Alisa went back upstairs to finish getting ready to go on their mission.

Nana was up and brewing coffee when they came back down. "I want to pray a Psalm over y'all before you head out. Alisa, why don't you run over to the RV and have Nicolas come to the house so I can pray over him too."

"We have to leave in five minutes," Alisa said.

"Then you best get to it." Nana was not accustomed to negotiating.

"Yes, ma'am." Alisa hurried out the door.

Nana poured a cup of coffee and handed it to Danny. "Have another cup before you go."

"Thanks." Danny took the cup.

"Did y'all get enough to eat for breakfast?"

"Yes, ma'am."

"Who's been eatin' this rabbit?"

"I had a bite. I thought the protein might help give me energy." Danny had indeed eaten a few bites, so it wasn't a lie, even if it weren't the whole truth.

"Alright then." Nana turned in her Bible to Psalm 91 and looked over the text as they waited for Nick.

Alisa soon returned with Nick following close behind.

Nana asked, "Where is JC and his boy? I've got to pray over them too."

Alisa looked confused. "You just said to get Nick."

"I'm old. I can't think of everything anymore. You're still young. Young folk have to look out for us old people, think of things when we forget."

Alisa huffed and started to go back out the door.

Nick said, "Hang on, Alisa. Nana, why don't you walk down to the barn and pray over all of us?"

"I ain't got no clothes on. I'm still in my housecoat."

Nick patted Nana on the back. "It's dark outside. No one will notice."

"Well, let me get my snake boots on and get a flashlight so I don't kill myself walkin' back to the house. Daniel, you carry my Bible down to the barn."

Danny smiled and took the Bible.

Once Nana had her boots on, the four of them walked down to the barn where the rest of the group was loading up into the truck.

Nana had Danny hold the flashlight while she read the Psalm. "He that dwelleth in the secret place of the most High shall abide under the shadow of the Almighty. I will say of the LORD, He is my refuge and my fortress: my God; in him will I trust. Surely he shall deliver thee from the snare of the fowler, and from the noisome pestilence. He shall cover thee with his feathers, and under his wings shalt thou trust: his truth shall be thy shield and buckler. Thou shalt not be afraid for the terror by night; nor for the arrow that flieth by day; Nor for the pestilence that walketh in darkness; nor for the destruction that wasteth at noonday. A thousand shall fall at thy side, and ten thousand at thy right hand; but it shall not come nigh thee. Only with thine eyes shalt thou behold and see the reward of the wicked. Because thou hast made the LORD, which is my refuge, even the most High, thy habitation; There shall no evil befall thee, neither shall any plague come nigh thy dwelling. For he shall give his angels charge over thee, to keep thee in all thy ways. They shall bear thee up in their hands, lest thou dash thy foot against a stone. Thou shalt tread upon the lion and adder: the young lion and the dragon shalt thou trample under feet. Because he hath set his love upon me, therefore will I deliver him: I will set him on high, because he hath known my name. He shall call upon me, and I will answer him: I will be with him in trouble; I will deliver him, and honour him. With long life will I satisfy him, and shew him my salvation."

Nana closed the Bible and bowed her head. "Lord, we humbly ask that you'll watch over all these, your children. You know their hearts and you know they're tryin' to do the right thing. And you know they love you. Psalm 91 said because they've set their love upon you, that you'll deliver them. I pray that you'll remember that promise today. Amen."

The rest of the group looked up and echoed Nana's amen.

JC inspected each person's gear, making sure their weapons were loaded, that their gear was secure, and that they had everything needed for the run. "Let's roll out. Jack, you're up front with me and Catfish. Everybody else is in the back."

Danny held Alisa's hand and pulled her up as she stepped on the bumper of Catfish's old truck. "Last chance to back out if you're afraid."

"Not on your life." She winked, then walked to the back of the truck bed and sat down.

Nick and Korey got in last and Catfish drove away.

Ten minutes later, they arrived at the trailer sales lot. The lock had long since been cut and the gate hung open. The faintest glimmer of daylight allowed them to see without the use of flashlights. Catfish backed up to the first available trailer and the security team made sure there were no hostiles.

Danny set his rifle on the open tailgate of the truck and took out the bolt cutters, just like in training.

JC walked up. "Let Alisa hang on to the cutters for a second. I want to make sure nobody is living in here."

Danny followed JC's instructions, retrieved his AK-47, and followed JC to the door. JC motioned for Nick to be part of the entry team, leaving Korey and Jack as lookouts for the perimeter. JC opened the door and shined the flashlight on the front of his rifle into the trailer.

Immediately, the sickening sweet smell of a rotting corpse hit Danny, causing his stomach to flip. He gagged as he turned away.

JC looked a little longer, as if he'd developed some immunity to the scent of death. "Beer cans and liquor bottles all over the place in here. Smells like somebody had their priorities screwed up for surviving the apocalypse."

"Or they decided to have one last hurrah," Nick said. "Looks like a foot sticking out over there, behind the kitchen. Do you want to go see if we can determine the cause of death?"

"Nope. Doesn't really matter. But we know we don't want this trailer." JC closed the door, and gave instructions for everyone as they did a perimeter sweep before looking through the rest of the trailers.

While the next two trailers didn't have decaying cadavers, they had been ransacked by partiers who'd left beer cans and drug paraphernalia lying about. The fourth trailer was a smaller one; Danny guessed it was about sixteen feet long. It appeared new and unbothered by partiers or looters. Catfish backed up to the hitch while Danny worked at cutting the lock. It was soon secured to the back of the pickup.

Catfish called out to Nick. "I'd imagine they'll have some fifth-wheel hitches around back or inside the warehouse. If we get one of them hitches, we can install it when we get home. We can run back over here in an hour or so. Get us one of them big boys over yonder."

Nick followed Catfish's eye to the large fifth-wheel trailers near the back of the lot. He looked over toward JC. "What do you think?"

JC looked the lot over. "Let's check around back. Danny, you and Alisa stay with the truck. Security team, follow me."

The security team walked cautiously around the corner of the building. Danny waited quietly next to the truck with Alisa and Catfish, with his AK at a low-ready position, listening for sounds of trouble.

Minutes later, JC appeared from around the corner and signaled for Catfish to back up the truck to his position. Korey, Nick, and Jack put the large hitch into the bed of the truck, then everyone loaded up and Catfish drove away.

Danny breathed a sigh of relief. The mission had gone smoothly. He hadn't been off the farm since Alisa's rescue, so he wasn't sure what to expect. They would be making more trips for more trailers that day, but he would breathe easier knowing that conditions didn't seem overly hostile.

The sun had cleared the horizon by the time they returned to the farm. They dropped the trailer off at the compound then drove the truck to the barn, where the more mechanically inclined folks like JC and Korey worked quickly to get the fifth-wheel hitch installed. Once it was done, the team loaded up for another trip. When they arrived back at the trailer lot, Catfish backed the truck up to a thirty-four-foot camper.

As they jumped out of the back of the truck,

Danny asked Nick. "That's almost as big as your RV."

Nick nodded. "Almost. And, it's brand new."

JC breached the lock without tearing up the door too badly. He had a quick look inside, then said, "Looks good. Let's get it hooked up and roll out."

Since the truck bed was covered on the return trip, Danny, Alisa, Nick, and Korey rode home in the trailer.

Once the trailer was back at the farm and parked in a good spot, Catfish said, "Be ashamed to not go get another one."

JC and Nick quickly agreed and the team was back on the road to get a third trailer for the compound.

When they arrived back at the sales lot, JC made sure the security team stayed vigilant. "Just because it went smooth the last two times doesn't mean you can let your guard down. Everyone stay alert!"

Again, the trailer was hitched up and quickly moved to the farm with no complications. Nana, Cami, and Pauline had lunch waiting for the team when they returned. They had a quick bite and headed right back out, bringing back one more small, eighteen-foot trailer and two more large fifth wheels for a total of six new trailers. It was decided by the scavenging team that the extra space would be utilized for storage or for other people who would be a good fit to live at Fort Jennie.

The plan had proceeded with no complications. The mission had not been very demanding physically, but Danny was bushed from the high level of stress involved in being on constant alert.

The sun was setting and he was ready for bed, but that wasn't going to happen. It was his turn to take night watch.

After a late dinner, Danny packed his gear for his shift and headed to the barn. "Where are you going?"

Alisa was fully dressed and following after him. "To stand guard, with you. I'm officially a soldier now."

Danny fought back a grin. "You're not officially a soldier now. I appreciate your concern, but you don't have to sit up all night with me. You have to be as tired as I am."

She shrugged. "Maybe we can take turns napping. You've had a long day. You'll never stay awake all night by yourself."

"Okay. I'll take you up on that offer, if you insist."

"I insist." She grabbed his arm and kissed his cheek as they walked. "It should have been Steven or Rocky taking the shift tonight, since they weren't out risking their necks."

Danny pursed his lips. "I can't complain. JC and Catfish volunteer to take a disproportionate share of the night-watch shifts."

"Catfish takes them so he won't be asked to do any gardening, wood chopping, or other manual labor."

Danny chuckled. "He's not lazy. He does a lot."

Alisa rolled her eyes. "Catfish does what Catfish wants to do, not exactly a team player."

"Yet, he's an invaluable member of the team." Danny opened the barn door and let Alisa climb the ladder to the loft first.

Alisa's voice sounded surprised. "Catfish! I thought you'd be sleeping in your new trailer. It's brand new. It has a bed, sheets, everything."

Danny soon cleared the top of the ladder to see Catfish lying on his cot in the loft.

Catfish pulled an old dirty quilt up over his shoulders. "I ain't in no hurry. Don't know how I feel about livin' in no shed on wagon wheels."

Alisa stood with her hands on her hips. "But the loft is the security lookout post."

"Ain't no bother to me. Jus' pretend I ain't here. If somethin' happens, I've got my shotgun right next to me. Give me a holler." He covered his head with the quilt as a sign the conversation was over.

Alisa looked at Danny as if to ask if he were going add anything to the conversation, but he didn't. Danny simply adjusted the radio and performed his comms check with JC, who was on call for the night. "Sweet dreams, I won't call you unless I need you."

JC's voice came back over the radio. "Okay, I'll be here. Over and out."

Catfish's heavy snoring provided a steady noise to keep Danny awake while it was his turn to keep watch throughout the night, but unfortunately, it did the same when it was his turn to nap.

The night progressed without incident, and the first break of dawn finally appeared. Danny roused Alisa from her sleep, and the two of them went back to the house and slept through the morning.

CHAPTER 16

Fear, and the pit, and the snare, are upon thee, O inhabitant of the earth.

Isaiah 24:17

Tuesday afternoon was spent getting the Reese family moved into their new fifth-wheel trailer. JC, Melissa, and Annie took another of the fifth wheels, leaving Jack in JC's old trailer all to himself. Alisa conscripted Dana into helping her move Catfish's things into the sixteen-foot trailer while he was feeding the hogs.

Danny followed JC as he walked the perimeter of the compound with the new layout. While not a fortified citadel, the close proximity would allow for all the shooters to be in one place in the event of an attack.

"What are you thinking?" Danny asked.

JC shook his head. "Just trying to come up with a plan to make this place a little harder."

"We're supposed to go get some fence, right?"

JC nodded as he continued to survey the compound. "Fence is good, but it doesn't stop bullets."

Danny looked at the two lines of trailers running between the house and the barn, forming a well-defined courtyard. "What do we have that will stop bullets?"

JC thought for a moment then smiled as he turned to Danny. "Dirt."

Danny looked at the ground. "Yep. Plenty of that. What are you going to do with it?"

"Dig a trench around the compound, maybe eight feet out from the trailers. Rocky has that front-end loader for his tractor. That will help us get it done pretty quickly. We'll pile the dirt up on the inside perimeter of the trench which will give us shooting positions all the way around the compound. If we can get a two- or three-foot trench, that will provide a two- or three-foot wall of dirt for protection on top. Maybe even top that off with another two feet of sandbags."

"You have sandbags?"

"Yep. Bought them after I heard about your dream. They cost next to nothing, but if they save our lives, they might be the most valuable thing we own."

"So we can start on that tomorrow, right?"

JC furrowed his brow. "I don't know. We're getting low on gas. That'll be a big job for the tractor. Catfish thinks he knows where some more fuel might be stashed. We'll probably have to make a gas run first."

"So that will be similar to yesterday's operation"

"Yep. You up for it?"

Danny paused. "I'm up for another run, but I'm not up for going through it with Alisa. Any chance Steven or Rocky will come?"

"No chance on Rocky. Steven is your buddy. What do you think?"

"Not a chance." Danny stuck his hands in his pockets. "Speaking of Rocky, is he moving into a trailer tonight?"

JC shook his head. "Not yet. Pauline needs to go through some things, decide what to bring, what to leave."

Danny held his hand out toward Rocky's house over on the adjacent hillside. "Their house is on the other side of the creek. It's not like they can't go over there ten times a day if they forget something."

"I know. I think she's stalling. I hope they get their act together before it's too late."

"When will you let me know about the gas run?"

"Let me look at the place on a map with Nick. If it looks good, I'll let you know before we turn in tonight."

"What's the place?"

"School bus depot, up in Pumpkin Town. According to Catfish, it sits back off the road a ways and probably wouldn't be found by looters. Either way, all we need is two or three buses to still have gas on the lot, and we'll have more than we can haul back."

"Is that far from here?"

"Thirty miles or so. Near Pickens."

"Pickens! We should try to contact Ranger Dave while we're there. Our radios should be able to connect with his if we're within a few miles."

JC shook his head. "It depends. If he has a really good antenna, maybe. Even so, we don't know how Ranger Dave will feel about us taking resources from his area of operation. It might be best to stay anonymous."

"We wouldn't have to say why we're there. We could say we're just passing through and that we appreciate his broadcast. It might be a good idea to make contact with him. We never know when we might need his help."

JC furrowed his brow. "That sounds great, Danny, but in reality, there's probably not much Ranger Dave could ever do to help us and vice versa. This is a tough world."

Danny lowered his head in disappointment. "Still, we could just say hi."

"We'll see. I'll talk to you later tonight." JC patted Danny on the back and walked toward Nick's RV.

Alisa and Dana walked up as JC was leaving. "What was all of that about?" Alisa asked.

"Nothing. JC is thinking of some ways to make the compound more secure. How did it go with Catfish?" Danny had no intention of telling her of another potential mission.

Dana rolled her eyes. "I think he'd be happier in a cave than a nice new trailer. I think he's part raccoon."

Later that evening, Danny got cleaned up and ready for bed. It had been a short day, since he'd slept all morning, but he was still tired from the scavenging mission and night watch the day before. Alisa sat on the bed reading her Bible by candlelight.

"I've got to run over and ask JC something. I'll be right back."

Alisa looked up from her Bible. "Can't it wait till morning? What are you going to ask him?"

"Guy stuff, I'll be right back." Danny wasn't going to lie to her, but he didn't want to have this conversation. He headed out the door before she had a chance to respond.

"Danny!"

He hurried down the stairs without looking back. When he arrived at JC's trailer, he wasn't alone. She had put her boots on and followed him over. Danny sighed as he knocked on the door.

JC opened the door. "Come on in."

Danny looked at Alisa and then turned to JC. "Any word on tomorrow?"

"It's a go. Nick, Korey, and Catfish are heading over to Catfish's place first thing in the morning to get two empty metal drums that he picked up from somewhere. They'll bring them back here, clean them out, and we'll all leave after lunch. It's a one-shot deal, and not that far, so we'll have plenty of time."

"I knew you were trying to sideline me, Danny Walker!" Alisa's face showed only excitement.

Danny wasn't sure if it was anger because he'd tried to cut her out of the mission, or happiness because she'd caught him. Maybe it was a little of both.

JC smiled as if he enjoyed seeing Danny squirm. "I guess you'll be on the team then?"

"Yes." Alisa crossed her arms and glared at Danny.

Danny turned to leave the trailer. "Never should have let her train with us."

Alisa followed. "See you tomorrow, JC."

"You guys be nice to each other. I need you both." JC chuckled as he closed the door behind them.

The next morning, Danny awoke, feeling rested and ready for the day. After breakfast, he and Steven went to collect firewood. It was the first time they'd really worked together since the disagreement over the trailers. Danny harbored no ill will, but it was a constant source of awkwardness.

Steven broke the silence. "So, does JC hate me? Does he think I'm a coward and I'm hiding behind my conviction?"

Danny shook his head. "I don't think so. He just wants to see everybody on board with the same plan. Having a divided camp is historically dangerous."

Steven pulled a small downed tree that was hanging over the ledge of the creek bank and began snapping the smaller limbs off. "I know, but there are going to be disagreements. I'm trying to understand your side's convictions, trying to be considerate . . ."

Danny cut him off. "Shhh. Listen!"

Steven looked offended. "What?"

"Vehicles, on the road. It's not Catfish." Danny dropped the wood he'd been collecting and began walking briskly up the hill toward the house. Steven did the same. Danny switched off the safety of his AK as he looked toward the end of the long gravel drive. An old Jeep and old Ford Bronco were turning in from the road and driving slowly toward the house.

"Run to the back door, get the girls, and tell them to gear up and be ready to fight. I'll go get JC and we'll talk to them. Stay inside, but be ready to come out shooting if you see us get in any trouble." Danny sprinted to JC's fifth wheel.

JC came out the front door just as Danny arrived. "I saw 'em. Lay that rifle under the trailer. Do you have a pistol?"

"No."

JC passed his Glock to Danny. "Stick this in the back of your pants and cover it with your shirt. I've got my .38. Let me do the talking. Just back me up if I need it. Jack is in the window with the .308. He'll be working on the guys farthest from us. You start shooting the ones close up."

Danny's heart raced as he followed JC to the front of the house where the vehicles had stopped.

"Remember to breathe. Hopefully, we can talk our way out of this." JC had slowed his walk to a calmer pace by the time he got to the men coming out of the vehicles. Four men got out of the Jeep, and two more came out of the Bronco. All were wearing a hodgepodge of camouflage pants and black Polo shirts, with an assortment of battle rifles, except for the man who got out of the passenger side of the Bronco. He wore khaki cargo pants, a black button-down shirt, a black tie, and a pistol belt with a drop-leg holster, and black leather gloves.

"Gentlemen, how can we help you?" JC was polite, courteous, and sounded very relaxed.

The man in the tie removed his gloves. "We represent the interim government, headed up by Regent Darren Schlusser. We wanted to stop by, introduce ourselves, and let you know that Regent Schlusser is committed to restoring order and rebuilding the American way."

JC's smile looked very genuine. "That's fantastic. Things were starting to get a little rough."

The man returned the smile and gave a signal for the men behind him to stand at ease. "It's going to be a long process, but the regent has a plan and the means to implement that plan."

JC stood in a very non-threatening way with his hands at his side. "You said interim government?"

"Yes, Regent Schlusser is just trying to fulfill his civic duty and provide a framework for government until such time that order has been re-established and free elections can once again be instituted."

"I'm just happy somebody out there is trying to put all of this back together," JC snickered. "We appreciate everything you men are doing."

"Thank you for that." The man stepped forward and offered his hand to JC. "I'm Sergeant Gorbold."

"JC, and this here is Danny. The pleasure is all mine." JC shook his hand exuberantly.

"Hi." Danny was confused. He couldn't tell if JC had really been taken in by these guys or if it was all an act.

"JC, we are going to be asking that folks who are getting by relatively well help in our efforts to alleviate the suffering of the less fortunate in our society." Gorbold looked over the compound.

JC looked at the trailers to see where Gorbold was looking. "Oh, ah, well," JC stammered as if he hadn't expected the question. "We just put our crops in. I'm sure we'll have extra this fall."

"Times are very tough out there, JC. Isn't there a little something you could spare now?" Gorbold sounded sincere.

JC took off his hat with one hand and rubbed his head with the other. "We might have a couple pounds of rice, maybe some dried beans that we could share. I'm hoping to have some fresh vegetables in a few weeks. It would be cutting it close for our little community, but like you said, it's tough for folks everywhere."

"Thank you. We're not asking for handouts. Whatever you can give will be credited to your account, and you'll be fully reimbursed when the new currency is issued."

"Oh, wow, that's great." JC smiled as if he were genuinely relieved.

Gorbold looked over toward the cattle. "Would you be willing to sell one of your cows?"

JC furrowed his brow. "I wouldn't know how much to ask, in the new currency, I mean."

"The administration is setting up standardized pricing until such time that the free market can take over."

"And it would be credited to my account?" JC asked.

"Yes."

JC looked over at the cattle and then back to Gorbold. "How would you get it back?"

Gorbold said, "We have livestock vehicles. I'll send one out tomorrow."

"I can slaughter it for you, first thing in the morning, if you can come tomorrow afternoon and pick it up. Unless you want it for breeding, of course."

"Slaughtered would be fantastic. If you wouldn't mind getting those rice and beans, we'll be moving along, for today."

"Oh, sure. Danny, give me a hand." JC walked toward the house.

Danny followed him inside.

As soon as the door was closed, JC pointed to Steven, Dana, and Alisa. "Get ready to move out. I'm going to send them to Rocky's, and we're going to circle around back and hit them when they leave."

Steven looked frantic. "What if they hurt Mr. and Mrs. Cook?"

"Steven, shut up and follow my lead. No time to talk this one over. I'm doing what we have to do to survive." JC went to the back porch and found some old containers that were slated to be used for gardening. "Danny, bring me a bucket of rice and beans."

Danny quickly complied. He ran up to his room and grabbed the bucket nearest to the door and brought them down.

JC opened it and hastily poured some of the beans and some of the rice out of several bags, tying them off, then placing the opened bags of beans and rice in a large trash bag. "Follow me back out."

Danny walked back out the door with JC, trying to remain calm. It had been easier to stay relaxed before he knew what they were getting ready to do.

JC handed the man the garbage bag. "I'm sorry about the presentation."

Gorbold opened the bag and looked inside. "That's very generous of you. The regent will be very proud to know folks like you still exist."

JC lowered his head in a gesture of humility. "Oh, we're around. Times like these, we have to work together." He looked back up toward the hill across the creek. "Folks over there are good Christian people. If they knew what you were doing, they'd be glad to help. Like most of us, I doubt they have much, but they might have a little flour and sugar they could give."

Gorbold placed the garbage bag of food in the rear of the Bronco. "Every little bit helps."

JC waved. "Folks over on the hill, Cook is the name. You tell 'em JC sent you. Tell 'em I said you're alright."

"We'll do that. Thanks again, you've been most helpful." Gorbold smiled as he got back in the Bronco and waved the vehicle forward.

JC slowly walked back toward his trailer as the Jeep and the Bronco drove back up the drive. "Go gear up and meet me on the back porch in thirty seconds. Just grab your vest and ammo. Your rifle is under my trailer I'll bring it with me," he ordered Danny.

"But . . ."

"No time for buts, Danny, Go!"

Danny focused as he turned toward the house, circled around back, and went inside. Alisa, Dana, and Steven were waiting on the porch with rifles, shotguns, and ammo.

Dana held up Danny's tactical vest. "Need this?"

"You're awesome." He took it, put it on, and quickly zipped up.

"What's going on?" Dana asked.

"Just be ready." Danny placed the Glock that had been in his back waistband into the holster on the front of the vest.

JC was at the back door in seconds with Jack close behind him. Jack had the .308 in his hands with his AR-15 dangling from a single-point sling in front of his tactical vest. JC handed the AK-47 to Danny, and handed an AR-15 to Steven. "This is Melissa's rifle. Don't scratch it; she'll kill you." JC repositioned his own AR-15, which he was carrying with a sling, and motioned for them to follow.

Dana followed close with Steven's pump-action shotgun. "What are we going to do?"

"Kill 'em." JC's answer was short.

"What about Nana and the Reese children?" Danny asked.

"Melissa is going to get Cami to tell the Reeses, then she'll take Annie over to Nana's. They'll all hunker down in the house until it's all clear. Don't worry about them; they'll be fine.

"Pay attention because there's no time to repeat

the instructions. When we get into position, you four are going to lay low while Jack and I get into a sniping position. We'll kill two men with the first shots. As soon as you hear us shoot, you guys open fire. If you can hit someone, great. If not, the most important thing is to make noise. Just keep shooting, reloading, and shooting some more. They're going to be focused on you and returning fire. So hide behind a tree, whatever, but keep shooting in their general direction. Your shots are going to keep them distracted so we can pick them off, one shot at a time.

"If it looks like they are going to be able to flank you and fix your position before we can finish them off, I'll yell 'retreat'. Jack and I will draw their fire and you fall back to the creek bank. Drop down inside the creek and wait for us to lead them to you. Then, you'll have to kill them before they get to the creek. We can't let them come across the creek. That's where the kids are. Everybody understand?"

Steven rushed to keep up with the fast-moving assault team. "If we kill these guys, aren't they just going to send more troops out to hunt us down?"

JC continued to lead the team back through the woods to a place where they could cross the creek at a hurried pace. "I didn't see or hear any radios. I don't think this bunch is that well-organized. Wherever their headquarters is, leadership will only know the general direction this squad was supposed to cover and that they never returned from their operation. For all they know, this team could have hit it big and decided to branch out on their own.

"Regardless of what the rest of their group looks

like, these goons are going to be back if we don't kill them now. Whether the total force is 100 or 1000, it will be six less in about ten minutes."

Once the team crossed the creek, JC put his finger to his lip. "No more talking from this point forward."

The team circled around from the woods behind Rocky's house in time to see two of the soldiers from the Jeep walking out of the Cooks' house carrying Rocky's rifle, shotgun, and several ammo boxes. They loaded them in the back of the Bronco and went back inside. JC whispered, "We'll hit them as soon as those two come back out. The second they come out the door, start shooting. Since those two will probably be carrying supplies, they'll have to drop what they are doing before they can return fire, so worry about the other guards first. Gorbold only has a pistol. He isn't as big of a threat at this range, so take out the riflemen first."

JC motioned for Danny's team to find large trees for cover as he and Jack melted back into the woods.

Danny's heart pounded as he pointed to Alisa and Dana, then pointed to the guard nearest them, signaling that both girls should center their fire on that guard. Then, he pointed Steven to the next nearest guard. Danny said a silent prayer, asking God to give him the precision to kill the guard farthest away.

Rocky was standing on the porch holding Pauline, who was crying as Gorbold stood nearby with a condescending look. It sounded as if he was lecturing them, but Danny couldn't make out what they were saying. He couldn't worry about that anyhow. Danny had to focus on the doorway and be ready to take his shot the second the men came outside. He began counting his breaths to make sure he was remembering to breathe. His eyes darted back and forth from his target to the doorframe. Each time he made minor adjustments to the aim of his rifle, he took the slack out of his trigger so he wouldn't jerk the rifle off target when he squeezed the trigger. Danny saw a foot come out the bottom of the doorway; he took a deep breath and pulled the trigger.

CHAPTER 17

Have not I commanded thee? Be strong and of a good courage; be not afraid, neither be thou dismayed: for the LORD thy God is with thee whithersoever thou goest.

Joshua 1:9

Danny's target dropped to the ground. He wasn't sure if it was from his own shot or if Jack or JC had eliminated the target. He had no time to consider it. He moved directly to the next armed guard, but that man also fell before Danny could take a shot. By now, the two men coming out of the house had dropped their supplies and were trying to get control of their weapons in order to return fire. Danny took a shot at the one nearest him. He distinctly saw the bullet hit the man in the upper leg. A bullet coming from JC's direction ran through the head of the other man, pushing a fountain of blood and brain out with it.

Danny took a second shot at the guard that he'd hit in the leg as the man was still trying to shoot back. Danny fired once, twice, three, four, and five times at the man, riddling his body with bullets. The man finally fell limp and Danny turned his attention to Gorbold, who had Pauline by the hair with one hand, and his pistol pointed at her temple with the other.

Gorbold called out. "This stops right now or the lady dies!"

"Please! Stop!" Rocky called out toward the woods.

JC emerged from the woods with Jack close behind him. Both had their weapons trained on Gorbold. JC continued to advance toward Gorbold who was backing toward the Bronco. "Put the gun down!" JC commanded.

Gorbold's voice grew more agitated as he backed away from JC who was getting closer and closer to him. "I'll kill her! I swear!"

POP! A flash shot out the barrel of JC's AR-15. Gorbold's wrist exploded and his pistol went flying. Blood gushed out of Gorbold's mangled wrist as he screamed. Blood was all over Pauline's head. Danny thought that perhaps the pistol had gone off and she'd been shot, but he doubted anyone who'd been shot in the head could scream the way she was screaming. Danny led his team in closer to kick the rifles away from the fallen men. JC stepped to Gorbold and hit him square in the nose with the butt of his rifle. Gorbold dropped backwards and JC jumped on top of him to zip tie his hands together. Next, he put another zip tie beneath Gorbold's armpit; evidently JC was using it as a tourniquet. Danny winced at the thought of what the unfortunate man was about to go through if JC had determined to keep him alive.

Jack walked around and double tapped all of the men who looked like they were beyond saving. Only one of the other five men appeared as though he was still conscious. Jack stood guard over him as he tossed a zip tie to Dana, who quickly secured him. Danny scanned the scene to make sure they hadn't missed anything.

Alisa was attending to Mrs. Cook. "I'm going to take her inside to get cleaned up."

"There might be someone inside," Danny protested.

"It's six people, the same six that were at Nana's." Alisa continued toward the door.

Danny looked over at JC who was sitting on top of Gorbold. JC nodded. "It should be fine, but you go in with her, Danny."

Danny went in first and cleared each room on the way to the kitchen. Alisa and Pauline followed behind. Pauline sat down at the table while Alisa got a towel and a bucket of water. Danny heard a commotion coming from outside. "Will you be okay?"

Alisa soaked the towel and wrung it out. "Yeah, go ahead."

Danny walked back out the door to see Steven and Jack restraining Rocky, who was yelling at JC.

"You sent those animals over here!"

JC put his hand in the air. "They were coming to you anyway. I just made them feel comfortable enough so I could hit them."

"You almost got Pauline shot! How did you know how we'd react?"

JC let his rifle hang by the sling. "Listen Rocky, you're okay, Pauline is okay and the threat is eliminated."

"For now! How long until the rest of them coming looking for these?"

"We'll cross that bridge when we get to it. At least, now we'll be able to get information on how many of them there are, where they're located and what they plan to accomplish.

Gorbold defiantly said, "You won't get any information out of us."

JC turned his attention to the man lying by his feet and began to laugh. He kicked Gorbold in his injured wrist, sending blood flying two feet across the yard and splattering it all over his boot. He hit the quick release on his single point sling and set his rifle against the tree in Rocky's front yard. He looked at Jack. "Let Mr. Cook go and drag this one back to the barn. Get him strung up on a beam."

Jack and Steven let Rocky go and each picked up one of Gorbold's feet to begin dragging him back toward the barn.

JC put his feet shoulder width apart and addressed Rocky. "If you want to take a swing at me, you come on. If not, shut your mouth and don't ever say another word to me about my decision here today. I just saved your tail."

Rocky still looked angry, but in no way looked ready to take JC head on.

JC looked Rocky in the eyes. "If you haven't learned anything from this whole EMP experience, you should have learned that sticking your head in the sand doesn't make problems go away. Just because you can't see the Boogie Man doesn't mean he isn't there. You better get on board or get ready to die a horrible death, because there ain't no in-betweens in this world."

JC turned to Danny. "Let's get our gear and drag the other one to the barn."

"What about the vehicles?" Danny asked. "We have to do something with them. Shouldn't we just drive him over in the Jeep?"

JC stopped to process the idea. He looked at the Bronco and the Jeep, then at the restrained man. "Nah, let's just drag him. I don't want to get blood all over the vehicles or our stuff that's inside. Besides, I want to drag this one, face down through the creek. It will be part of his condition process. Dana, check the Bronco and see if the keys are in it."

Dana walked over and looked. "Yep."

"Good, what about the Jeep?"

She checked that as well. "This one too."

"Great. You drive one of them back and have Alisa drive the other. Pull them around to the back of the barn so they won't be visible from the road or the driveway."

"Okay, we'll see you there" Dana said.

"What about the dead?" Rocky asked.

"Make yourself useful. Build a fire pit to burn

them on." JC said without turning to look at him.

Rocky huffed, but followed JC's directions.

The man JC and Danny pulled by the feet across Rocky's yard and down the hill had an entry wound in his side, another in his thigh, and another in his shoulder. Danny wondered how the man could still be alive. At first he had considered him fortunate to have survived, but as the man screamed and yelped at the pain of having the dirt, grass and rocks rubbed against his open wounds, Danny thought those who Rocky would be putting on the burn pile were better off. The man was unconscious by the time they got him to the creek, but came back around after getting his mouth full of water. He looked very near death once he was in the barn. The girls pulled around with the vehicles about the time Danny and JC arrived with the wounded man. Steven and Jack were resting from having dragged Gorbold to the barn.

JC left the wounded guard to throw a rope over the beam. He tied one end to Gorbold's foot and hoisted him up in the air by one leg. He tied the other end of the rope to a support beam and let the sergeant dangle. JC resumed his gullible hayseed routine as he addressed Gorbold. "We thought you were here to help. I couldn't believe my eyes when I saw you taking those good folks' guns. And to think, I was gonna skin a cow for you. I hope you're ashamed of yourself.

"If you want to make it up to me, and I'm sure you do, just tell me how many people are in this new government, and where they're stationed."

Gorbold grunted in pain as he swung upside

down by the leg. "You're going to kill me anyway."

JC chuckled. "That might be true, but I can promise you, there are different ways to die. There's fast and painless, and then . . ." JC ripped open the man's shirt, took out his knife, and ran it across Gorbold's chest, making an even laceration so that blood ran down from his chest into his mouth and nose causing him to choke and spit in order to breath. "Then, there's the other way to die."

Alisa turned away and Dana excused herself from the barn. JC noticed and said, "Danny, why don't you and Steven take the girls back to the house. Get some water, and first aid supplies, we might need to keep the guard alive for a while longer. See if you can find some apple sauce or something easy to digest. He probably needs something to eat. He's lost a lot of blood."

"Okay." Danny wasn't in the habit of arguing with JC anyway, but particularly not when he was in the middle of extracting information.

Before they reached the house, Catfish's truck turned into the drive. Danny nodded to Steven. "Can you guys get those things together for JC? I need to fill Nick in on what happened."

"Sure." Steven said, then went in the house with the girls.

Catfish pulled up to Danny. "What in tarnation is a goin' on around here?"

Danny debriefed Catfish, Korey and Nick.

"Is everyone okay?" Korey quickly exited the vehicle.

"No one was hurt, at least no one from our compound," Danny explained.

Nick looked deeply concerned. "Any idea how many more there are? Where's their camp?"

Danny shrugged. "JC has the squad leader hanging like a Christmas ham in the barn right now, trying to find all that out. One of the guards is lying on the floor, barely conscious, but I don't know if he'll live long enough to interrogate."

"I've got some advanced medical supplies. If all his organs are intact, I can probably keep him breathing. Then, I've got enough pain killers to cut him a deal, because I'm sure he's feeling it." Nick headed off toward his RV.

"I'm going to check on my family." Korey started toward his trailer.

"JC moved them all into the house," Danny called out.

Korey changed course and b-lined for the house. "Thanks!"

"I turn my head for five minutes and the whole operation goes to the devil. Don't reckon we'll be goin' to get no gas today." Catfish cut the engine.

Danny looked over toward the barn to see if he could see the Jeep and the Bronco. "We might not need to."

"What are you figurin' on?" Catfish got out and closed the door.

"Come on, I'll show you." Danny led the way toward the barn. As they got closer, tortured cries could be heard coming from inside.

Catfish shook his head. "That JC sure knows how to make em' squall."

Danny tried to ignore the pleas coming from inside. He opened the door to the Bronco and turned the key. "About three quarters of a tank."

Catfish was already doing the same thing with the Jeep. "'Bout the same here. We probably get about fifty gallons between the two of 'em."

JC walked out back. He was sweating heavily.

Danny said, "Looks like a tough job."

"Easier than his." He pointed the knife back toward the barn. "How much fuel in the vehicles?"

"Both about three quarters full," Danny answered.

JC nodded. "That sounds about right. Gorbold says there's roughly fifty men in Greenville, another seventy-five to a hundred in Spartanburg. Charlotte is the hub for this new government. It supposedly has a couple thousand and is growing by the day."

"I thought he wasn't going to tell you anything," Danny quipped.

"Guess he had a change of heart." JC wiped the knife off on the bottom of his boot.

"Them other ones, up yonder in Greenville, they know where these ol' boys was?" Catfish spit tobacco to the side, away from where Danny and JC were standing.

"They have a mapped out route of the areas they were supposed to go to. If he's telling the truth, they'll know where they disappeared, down to an area about two miles wide by ten miles long," JC answered.

"If they come round here, and see us set up like Fort Apache, I reckon we'll be prime suspects." Catfish stuck his hands in the top straps of his overalls.

Danny looked at JC. "So what do we do?"

"I guess we get set up like Fort Apache, right?" JC looked at Catfish.

Catfish chuckled and then spit again. "I reckon so."

JC blotted the sweat off his face with his shirt tail. "I left Rocky on less than desirable terms. Danny, why don't you get Nana to cook up something nice for him, then take Alisa up there to check on him and Pauline? Talk to them, try to smooth things over for me, then see if you can get him to hook up his front-end loader and start digging this trench. We've got the rest of the day to get ready for the goons. Tonight, when Gorbold doesn't come home, they'll start looking for him. They might be here tomorrow or they might be here next week, but sooner or later, they'll be here.

"Jack and Catfish will help me get the gas out of these vehicles, then figure out where to hide them."

Catfish cut JC off. "You drive 'em into the lake. Straight off the boardwalk."

"You thought of that pretty fast," Danny commented.

Catfish started walking back toward his truck. "Won't be the first time."

"There's no chance we might need them later? Wouldn't it be better to keep them somewhere so we could get to them in an emergency?"

JC shook his head. "Those vehicles will stick out like a sore thumb when the goons come looking. Anywhere we put them is going to be a potential problem. Plus, in Regent Schlusser's mind, as long as they can't be found, there's always the chance that Gorbold and the others went AWOL."

"Yeah, I guess that makes sense," Danny agreed.

An hour later, Nana insisted that she walk over to Rocky's house to take her pot of homemade rabbit dumplings. Danny had sampled a few, but was still hoping that they'd be invited to eat with the Cooks.

Pauline opened the door when they arrived. "Come in."

"How are you holding up?" Alisa gave Pauline a big hug.

"Better. That was quite a morning. Of all the things your mind tries to prepare you for . . . I never expected a bunch of thugs putting themselves out to be a legitimate government to show up on my doorstep."

Danny snickered. "Yeah, I thought those days were over with."

"Well these here dumplins will have you feelin' fit as a fiddle." Nana took the pot to the kitchen.

"Where's Rocky?" Danny inquired.

"Out back, building a fire, to get rid of the . . . the bodies." Pauline turned her head. She was a sweet woman, kind and gentle, but she wasn't cut out for the apocalypse.

"I'll go give him a hand if you ladies want to set the table." Danny didn't mind pitching in, but he wanted it to be understood that he expected some rabbit dumplings if he was going to be dragging dead bodies up on a wood pile.

Danny headed out back to find Rocky. "Hey, need a hand?"

Rocky had a sufficient amount of wood

collected, but hadn't gotten around to moving the corpses yet. He cracked a faint smile and gave a nod. "Sure, thanks Danny."

Danny grabbed the arm of one of the fallen guards. "Did you go through their pockets?"

Rocky shook his head as he grabbed the man's other hand to drag him over to the wood pile.

They stopped at the pile and Danny bent down to unzip the man's tactical vest, remove his belt, and boots. "AK-47 magazines in his vest. All full. This is like Christmas."

Rocky evidently hadn't become quite as battle-hardened as Danny. This was Danny's fourth engagement and he was losing all sympathy for his assailants. If they were evil enough to try to hurt him or the ones he loved, he felt no remorse for sending them on down the line. While not quite up to the task of assisting JC in the information gathering process, Danny was quickly adapting to this uncivilized environment and lost no sleep over whatever had to be done to the aggressors who were reluctant to share what they knew. Danny riffled through the man's trousers, extracting a knife and a tactical flashlight. The shirt and pants were too blood stained to be of any use.

"Okay, let's get him up on the wood pile." Danny took the man under the armpits and nodded for Rocky to grab the legs so they could hoist him up.

Next, they proceeded to do the same to the three other men. Danny took the vests of the four, all of which had full magazines for their rifles, since the attackers had all been eliminated before they had a chance to reload. Some never got off the first shot. Danny and Rocky collected the weapons strewn about in Rocky's yard which had become a make-shift battlefield. They picked up one M1A which used the same ammo as JC's .308 deer rifle, two AR-15s and two AK-47s.

"Looks like you have your pick for a new battle rifle," Danny said.

Rocky looked the selection over. "I like that M1A. Classic. How many magazines of ammo did you find for it?"

"Four in the vest. One in the rifle. They look like twenty round mags, so assuming they're all loaded to capacity and he didn't get off a shot, you'd have about a hundred rounds. But JC stocked up a lot of .308."

"Yeah, but he's ticked off at me. I don't think he'll be in any hurry to fork over a bunch of ammo to me."

Danny started shaking his head the second Rocky started talking. "Not at all. JC would be more than happy to give you ammo. Even if he were mad, this is mutual survival, we depend on each other. JC isn't mad. Frustrated would be a better word. One thing we all have to understand is that he was a New York cop. He's seen the full depravity of human nature and understands how low it can go, if not arrested by people willing to stand in the way of evil. Then to have to babysit the rest of us until we come around to realize what we are up against makes his job harder."

Rocky crossed his arms as he listened to Danny. "Pauline and I haven't acted very appreciative of his efforts. I suppose he had to deal with that as a New York cop also."

Danny patted Rocky on the back. "I don't think he got into law enforcement hoping for accolades from the public. But, it would be easier on him if he didn't feel like he had to fight the bad guys and the folks right here in our own compound."

"I think Pauline and I are waking up to the facts that it really is going to be as bad as JC has been saying. We'll probably move into the trailer this evening, if we're still welcome."

"You are absolutely welcome. In fact, we'll help you move. JC was hoping you wouldn't be too mad and that you'd give us a hand digging a trench around the compound this afternoon. He thinks the rest of these heathens may be coming sooner rather than later."

"I'd be more than happy to. It'll give me a chance to sort of redeem myself. Thank you, Danny." Rocky pulled out a box of wooden kitchen matches. "Would you like to do the honors?"

Danny took the matches. "Sure. Can we wait till after lunch? It's not exactly going to smell like barbecue pork."

"Hmm. Good call. Let's get washed up." Rocky put his hand on Danny's shoulder as they walked around to the rain catch barrel.

After lunch Danny walked out back to light the fire. He took out a match and struck it. As he looked at the corpses piled on top, he remembered the two men in the barn. He blew out the flame and tossed the smoking match on the wood pile. "Better see if

JC has anybody else who needs to go in the oven. We certainly don't have time to be collecting more wood."

Danny grabbed the two AKs and the two AR-15s, along with the vests and peeked his head in the back door. "Alisa, Nana, I'm going to head on back over to the house. I'll see you in a bit."

Danny dropped the weapons and vests off at the common area in the compound courtyard then headed on down to the barn. JC was coming out with Nick.

"We collected the rifles, stacked the wood and got the four bodies from Rocky's up on the pile. Do you have anyone else who needs to be disposed of?"

JC nodded. "Yeah, Gorbold is ready. The other one needs a few minutes. Nick promised him a comfortable passing in exchange for more info about what type of hardware we should expect."

Nick's face looked somber. "I gave him enough morphine to ease him on out of this world. He wasn't going to make it anyway."

JC added. "Catfish can drive them over when they take the vehicles to the lake. Any word on the trench?"

"Rocky is going to do it. He feels bad about how he acted toward you."

JC waved his hand. "We're all under a lot of stress. Stuff like that is going to happen. I'm glad he's coming around. Do you think he's seen the light? Will they move down here now?"

"Yeah, said he's moving tonight."

JC nodded. "Good. What rifles did you pick up?"

"An M1A, which Rocky is keeping so he'll have a battle rifle, two ARs and two AKs."

"I guess you were happy about the AKs. More ammo." JC smiled.

"Yeah, they had about eight full thirty-round AK mags in their vests. I left them up at the picnic table."

JC walked over toward the Bronco and opened the tailgate. "We found two metal ammo cans in the back. Looks like about 500 rounds of 5.56 and another 500 rounds of 7.62x.39."

"No kidding?" Danny's face lit up.

"We didn't see any .308. That probably means they're not very well supplied with that caliber at their base." JC popped open two more ammo cans. "We also found four flash bangs and four fragmentation grenades in the truck. It will all come in handy for what we've got coming at us."

Danny quickly remembered that this whole episode was not a total windfall. Any assets they had just gained would likely be spent in the days ahead. But, better to have it than not. "What are we going to be up against when they hit us?"

"There's a Hummer with a .50 cal in Greenville. I would imagine they'll be rolling in that when they come looking. They had a couple MRAPs in Charlotte, but those are stationary, at least for the time being."

"Sounds like this guy is building up some serious military hardware."

JC nodded. "Yeah, he's using his muscle to extort food, fuel and supplies. Then, he can trade that for whatever he needs. Imagine you're a soldier that had the good sense to get out of dodge before everyone at your base started eating each other. That vehicle you bugged out in isn't going to do you any good if you don't have fuel. And it will be even more useless if you starve to death. He's slowly putting together an infrastructure to be a complete war lord." JC closed the ammo cans and picked up two of them.

Danny picked up the other two and followed JC toward the trailers. "So you're expecting roughly fifty men to show up in various vehicles and a Hummer with a .50 cal?"

JC thought as he walked. "All fifty of the men at the Greenville outpost probably aren't infantry. You probably have ten to fifteen fobbits."

"Fobbits?" Danny had no idea what he was talking about.

"FOB is military for forward operating base. A fobbit is someone that never leaves the base. If this guy is running his organization like a military, which from the looks of Gorbold, he probably is, then the FOB likely has a few people dedicated to the DFAC, a couple mechanics and various other support positions that won't be involved in the search for the missing team."

"DFAC?"

"Dining Facility."

"Oh, okay. So we should expect thirty-five to forty men?"

"It's hard to say, but that's how I would work it if I were him." JC placed the ammo boxes on the picnic table next to the guns. "I'm going to give Korey one of these ARs. I guess give the other one to Steven, and give Dana an AK. And don't worry, I'm putting you in charge of the ammo for the AK. But at least give her fifty rounds to practice with. She might be the one who pulls the trigger on the guy who was getting ready to kill you. Unless you want to switch over, then give Steven an AK and you take the AR."

"I'm happy with my rifle. I guess I'm getting a little attached to it."

JC snorted. "You've been through a lot together. You should be."

Rocky came slowly down the drive in his tractor with the front-end loader attached. He drove up near where Danny and JC were and cut the engine. He waved as he jumped off and walked over. He held out his hand as he approached JC. "I was out of line earlier. I hope you'll forgive me. I appreciate all you've done to help keep us safe."

JC shook his hand and smiled. "Don't even worry about it. We all get stressed out from time to time. Especially in this environment."

"It's no excuse, but thanks for being so gracious." Rocky adjusted his hat.

"I've got some ammo for your M1A, so make sure you stop by at some point this evening," JC said.

Rocky looked at Danny. "I'm going to need some help. A front-end loader is more for moving than digging. I'm pretty good with it, so I can definitely make the most of what I have to work with, but if I had a couple guys with shovels in front of me, it will look a lot more like a trench. We'll get a much cleaner line."

"Sure, I'll get Steven."

JC nodded. "Me and Jack were planning on filling sandbags with the loose dirt, so we'll be there if you need us."

"Sounds good. I guess between the three farms, we should have plenty of shovels." Rocky turned to walk back toward his tractor.

JC patted Danny on the back. "Good job ironing that out for us. Sometimes we just need a peacekeeper. Take your ammo and weapons to the house. I'll get those grenades put away and I'll meet you down at the barn.

Danny did as JC had instructed. Inside, he ran into Alisa. "Fresh weapons and ammo, coming through."

"Awesome. You have more ammo for your AK?"

"Yep. And rifles for Dana and Steven. I've got to get them put up and start working on the trench. We can use all the help we can get. Can you round up Steven and Dana and have them meet us out front?" Danny paused to give her a kiss. His hands were full, so he couldn't give her a hug like he wanted. "You did a good job this morning. You're certainly no victim."

She wrapped her arms around him and kissed him again. "Thanks. I needed that. It was frightening, but I faced my fear and I got through it."

Catfish, Nick and Korey disposed of the vehicles after the gas had been siphoned out. Catfish also took care of setting the bonfire behind Rocky's house which disposed of the bodies. As Danny worked, he would occasionally get a whiff of the burning corpses, which made his stomach feel sour.

Pauline Cook made a priority of moving their belongings to one of the fifth-wheel trailers, while Rocky was busy utilizing the tractor. Tracey and young Jason Reese helped Mrs. Cook, while Melissa kept an eye on the two little Reese girls, Kalie and Emma.

The rest of the day was spent digging the trench, filling sandbags, selecting defendable firing positions and digging out fox holes for positions around the perimeter of the compound. Locations, chosen by JC and Nick, to be firing positions were dug out to a depth of three feet, then shielded with sandbags, three deep to reduce the odds of the person in that spot being hit by the .50 caliber machine gun.

As tired as he was after the day was done, Danny still didn't feel sleepy. The apprehension of what was coming served as an unwanted stimulant that made a good night's rest evasive.

CHAPTER 18

And call upon me in the day of trouble: I will deliver thee, and thou shalt glorify me.

Psalm 50:15

On Thursday, Danny and the others hurried through breakfast. Nana heated up the morning meal which was served at the picnic tables in the common area, with the help of Cami and Tracey. It was the first time everyone had eaten breakfast together in the courtyard.

There was no delay after eating. JC and Nick coordinated training for the compound, making range cards for each of the five primary firing positions and making sure the people assigned to each position could hit a man-sized target anywhere within their lanes of fire.

Danny and Steven assisted JC in digging out a

shallow trench which would conceal fishing wire that would be used to trigger booby traps constructed from the four live grenades found in the Bronco. The four devices were to be placed at defensible positions along the gravel driveway, which was the most likely avenue of approach. Each of the four grenades could be triggered by pulling a length of the fishing line from inside the front firing position, a fox hole which JC called the Pinnacle.

Of the four functioning radios, three were carried at all times by Nick, JC and Danny. The fourth was always in rotation to be recharged at the solar shed located in the center of the compound. A strict schedule was followed by JC, Danny and Nick so that no one's radio was ever discharged by more than half. In the event of an attack, Korey was to get the fourth, as he and ten-year old Jason were responsible for manning the fortified firing position behind the barn, called the Delta. Danny's position, which was a fox hole located directly in front of the house, was called Alpha and would be defended by him, Alisa and Dana. JC, Jack and Steven would cover the Pinnacle, just a few yards down from Alpha position in the direction of the barn. Nick and Cami would cover Bravo, which was the heavily sand-bag-covered fox hole nearest to the front of the barn. Catfish and Melissa were assigned to Charlie position, the fox hole behind the house. Charlie position would not have a radio for communication, so in the unlikely event that it were to be hit directly, Melissa was instructed to blow a whistle, alerting JC who could then coordinate and direct fire from Alpha and Delta to assist.

Should the compound come under fire, Pauline, Nana, and Tracey would take the three young girls, Annie Castell, Kalie and Emma Reese, to hide under Nana's bed in the house. Being under the bed would keep the children low which would minimize their exposure to stray bullets and the mattress over top of them would offer some level of protection from shrapnel and debris. Nana, Pauline and Tracey would be armed and prepared to defend the children to their last breath, should the compound be breached and the house taken by Regent Schlusser's goons.

A minimum of three people stood guard at all times, with one watching the rear of the compound and two others in positions where they could see the sides and front of the compound, particularly the gravel driveway and road beyond. Lookouts who didn't have radios were given whistles so they could summon a person with a radio if they were to see something.

From this day forward, everything would change and survival would become exponentially more difficult. Security would become the largest consumer of labor in the compound, but all the other tasks and chores still had to be covered.

Danny, Alisa and Dana finished adding the third row of sandbags to Alpha position as he felt the first rain drop.

"Great. As if this chore couldn't get any worse." Dana huffed.

"We're almost done, so it's not so bad." Alisa

tried to lighten the mood.

"It will be worse for whoever has to stand guard in the rain." Danny pushed against the top row of bags to test their stability.

"Stand guard in the rain? Are you crazy?" Dana leaned her shovel against the wall of the trench and crossed her arms.

"Rain doesn't stop the enemy, so it can't stop us either." Danny had been thrust into something of a leadership position. While it had never been directly expressed, it was implied by JC who held Danny responsible for the actions of Alisa, Dana, and even Steven. The three of them generally accepted the implicit authority, either because they genuinely respected Danny or because they didn't want to get chewed out by JC for anything, especially insubordination.

"So, who has to stand guard in the rain?" Dana frowned.

"You two can flip for it." Danny kicked the dirt off of his shoes as if he were leaving.

"Danny! That's not fair!" Alisa protested.

He chuckled. "Just kidding, we'll draw straws. Short straw loses."

Alisa stuck her finger in the air. "What if we put some boards over top of the dugout? We could cover the boards with some trash bags, then put sandbags on top of that. It would cover it from the rain, and keep grenades from being able to drop right in our fox hole."

Danny nodded. He wondered why JC hadn't thought of such an implementation. "Really good idea, Alisa. You guys start filling sandbags for the top and I'll go see what materials I can find."

"Why are we filling the sandbags?" Dana sounded cranky.

"Because I need to tell JC, so the other positions can build roofs also." Danny walked up the steep ramp they had dug into the fox hole as an entrance.

"Okay, but get the stuff for our roof before you go telling everybody else," Alisa said.

Danny turned and winked at her. "Another great idea."

Danny gathered some trash bags from the back porch, then headed down to the barn to scavenge some boards. He brought them to Alisa and Dana, then went to find JC and Nick. Both were standing just inside the solar shed to avoid the light drizzle of rain, discussing the plan and speculating the different ways the compound was vulnerable to attack.

"Hey guys." Danny waved as he approached. They made room for him in the entrance of the shed. He stepped inside, then filled them in on what his team was doing for a roof.

"Why didn't we think of that?" JC looked at Nick.

Nick threw his hands up. "Simple solution. I'll look for some extra materials and tell the teams working on the other locations. Tell Alisa that was a fantastic idea."

The day wore on and on, but there was no sign of anyone looking for the missing patrol. Danny allowed himself to hope that perhaps the leaders in Greenville would just write them off as having gone AWOL. Or perhaps, they just weren't in the position to expend more resources to look for the missing members of their regiment. But he knew better. If this man, Schlusser, was to have any kind of respectability in the area at all, he couldn't let the disappearance of six men go without an investigation, both for his image to the public and, more importantly, for the perception of his own men. There's not much of a chance to set oneself up as a war lord if one's own men detect even the faintest notion of weakness. And it was this understanding that promised Danny yet another fitful night of sleep.

Danny woke up to the sound of knocking at his bedroom door. He instinctively reached for his rifle.

Dana's groggy voice came through the door. "You're on watch."

"Thanks," Danny called back. The watch shifts were intentionally mixed up to start and end at different times for the three main observation posts, the Pinnacle, Bravo, and Delta. This would keep any opposing force who might have the compound under observation from being able to time an attack to the changing of the guards.

Danny quickly got dressed and made his way to the Pinnacle. While JC had simply named the key position, Pinnacle, the foxhole had quickly become known as the Pinnacle. Danny keyed his mic when he arrived. "I'm at the Pinnacle."

"10-4, I'll bring you a cup of coffee when it's ready. I'm sure you could use it." JC's voice came over the radio.

Danny thought about the coffee. He most

certainly could use a cup. He scanned his lane of fire for activity. He practiced looking at the range card and finding objects out in his field of vision. He looked at the tree, near the gravel drive, which was a little less than halfway out to the road. "Seventy-five yards." The same tree was only fifty-five yards from Alpha, so he had to make sure he wouldn't rely on the information from the range card in Alpha if he were to be in another location when the compound got hit. Danny continued to review the card and the distances, making a mental note of how much the bullet would drop, traveling to the various positions between the Pinnacle and the hedgerow, which marked the likely end of the effective range of his rifle from this position.

Somewhere along the way, Danny's mind began to drift back to school, his apartment in Savannah and stealing a kiss from Alisa at the service station in the back of Lilly's restaurant. How had his normal life been ejected from such an average existence into this tumultuous world of disorder? By the abandonment of God. That's how. America had pushed and pleaded with her creator to be left alone for nearly four decades. And being the gentleman that he was, God had finally granted that request. Danny sighed as he ran his finger under the Velcro strap on the front of his tactical vest, always double checking that he'd put the magazines in the pouches correctly; opening on the bottom, with the bullets facing right.

"Coffee's ready." JC's voice startled Danny and he jumped.

"Oh, thanks. That's great." He took the cup and

sipped the warm beverage. The smell alone rejuvenated him.

"They say war is 99 percent boredom and 1 percent sheer terror." JC surveyed the field before them.

Danny nodded. He knew something of the terror after four firefights and a rescue mission. "And anticipation. They forgot to add that. It kind of gets in the way of being able to enjoy the boredom."

"Yeah." JC snorted. "Nana is working on some pancakes. I'll bring you a plate when they're done. And, I'll watch your post so you can eat without staring at an empty field."

"Thanks." Danny took another sip of coffee. "Looks like rain again."

JC looked at the gray sky. "Maybe. It was like this all day yesterday and all we got was a few sprinkles. If we don't get some rain soon, we won't have any crops to defend."

"Rain or no rain, cloudy days make me feel sleepy."

"Well don't go to sleep on watch. You'll get a court martial." JC winked as he left the fox hole.

Danny gave JC a wave as he left the fox hole. JC had a tough side that was harder and colder than steel, but he had a humane side, compassionate and caring; very uncommon features, especially in this post-apocalyptic landscape. Danny had an extremely high appreciation for both of those sides.

Half an hour later, Danny had breakfast and another cup of coffee. JC watched the Pinnacle so Danny could get a bathroom break, then it was back to the grind.

Just before noon, Alisa scampered into the fox hole and gave Danny a kiss. "Having fun?"

"Loads."

"Well, your shift is almost over, and, I brought you a friend."

Rusty looked into the fox hole and wagged his tail, but didn't seem willing to come inside just yet.

"Hey buddy." Danny gave him a scratch.

Suddenly, Rusty froze. He walked away from the entrance to the fox hole and over to the ledge of the trench.

"He wants nothing to do with that filthy hole." Alisa giggled.

Danny was much more serious. "He hears something. Be quiet."

The gravity of the situation quickly registered with Alisa as she froze and listened with Danny.

Danny peered through the hedgerow but saw no evidence of any vehicles on the road. Still he keyed his mic. "JC, Rusty hears something, tell everyone to be on alert." Danny let go of the button. He turned to Alisa. "Run and get Dana, tell everyone to get to their battle positions."

Alisa took off without saying a word. Danny slowly emerged from Pinnacle to make his way toward Alpha. JC and Jack were coming down the ramp as he was coming out.

"You think it's something?" JC asked in passing.

"Yep." Danny quickened his pace. Just before he reached his fox hole, Danny saw a '78 white Ford F150 four-wheel drive, coming down the hill, moving slowly on the other side of the hedgerow. He pressed the talk key. "We've got company."

He moved faster toward Alpha position, still looking at the truck through the hedgerow. Another old truck was following the Ford. Maybe an old Chevy. Danny keyed the mic again. "Multiple vehicles traveling in our direction."

Just before he jumped in the fox hole, Danny saw the dreaded Humvee with the large machine gun mounted on the back. He pressed the key once more. "This is it. Get the children inside and everybody man your station. We've got several vehicles coming in, including the Hummer with the .50 cal!"

Danny took aim. It had already been discussed that they would not try talking themselves out of the situation. Everyone was to commence firing the moment they felt like they had a kill shot. The white Ford turned on to the gravel drive first. Danny could see the driver from a distance and tried to make a running calculation of the bullet drop. He aimed high to compensate and pulled the trigger. The driver hit the brakes and began to back up. Danny fired again and the truck began to careen backwards toward the hedgerow. The driver was no longer in control of the vehicle.

Alisa found her position right behind Danny, and Dana arrived soon after. Danny began firing at the men exiting the Ford. One jumped out of the cab and six more came out of the bed of the truck. Alisa and Dana opened fire, as well as the shooters from Pinnacle and Bravo, killing or injuring four more men. The second truck was trying to back out of the drive, but was blocked by the Humvee. Danny focused his fire on the driver of the retreating

Chevy. Once the second driver was taken out, more men tried running for cover fleeing from the cab and the bed of the Chevy. Shooters from the compound quickly eliminated six more men.

Then, the Humvee pushed in and the gunner up top opened up, spraying the compound with heavy fire. Danny grabbed Alisa's arm and pulled her down inside the fox hole, away from the gun port they'd been shooting out of.

JC's voice came over the radio. "I need you guys to keep making noise. Jack can take the gunner out, but he needs cover fire so they can't pinpoint his location."

Danny looked at Alisa and Dana. "Just stick your guns out the hole and fire in their general direction."

"What are you going to do?" Alisa asked.

"I have to try to pin them down, so they don't try to fix our location. While no one is looking, their troops could be moving up the creek to flank us." Danny peeked out and watched the gunner. He listened for when the heavy fire swept by, then popped out and started taking shots at the men all around. He heard the shot from the .308 that dropped the machine gunner. "Good shot, Jack." Of course Jack couldn't hear him, but he said it anyway.

Pinnacle, Bravo and Alpha all opened fire on any target they could see until the machine gunner was moved out of the way and replaced by another man. "Let's run that drill again." JC's voice came back over the radio.

Danny tried to perform the same maneuver, but now, more enemy shooters had emerged from a fourth vehicle, an old white van, and were focusing fire on his gun port. Danny keyed his mic. "They're pinning us down! I can't do much."

"You have to keep shooting." JC called back.

Nick's voice came over the radio. "Rocky is hit. Looks like the .50 got him. He's hurting pretty bad. Cami is going to see what she can do, but I need someone else up here to help me lay down fire. Korey, can you get to me?"

"And leave Jason here alone?" Korey's voice sounded worried.

Nick's voice came back. "If we don't hold this fort, you can't help him anyway. He's got a whistle. Tell him to blow it if he sees anything and you'll come running."

"Okay," Korey responded over the radio.

Danny continued to look for opportunities to shoot, but by this time the men were well hid in the hedgerow and not nearly so easy to spot. He continued to stick his head up and then back down. He felt like he was in some morbid version of whack-a-mole. Finally, on one of his trips to peer out of the hole, he saw a distinct muzzle flash. What was even better, he knew exactly which tree the flash came from. It was one of the trees on the range card and he knew exactly how far away it was and precisely how high he had to shoot to get the bullet to drop to the target. He raised up and fired. He hesitated too long to see if he'd hit his mark as a bullet smashed into the sandbag right by his cheek spraying dirt into his eye. He ducked down to wipe the dirt.

"Danny! Are you hit?" Alisa squealed.

"No, it's just dirt in my eye."

Dana handed him a jug of water. "Here, rinse it out."

Nick's voice came back over the radio. "Korey, where are you man? I at least need somebody to shoot while I change mags."

JC echoed Nick's request. "Korey, we need you at Bravo. Are you there? Just tell me what's going on."

Once Danny had his eye cleared, he took over shooting out the port. Alisa had covered while he cleared his vision. Danny saw the muzzle flash from the same tree. He took cover, visualized himself taking the shot, and then with lightning speed, he took the shot again. He didn't wait to see if it hit, but somehow he knew he'd eliminated the target. Danny ducked down and let Dana cover as he changed magazines.

JC's voice came back. "Nick, how is Rocky looking?"

"Not good." Nick replied.

"Look behind you and see if you can get a visual on Korey," JC said.

"Negative." Nick's voice came back over the radio.

JC's voice responded, "He's either down or they're in his fox hole. I'm sending Steven to tap Catfish to come to you. As soon as he gets back, I'll go see where Korey is."

Dana snatched the radio from Danny. "Steven, keep your head down. I love you!"

Danny hated what was happening. Rocky was down and in bad shape, Korey wasn't responding to the radio, and there was no end in sight. Every time Jack took out the machine gunner, it bought the compound less than a minute of respite before the heavy machine gun fire resumed at the hands of a replacement gunner.

Nick's voice came back over the radio. "You better get Catfish over here fast. I just took one in the right shoulder. I'm done shooting for the day. I can pull the trigger with my left hand, but that's about it. I wouldn't hit the broad side of the barn."

"10-4. Have Cami take care of you. If she can't help Rocky, just let him go. We can't lose you both," JC called.

Steven's voice came over the radio. "Hey, I found Korey, he's gone. I've got his radio. What should we do about Jason?"

JC called out. "Let's keep him alive and worry about grieving later. That's what Korey would want us to do. Get back over here. Is Catfish heading to Bravo?"

"Yes." Steven said.

"Why don't you head on over there with him. Jack and I can cover the Pinnacle."

"Okay."

Danny continued to return fire, but there was very little progress. The simple fact was that the compound was outmanned and outgunned. "Alisa, I need you to start reloading magazines for me. I'm getting low."

Alisa wasted no time opening the ammo box and beginning to fill Danny's spent magazines. The sound of the .50 caliber bullets raining against the dirt wall of the trench shook the earth, kicking up such a cloud of dirt and dust that it was difficult for Danny to even see a target on the rare occasions that he could stick his head out long enough to take a shot.

JC called back over the radio. "Catfish, Steven, are you guys in position?"

". . . here but the boy done got shot." Catfish was speaking before hitting the key so it was cutting off the first few words of his sentence.

Dana screamed. "Steven!"

"Where is he shot?" JC called.

". . . leg, right where he got shot last time." Catfish was still talking before keying his mic.

"Is it bad?" JC asked.

". . . worse, but he's still conscious."

Dana took Danny's radio again. "Steven! Can you hear me?"

Steven's voice came back. "Same leg, same spot. What are the odds?"

"Quit trying to be funny and get somewhere safe!" Dana barked.

Danny was happy that Steven was still alive, but the reality was that they were getting eaten alive. It wouldn't be long until the goons made an advance to breach the compound. At this rate, it wouldn't be long at all.

Dana handed the radio to Alisa. "I've got to go check on Steven. He's probably bleeding really badly."

"Cami will look after him. He made it to Bravo. No sense getting yourself killed." Danny took another quick shot into the cloud of dust that was now acting as concealment for the invading force.

Dana protested. "No, Danny, I have to go."

Danny took another shot, then ducked back down. "No, Dana, you're not going. What we really need right now is another one of your miracles."

"My miracles?"

"Yeah, for whatever reason, God chose me to have dreams and visions. He chose Alisa to interpret those dreams and I think he may have given you a special gift to pray for miracles."

"Oh no. I pray for stuff all the time that doesn't happen." Dana shook her head.

Danny took a deep breath, took another shot, and then continued speaking. "Last time when Steven was shot, you prayed. And like a minute later, Catfish showed up with his truck. You know it was a miracle."

"That was one time." She took a quick peek out the gun port, then fired her rifle.

Alisa handed Danny three of the reloaded magazines. "Dana, Danny is right. If we don't get a miracle, we're probably all going to die. Do you think God saved us from the bandits on the way here and delivered me from the hands of the kidnappers only to let us die in this dirt hole?"

Dana took another shot then ducked back down. "Okay, but you pray with me. I don't think I'm anyone special and I don't think God hears me anymore than anyone else."

Danny fired several shots then changed magazines. "Okay, quick prayer. We'll all pray."

Alisa began. "God, we're in big trouble. We really need your help. Please save us."

Danny went next. "God, you've delivered us

before. We know you created the heavens and the earth. It would be a simple thing for you to save us again. Yet not our will, but yours be done."

Danny tapped Dana on the shoulder as he stood back up to fire three more quick shots.

Dana prayed. "God, I love you so much. And I thank you for saving my soul, so that whatever happens on this earth, I know I'll be with you in the end. Maybe today. But I'm scared God. I'm afraid, and I love Steven." She broke down into a violent sob. "Please God, please save us one more time."

Danny pursed his lips. Her earnest plea brought a tear to his eye. He wiped his eye and continued returning fire.

JC called out over the radio. "Danny, do you think the girls can hold Alpha if you come over here? I'm going to send Jack down to help Catfish cover Bravo."

Danny looked at Alisa and Dana. "Can you guys do it?"

Alisa nodded. "Don't forget your magazines."

Danny began stuffing the reloaded mags in his pouches on the front of his vest. "You be safe. Quick bursts, then duck back down."

Alisa held his face with both hands and kissed him. "I love you, Danny Walker, you come back to me, okay?"

He handed her the radio then gave her one last quick kiss. He knew it could be their last but he quickly chased that thought from his mind.

Danny low-crawled up against the sandbag wall of the compound to the Pinnacle.

"How are you set for ammo?" JC asked when he

arrived.

"Alisa just reloaded a bunch of mags for me."

A loud whistle rang out from behind the house. The whistle was followed by several shots.

JC lowered his head as he sighed. "That was Melissa. If she blew that whistle, that means she's got troops over there trying to flank us." JC keyed his mic. "Jack, sorry son, I've got to move you again. Mom's got company and I need you to get over to Charlie. You should have two radios, so take one with you."

JC set the radio back down and leveled his rifle at the dust cloud to begin assaulting the void once more. "I have to be honest with you, Danny. We can't see what we're shooting at, they've got us out gunned, we're dropping like flies, and we're eventually going to run out of ammo. This probably isn't going to end well."

Danny took his turn to fire at the billowing veil of dirt. "It ain't over till it's over."

JC snorted. "I like your optimism."

Danny took another shot into the shroud of dust. This dust was brown and dirty, not like the blood red dust he'd seen in his dream. But nevertheless, this was indeed, the dust of war that the vision had foretold. He could feel it. The cloak which hid his attackers was the very same curtain of war. Would God give him a vision for which he could do nothing but perish? Why would he bother warning Danny through the nightmare if it were only a prophecy of his demise?

Danny ducked down as he heard what sounded like heavy debris raining down on the bunker.

Typically a succession of rounds from the .50 cal hitting nearby would kick up a shower of dirt and debris but it would quickly subside. Then he smelled it. "Rain."

It was raining again. The clouds that had made the morning so dreary were now a blessing from God that would soon settle the haziness from the dust being kicked up by the guns. Danny looked through the gun port and could finally make out the figure of one of his assailants as the murk dissipated. He took a shot, and then another, finally making his first kill in over two hundred rounds.

JC picked up the radio. "Let's hit 'em hard gang. We've got a window."

Danny took turns with JC. There was another brief hiatus from the deluge of the .50 caliber machine gun. Danny and JC seized the opportunity as did the other teams. It was short lived, but two more men fell. Less than thirty seconds later, there was another intermission from the large machine gun.

"Wow, Jack is really hurting these guys." Danny smiled at JC. The sudden excitement that they might actually live was overwhelming.

JC likewise couldn't contain his emotions. He grinned. "It ain't Jack. He's got the .308 over at Charlie. Maybe the gun is overheating and seizing up."

Danny leaned out for another shot and watched yet another man get picked off from the machine gun station. "Nope. Somebody is killing them."

JC exchanged places and took another volley of shots. "There goes another one! Someone is picking them off as fast as they can clear the body and get another gunner up."

JC took two more shots. "Here comes another machine gunner. I gotta watch this."

"Don't get shot!" Danny warned.

The bullets from the .50 swept across the wall of the compound then suddenly ceased, again. "There's a sniper behind them!" JC sounded ecstatic.

"Who?" Danny was filled with hope. He had a new lease on life.

JC shook his head with an ear-to-ear grin. "I don't know. It ain't nobody from our compound. But whoever it is, he's good. And what's more, I don't think Schlusser's goons have figured out the shooter isn't in our compound. So we have to keep giving this guy cover fire. We can't let the goons figure out what's going on." JC keyed the mic. "All teams keep laying down heavy fire. Don't worry about accuracy, just keep making noise."

Danny and JC continued to shoot. Danny tried to keep the rounds going in the general direction of the enemy, but focused on shooting. One after the other, the machine gunners kept falling. Soon, the enemy force was dwindling. Danny saw a man make a motion and yell something indiscernible, then the remaining men began piling into the van and the Hummer.

"Oh no! They ain't going nowhere." JC keyed the mic. "Catfish, get your truck and get it up front. We can't let these clowns get back to their base. Jack, grab the ammo from Charlie and meet Catfish at the truck. Alisa, bring the ammo from Alpha, we'll reload magazines on the road." JC tossed the radio on the ground and jumped out of the fox hole. "Come on Danny, we have to pull those grenades. We might use them yet."

Danny slung his rifle and followed JC. The attackers were pulling away and someone was still firing at them from the other side of the road as they fled. Catfish was around front in about a minute, but the van and Hummer were long gone.

JC jumped in the bed of the truck. "Let's move Catfish. They're not expecting us to chase them, so they'll slow down a few miles up the road. They're heading to Greenville, so we know where they're going."

Danny, Alisa, and Jack all piled into the truck also.

"Hang on to your horses." Catfish gunned the old pickup causing it to fling the freshly made mud several feet into the air as he sped off.

Danny held tightly to the edge of the truck bed. "Where's Dana?"

Alisa braced herself for the bumpy ride as well. "She had to go check on Steven. I told her to go ahead."

Danny smiled. "I think we have enough people for the clean-up run."

Catfish quickly navigated around the Chevy which had been abandoned in the drive. The Ford was well out of the way as it had rolled to a stop against the hedgerow. The tires squealed as he took the turn onto the road.

JC banged on the side of the truck. "Stop!"

Catfish hit the brakes. "What is it?"

Two heavily camouflaged men came running out of the field with their rifles held over their heads as a signal that they meant no harm.

"Dad!" one of them yelled.

"Chris?" JC stood up in the back of the truck.

Chris and the other man ran up to the truck.

"Get in!" JC grabbed his long lost son's hand and hoisted him into the truck.

Chris helped the other man into the truck. "This is my Air Force buddy, Clay."

JC slapped the side of the truck again. "Go! Go! Go!"

Catfish sped away again while JC embraced his son, sitting in the back of the truck bed. Danny turned his head when he saw JC sobbing over the reunion with his first-born. That was the tender side of the man that he admired so much.

Alisa continued to reload magazines, and so did Jack, after a quick hug from his older brother.

Chris had to yell to be heard over the wind blowing past the speeding truck. "We hit the center of the Hummer's window, which shattered it. So they can't see out. They'll either have to pull over to kick out the windshield or the driver with have to navigate the vehicle with his head stuck out the window."

"That's my boy!" JC held up one of the grenades. "Both of those options provide a nice opening for gift deliveries."

As the truck peaked the next hill, Catfish knocked on the back window to get the attention of the passengers in the bed of the truck. Danny looked to see what he wanted. Catfish was pointing straight ahead. Down the hill, perhaps a mile and a half in front of them, Danny could see the Hummer following close behind the white van.

Chris lowered the legs of the bipod affixed to his rifle. It was a camouflaged tactical rifle with a fancy looking scope.

"What's that?" Danny asked.

".338 Lapua. It was beast to pack here all the way from San Antonio. But it helped get us here alive." Chris popped up and set the bipod legs on top of the truck cab. Clay got behind Chris and sat with his back against Chris' legs to keep him from falling backwards.

Danny turned to look at the Hummer that they were slowly gaining on. They had spotted the truck and someone was attempting to get in position to run the .50 cal.

Chris's rifle rang out and the man in the Hummer slumped over the handle of the large gun. Danny waited to see if someone would come out to replace him. No one did. Either there was no one else in the Hummer to replace him or no one with the courage to face off against Chris.

Chris kept his rifle mounted on the roof of the cab. JC opened the back sliding window and instructed Catfish of the plan. It took a while, but Catfish finally caught up to the Hummer, most likely because of the visual impairment of the driver, as the vehicle could have easily outran Catfish's old truck. The van, however, looked as if it were topped out.

JC looked at Danny. "When you see me let go of the grenade, start counting off the time, one

Mississippi, two Mississippi, got it?"

Danny nodded. "You don't know how long the fuse is set for?"

"Probably five seconds, but every second counts."

Catfish slowly edged up to the Hummer. The driver had indeed been driving with his head out the window, but was forced to bring his head back in as Alisa and Jack took shots at him. But the window was still down, providing JC the opportunity to toss the grenade into the cab. JC stood next to Chris and launched the grenade. It bounced off the shattered windshield and in the direction of the passenger's seat.

Danny closed his eyes as Catfish hit the brakes. "One Mississippi, two Mississippi, three Mississippi, four Mississippi, five Mississippi, six . . ."

BOOM! The Hummer careened off the road and came to a sudden stop after running head long into a group of trees.

JC slapped the side of the truck and yelled to Catfish, "Keep going we have to catch the van!"

After Catfish slowed down to avoid the explosion in the Hummer, the van had now gained over half a mile on Danny's group and was putting more distance between them every second. The van made a quick turn onto Dobbin's Bridge Road. Catfish followed, then veered off into the neighborhood.

JC yelled, "What are you doing?"

Danny slid closer to the cab so he could hear Catfish's reply.

Catfish yelled back. "They've got to get to 29 if they're headin' to Greenville. Monitor Drive will get us there faster!"

"Then you'll be in front of them. That's not what we want!"

"We'll just wait for 'em, then." Catfish sped through the neighborhood and parked behind the burned out gas station on the corner of Monitor. "They'll be comin' round any second. Y'all best get in position."

JC shook his head. "I guess Catfish is running this op. Come on."

Danny and the others all found positions behind the bushes lining the gas station parking lot, lying in wait for the white van.

JC quickly asked Danny, "How many seconds on that last grenade?"

"Five and a half."

JC took off running in the direction that the van would be coming. He swiftly cleared an empty lot and disappeared into a cluster of bushes, trees and tall grass.

Seconds later, Danny saw the van coming in their direction. Just before the van reached the brush where Danny had last seen JC, a grenade went off right in front of the van. The vehicle swerved into the parking lot of the auto repair shop on the other side of the street. It came to a stop as it smashed into several cars in the lot.

Chris and Clay led the assault on the van as they ran toward the vehicle with weapons leveled at the doors. Finally, the back doors swung open, and three men ran toward the side of the building for cover to evade Danny's group, who were approaching from the front of the van.

Danny saw JC bolt from the bushes, across the street firing at the fleeing men.

Chris and Clay first cleared the driver's side of the van. Clay double tapped the driver making sure he wouldn't regain consciousness at an inopportune time for the team. Next, they made sure no one else was in the back of the van.

Danny waited for their signal, then assisted Chris and Clay as they pursued the fleeing goons. Jack and Alisa were close behind him. The men from the van took cover behind a red convertible at the corner of the building and began firing on Danny's team.

Chris looked to his father for direction who made a couple of hand signals that Danny wasn't familiar with. Chris called Danny over behind a silver PT Cruiser for cover. "You guys keep shooting at them. Keep them busy long enough for Clay and I to get around the back side."

Danny looked at Jack and Alisa. "Okay, we can handle that."

Chris and Clay stayed low to hide behind the other cars as they made their way around to the opposite side of the building. Danny, Alisa and Jack took turns firing volleys of shots toward the goons. JC also took several shots from another position to help keep the men distracted. This went on for roughly a minute, then Danny heard the shots coming from the back of the building.

"That's our cue." Danny led his team, shooting as they walked toward the red convertible. JC also converged on the location, helping to finish off the three men that Chris and Clay had attacked from behind.

JC let his rifle hang from the single-point sling. "Good work guys, let's see if that van is still drivable and get out of here."

Danny was confused. "Won't that lead the others to us?"

"That Hummer had a radio antenna. Schlusser already knows who we are and where we're at. It's just a matter of time until he gets organized and comes after us. And when his boys get here, we'll need every asset we can get. If they hit us with forty guys and couldn't take us, you can bet there will be a heck of a lot more than that next time." JC's tone was grim.

Chris hugged his dad again. "It's good to see you."

"You, too." Despite the dreadful prognosis of the immediate future, JC cracked a smile as he embraced Chris. "Let's get this op wrapped up so we can get home. I'm dying to hear about your trip. I bet it was a doozy."

Jack jumped in the van, the engine was still running. He put it in reverse and backed away from the row of parked cars which had stopped it.

Catfish put a hand in the air. "Might want to make sure you don't have no gas leaking 'fore you take that thing out for a spin." Catfish got down on his stomach and checked for leaks. "Looks alright."

Jack proceeded to back the van out. The front fender scraped against the tire rim as the shredded rubber of the blown out tire flipped past the folded metal. The constant metal on metal sound was interrupted by the rhythmic "ffflump, ffflump, ffflump" of the separated tread.

Catfish pointed to the back. "You youngins scratch around in the back, see if you can't find a spare tire. It might be up underneath the vehicle. I'll see if I ain't got somethin' to rectify this fender."

Danny and Alisa located the spare tire, but it was flat. Still, Danny knew something had to be done with it so he removed it from the van and rolled it up to the front where Catfish was beating the fender with a hammer. "That's a pretty low-tech solution."

Catfish looked at him for a second. Finally he said, "I reckon it was low-tech problem, then." He continued bashing the fender with the hammer until it was well clear of the wheel well.

JC looked at the tire. "That thing ain't going to do us much good."

Alisa looked around at the cars in the lot. "If we can find a girl's car . . ."

"A girl's car?" Danny cocked his head to one side as he tried to figure out what was coming next.

"Girls hate to change tires, or, we're just smarter as a sex, but either way, lots of girls carry Fix-A-Flat in their cars so we don't have to stop and put the spare on. If we can find a girl's car, we'll probably find some Fix-A-Flat."

Danny rolled his eyes. "Great idea, but I'm not sure your theory of us having a better chance of finding a can in a girl's car is going to hold up."

Danny took the tire tool from the van and began smashing out any windows that weren't already broken, then checked the glove boxes and the trunks.

Alisa borrowed Catfish's hammer and began a separate search, starting with a Volkswagen Beetle. "Oh Danny, guess what I found," she called out in a sing-song voice.

JC took the can. "Let's see if it works before you start gloating." He shook the can as required by the instructions, then screwed the short hose on the valve stem of the deflated spare. In seconds the tire inflated.

Jack, Chris and Clay worked together to get the shredded tire off and the new tire on.

Danny peeked into the back of the van while the lug nuts were being tightened. "Looks like we've got some more ammo."

JC looked over his shoulder. "Good, we're gonna need it."

Jack, Chris and Clay loaded into the van.

JC waved at Danny. "You guys ride back with the Fish. I'm gonna ride with my kid. It's been a while. We'll lead, you follow, so you'll know if we have any trouble on the way back. We'll stop at the wrecked Hummer. It'd be real nice if we can salvage that. If not, we at least need to get that .50 cal."

Alisa slid into the front seat of Catfish's truck to sit in the middle and Danny took the passenger's side.

Catfish started the engine and followed the van. "I best not never catch none of you youngins referin' to me as 'the Fish'. If JC was any younger, I'd tan his hide."

"I'll tell him you said that," Alisa said with a coy

smirk.

They arrived at the Humvee minutes later. While the heavy steel front bumper was slightly dented from the impact, the tree had suffered the most damage. Inside the cab was a different story. The first ninety-five percent of the driver's body came out in one piece. The other five percent of it was strewn about the inside of the cab, like a gut pile in a tornado. The seats were shredded, the radio was in three pieces, the speedometer was missing most of the glass, and it was stuck on thirty-five.

JC looked at the bloody mess and curled his lip before jumping into the driver's seat. He pushed the clutch, put it in neutral and turned the key. Despite the catastrophic damage caused to the interior of the cab by the grenade, the engine fired right up. "At least the government did something with all that tax money, that didn't turn out to be a total waste. Looks like they bought a Hummer that can stand up to an EMP and a grenade."

Chris looked the vehicle over. "And all for the low, low price of $220,000."

"You want to ride with me, Chris?" JC asked as he put the Hummer in reverse.

Chris looked in at the mangled seat with bits of flesh and blood all over. "If you don't mind, I'll just ride back with Jack. I missed my little brother too."

JC smirked. "Yeah, sure thing, kid."

The van led the convoy, with JC driving the Hummer behind the van, and Catfish at the end.

As they pulled into the driveway, Danny was instantly reminded of the carnage they'd left behind. He exited the truck to the sound of wailing and crying. Tracey, Jason, Emma and Kalie were all on their knees in the grass, circled around Korey's bloody body.

Pauline sat at the edge of the Bravo fox hole, with her dead husband's head in her lap. Weeping with a loud sorrowful howl.

Danny dropped his head. As much as he wanted to go make them all feel better, he couldn't. And before he did anything, he needed a glass of water. The stress of the battle and subsequent assault had taken everything he had. He needed some water, and he needed to sit down, if only for a few minutes. The sudden heaviness hit him like a ton of bricks as he walked up the stairs to the house. Alisa followed close behind.

Danny turned to see two-year old Annie bolting toward JC as he got out of the Humvee. She clung to his leg, crying. What an awful thing for a little child to see. What a horrific event for a little girl to live through. Even so, she was much better off than the Reese children. Their pain was only beginning.

Danny looked at the front window of Nana's house. It was shot out and there were bullet holes all over the house. He opened the door to find Steven stretched out on the couch, towels under his leg, Nana cleaning the wound and Dana assisting her. "How is he?"

Dana forced a smile. "Oh you know, Nana got him drunk, on top of the loss of blood. He babbled on some nonsense for a few minutes, then passed out. He should be okay though."

Danny was relieved that Steven was going to be okay. He wondered what a messed up world it was that this was the second time he'd seen Steven, in exactly the same position, the same condition, and the same bandages on the same leg. "I guess this is the new normal," he muttered as he made his way to the kitchen. The walls of the living room were riddled with bullets, some of the pictures on the wall were busted. The old TV that hadn't worked since the EMP was also ripped apart.

Danny got his water from the old metal pitcher and went to sit down in the dining room. Nana's china cabinet had a few holes in it and some of the plates were busted and broken, but many others were still intact.

Alisa got a glass of water as well and sat down at the table next to Danny. "I'm so tired all of a sudden."

"Post-adrenal dump crash," Danny said.

"Did you learn that in college?" she asked.

He fought back a laugh. "No, I made it up. But it kind of fits, right?"

"I'd slap you if I wasn't having a post-adrenal crash."

"Post-adrenal dump crash."

"Whatever. You made it up." Alisa put her head down on the table.

Danny put his hand on the back of her neck. "I'm glad we made it. I love being married to you and I'm thankful for every day I have with you."

She lifted her head to turn toward him and put her head back down on her hands. "Thanks. Me too."

Melissa walked in from the porch. "Hey, Cami sent me up here to ask for some more towels."

"There's a tiny hall closet, it's behind the bathroom door. How is Nick doing?" Danny asked.

"He lost a lot of blood, but Cami got the shrapnel out of his shoulder and arm. It was a 5.56 hollow point. It made a real mess. He's resting, but I think he'll be alright."

"There's a bottle of Jack Daniel's on the kitchen counter if Nick needs it." Alisa sat up for a moment.

"Nick has morphine, so he's going to be okay. But don't tempt me with it." Melissa snickered. Then, her face went solemn. "And poor Tracey, she's got all those kids alone now. Not even morphine can take away the pain she's going through. I don't know what I would do if JC hadn't made it." A tear ran down Melissa's face.

Danny bit his lip. "We'll all make sure Tracey doesn't have to raise her children alone."

Melissa nodded and forced a smile. "Yeah, I'll certainly do what I can. It could have just as easily been me in her shoes. Well, I better get those towels. See you guys later."

The next day Danny asked God for the strength to complete the macabre tasks of the day. It would be his duty to select a grave site for Korey and Rocky. Of course he would need to find a serene location that could accommodate additional residents. It was highly unlikely that they would be the last members of the compound who would have to be buried. Danny knew that it was very possible that he could be selecting his own final resting place, or worse, Alisa's grave. Nothing good could come of dwelling on such things, so he got busy doing what needed to be done. A quiet place down near the creek was the perfect spot. A grand oak offered shade and sanctuary. The plot could easily be expanded. Next, Danny got JC to assist him in operating Rocky's tractor to dig out the two graves. Between the two of them, they soon had all of the buttons and levers figured out.

Chris and Clay were granted a twenty-four-hour period to rest and recuperate, before being expected to chip in with chores and security shifts, but they knew the hardship that had been brought on the compound by the two deaths and the injuries, so they insisted in helping out. The two of them along with Jack, took care of gathering wood and burning the bodies of the assailants scattered about the entrance of the driveway.

Nana, Cami and Melissa tended to the wounded and took care of cleaning the bodies of Korey and Rocky for the funeral service to be held that sorrowful Saturday afternoon.

Alisa and Dana took care of preparing the food for the day and trying to clear out some of the debris from Nana's house caused by the previous day's battle. They picked through the dishes in the china cabinet, throwing out the broken pieces and seeing what was usable.

Catfish handled the vehicles, driving them to the back of the compound and assessing them for mechanical damage from stray bullets.

With everyone working together, most everything got done. And late that afternoon, Steven led the memorial service, at the grave sites down by the creek. He was much too weak to walk on crutches, so Danny, Chris, and Jack carried him to the wheel barrow and took turns pushing him to the old oak tree.

Steven prepared a short sermonette focused on the hope of the resurrection. Everyone attended, except Nick, as he had lost a lot of blood the day before and would be recuperating for a few days.

Tracey, Jason, Kalie and Emma held each other close, comforting one another by Korey's grave.

Pauline looked the worst of all, holding a small bouquet of wild flowers limply in her hand. Rocky was all she had, so hers would be a tough row to hoe.

Steven read a short passage from John 11. "Jesus said unto her, I am the resurrection, and the life: he that believeth in me, though he were dead, yet shall he live: And whosoever liveth and believeth in me shall never die. Believest thou this?"

Danny half listened to Steven's memorial message, but he couldn't stop his mind from wandering. He held Alisa's hand tightly, glad that it had not been his beloved that they were burying this day, and feeling a little ashamed for thinking such a thought.

"Ichabod," he said, just above a whisper. Despite the losses, he and the surviving members of the compound had been victorious against the assailants who attacked them. They had stood the test, held their ground, and defended what was theirs; but as he looked around at the suffering and the carnage all about him, he certainly saw no glory in it. And with a mantle of grief hanging over the compound, both for the lives lost during this assault and for the brutality that was sure to come, there would be no glory any time soon.

NOTE FROM THE AUTHOR

Don't Panic! Inevitably, books like this will wake folks up to the need to be prepared, or cause those of us who are already prepared to take inventory of our preparations. New preppers can find the task of getting prepared for an economic collapse, EMP, or societal breakdown to be a source of great anxiety. It shouldn't be. By following an organized plan and setting a goal of getting a little more prepared each day, you can do it.

I always try to include a few prepper tips in my novels, but they're fiction and not a comprehensive plan to get prepared. Now that you're motivated to start prepping, the last thing I want to do is leave you frustrated, not knowing what to do next. So, I'd like to offer you a free PDF copy of *The Seven Step Survival Plan.*

For the new prepper, *The Seven Step Survival Plan* provides a blueprint that prioritizes the different aspects of preparedness and breaks them down into achievable goals. For seasoned preppers who often get overweight in one particular area of preparedness, *The Seven Step Survival Plan* provides basic guidelines to help keep their plan in balance, and ensures they're not missing any critical segments of a well-adjusted survival strategy.

To get your free PDF copy of
The Seven Step Survival Plan, email me,
prepperrecon@gmail.com
with **Seven Step Offer** in the subject line.

Thank you for reading
Ichabod
Seven Cows, Ugly and Gaunt: Book Two

Reviews are the best way to help get the book noticed. If you liked the book, please take a moment to leave a five-star review on Amazon and Goodreads.

I love hearing from readers! So whether it's to say you enjoyed the book, point out a typo that we missed, or ask to be put on the notification list for future books, drop me a line.

prepperrecon@gmail.com

Stay tuned to **PrepperRecon.com** for the latest news about my upcoming books, and great interviews on the Prepper Recon Podcast.

Keep watch for

A Haunt for Jackals
Seven Cows, Ugly and Gaunt: Book Three

If you liked *Ichabod*, you'll love my previous series

The Days of Noah

In The Days of Noah, Book One: Conspiracy, The founding precepts of America have been destroyed by a conspiracy that dates back hundreds of years. The signs can no longer be ignored and Noah Parker is forced to prepare for the cataclysmic period of financial and political upheaval ahead. Watch through the eyes of Noah as a global empire takes shape, ancient writings are fulfilled, and the last days fall upon the once great, United States of America. Start reading today.

Coming Soon!

The Days of Elijah

This follow-up series to The Days of Noah chronicles the struggles of ex-CIA analyst and new believer, Everett Carrol, as he tries to survive the total onslaught of ruin brought on by the tribulation, a coming period of wrath promised by the Bible to be unparalleled in destruction and suffering.